"I don't want to go!"

Katie was obviously panicked by the idea of losing her protector. Eric looked helplessly at Aurora. Though she'd offered to help him with Katie, he suddenly felt ridiculously presumptuous. Such a beautiful woman surely had other ways to spend her time.

"Why don't you let Katie stay here for the afternoon?" Aurora searched for the right words. "I want her to stay," she assured Eric, catching Katie's hand and drawing the child to her side. "We'll be fine."

"If you don't mind...." Eric said, inwardly kicking himself for the sense of relief he felt.

For one preposterous moment Eric considered going down on his knees before the gorgeous doctor to ask her to marry him, promising her all of his worldly goods—and only as much of his company as she wanted to put up with—if only she would become his daughter's mother....

ABOUT THE AUTHOR

The writing team of Karen Parker and Mary Scamehorn has been together since 1983. Their first eight books were published by Dell under the pseudonym of Blair Cameron. *Shadows of the Past,* their third book as Kathryn Blair for Harlequin American Romance, is a dramatic and touching story about overcoming the burdens of yesterday's trials and learning to look to the future for growth, peace and love. Both authors teach school and make their homes in Tacoma, Washington.

Books by Kathryn Blair
HARLEQUIN AMERICAN ROMANCE

Don't miss any of our special offers. Write to us at the following address for information on our newest releases.

Harlequin Reader Service
P.O. Box 1397, Buffalo, NY 14240
Canadian address: P.O. Box 603,
Fort Erie, Ont. L2A 5X3

KATHRYN BLAIR

SHADOWS OF THE PAST

Harlequin Books

TORONTO • NEW YORK • LONDON
AMSTERDAM • PARIS • SYDNEY • HAMBURG
STOCKHOLM • ATHENS • TOKYO • MILAN

For Kirsten, my precious daughter.
—Karen

Published August 1991

ISBN 0-373-16403-3

SHADOWS OF THE PAST

Chapter One

"Dr. Duvall! Dr. Duvall!" Katie Thorpe's high voice pierced the silence of the sunny day as Aurora Duvall reached the top of a grassy knoll in the hillside cemetery.

Quickening her steps, Aurora hurried to meet the young girl who'd broken away from the group of mourners under a canopy at the grave side to run toward her.

"What's wrong, honey?" Aurora asked with concern as Katie wrapped her arms around her and sobbed. Aurora's arms encircled the slender body, tentatively at first—then, as a wave of compassion for the newly motherless child surged through her, she gathered her closer. Long-suppressed maternal feeling welled up inside her, until she felt as though she were dissolving in the potent emotion.

"Don't let my dad send me away," the thirteen-year-old pleaded, looking anxiously toward a tall, dark-haired man who had just started walking across the lawn in their direction. "Don't let him make me go!"

"I'll talk to Eric," Aurora's friend Brook Oliver put in hastily, a worried frown creasing his brow. "Do you think you can bring her along?"

Aurora nodded. "Just give us a couple of minutes." She waited until the stocky man had intercepted Katie's father and the two men had turned to walk back to the grave site before asking, "Send you away where?"

"To Texas! With them!" Katie turned to point an accusing finger at a smartly attired man and woman standing together beside the freshly dug grave. "My Aunt Carla and my Uncle Tom."

"Your father wouldn't send you away...." Aurora said softly, smoothing down the distraught child's smoky-brown hair.

"He's going to! Can't you stop him?" Katie implored. Stepping back, she raised her tear-streaked face to look directly at Aurora. "He doesn't want me here!"

"That can't be true," Aurora objected, letting her empty arms fall to her sides.

"Will you tell him that I can't go? That I have to stay here?" Katie begged, her deep blue eyes brimming with more tears. "Will you tell him now?"

"I can't do that, dear. This isn't the time or the place—"

"I don't have much time," Katie broke in desperately. "Can you and Uncle Brook come to the house? Talk to him there?"

"Yes...if you'll go back to your father now and stand beside him during the service. How about it?" Aurora asked. Taking a tissue from her handbag, she offered it to Katie.

"Okay," Katie agreed hoarsely, wiping her cheeks on the tissue then tucking it into the pocket of her gauzy white dress, "but I really don't want to be here at all."

"I know, honey," Aurora whispered, feeling tears start behind her own lids as she gathered the child to her for a final hug, "but you can get through this. I know you can." Keeping an arm around Katie's slim shoulders as they walked back to join the small group at the grave, she gave the child a reassuring squeeze before leaving her with her father and stepping in beside Brook.

As the service began, Aurora anxiously watched Katie. She still didn't know what was at the root of the Thorpes' family problems, but she did know that Katie and her father were caught up in an unusually tragic situation.

Imperceptibly Aurora shifted her weight, feeling uncomfortable with the idea of invading the well-known man's privacy. But his daughter had asked for her help and she wasn't going to let her down. During the term that she'd been the consulting physician at the Seahurst Academy for Girls, she'd thought that she and Katie had become quite close, so the shocking events of the past few days had left her with a sense of guilt that she couldn't shake. When Brook Oliver, the director of Seahurst's Middle School, had assigned Katie to the job of student infirmary assistant and had asked Aurora to take a special interest in the girl, she should have asked him why. In light of Katie's mother's sudden death, she felt negligent.

"Ashes to ashes, dust to dust..." A few of the minister's familiar words penetrated Aurora's consciousness before she became lost once more in her troubled reflections. Although Katie had welcomed Aurora's special attention, she'd seemed perfectly normal and had never given any indication during the casual talks they'd shared that she had any serious family problems.

Glancing sideways at Brook, Aurora felt a stab of annoyance quickly tempered by sympathy. Obviously he was close to the Thorpes, far more so than she'd imagined. When he'd called the day before to ask her to come to the funeral with him, he'd sounded as if he'd been crying. And when he'd picked her up this afternoon there'd been such a look of abject grief in his ordinarily cheerful blue eyes that she hadn't even attempted to start a conversation. Still, if he'd supplied her with some parental background on Katie, perhaps she could have said or done something that would have helped prepare Katie for this ordeal.

The mercifully short, grave-side service was drawing to a close. Even under the dark green awning, the late-afternoon sunshine of the faultless Southern California day could be felt. Its strong beams penetrated the canvas, casting a strange pallor upon the congregation. Feeling hot and sticky in her black silk dress, Aurora longed for a brisk breeze to lift the heavy fall of hair from the back of her neck for even a moment, but the air remained deathly calm.

After Katie and her father had each stepped forward to place a rose on the bronze coffin, Brook moved toward them, but Aurora held back. The poignancy of the awful moment—the time of absolute parting—hit her hard. Her mind slid back thirteen years, and she relived again the gut-wrenching trauma of loss that she knew she had never...would never...recover from.

Forcing her mind away from such thoughts, she turned her attention to Katie's father, Eric Thorpe. She'd never met the man, so she hadn't known what to expect. He was tall and lean. Even from the back he was attractive, but his face was almost irresistibly compelling. Framed by close-cropped black hair that was brushed back on the sides, his high forehead rose above brows that were dark slashes shadowing his deep-set black eyes. Divided by a sharp Roman nose set above clearly delineated lips, his tanned face was saved from being narrow by a low, square jawline that jutted back from his slightly prominent chin. He had the look of an ascetic, and she could easily picture him in the austere robes of a charismatic monk. But his beautifully tailored dark suit, white shirt and somber tie suited him as well. Far from being a monk, she reminded herself, he was a grieving widower.

She watched as Brook took each of the chief mourners in his arms for a consoling hug before a few of Katie's girl friends from the academy shyly stepped forward to gather around her. Prepared to go to Katie if she showed any signs of breaking down again, Aurora noted that both the young girl and her father continued to demonstrate the amazing control they'd shown throughout the service. White-faced and uncharacteristically tense, Katie had stood dutifully at her father's side, yet strangely apart from him.

Aurora's eyes narrowed in assessment. Katie's outburst hadn't been a momentary overreaction to a minor misunderstanding. Something was seriously wrong between Katie and her father. Their grief, which in the normal course of things should have drawn them together, was pushing them apart... or, worse yet, she suspected, intensifying a long-standing estrangement.

AFTER LEAVING the cemetery, Aurora sat beside a subdued Brook as he drove his all-terrain vehicle along the winding seacoast road toward town. The beauty of the scenery that had enticed her to set up practice in Seahurst was lost on her today, though, as they swept wordlessly past the enchanting vista. Preoccupied, she dwelt on the haunting memory of Katie's frightened eyes, and the overpowering sensations that had engulfed her when the child had come running to her for help. Without warning, Aurora burst into tears.

"Want me to pull over?" Brook asked in alarm as she fumbled in her handbag.

"No," she answered angrily, wiping her nose with a crumpled tissue, "but you owe me an explanation."

"Of what? The Thorpes?" the blond man countered. "The papers and the newscasters said it all." He set his round jaw grimly as he recited, "'Stacia Thorpe, forty, wife of Eric Thorpe, playwright, author of the comic hit play

Where Did I Go Wrong? and its sequel, *Sorry I Asked*, as well as numerous other popular screenplays, jumped to her death from the Golden Gate Bridge. Stacia Hudson, before her marriage to Thorpe, was a talented and successful New York stage set designer best known for her use of vibrant primary colors.' Quote and unquote.''

Pregnant wife of—Aurora silently added what everyone who had access to the local medical community grapevine knew from the autopsy findings. At least that tidbit hadn't made the news yet. For Katie's sake, Aurora hoped it never would. Still, she couldn't shake the feeling that for some reason the pregnancy had been the catalyst that had moved the woman to end her life.

"That's all?" she asked.

Brook shrugged. "It's not my story to tell. But I do hope you'll hang in there and help Katie through this."

"I'm going to try," Aurora acknowledged, "but she seems to think her dad's going to send her away with her aunt and uncle. Do you know anything about that?"

"No...Ric hasn't mentioned it to me. Maybe he thinks it would be good for her to get away for a little while."

"She doesn't want to go. She made me promise to talk to him about it."

"That's a good idea," Brook approved. "But go easy on him, will you? He's been under terrific emotional strain."

"I'm sure he has, but Katie's in bad shape, too. I suspect she feels she's lost control over her life," Aurora said, wondering if, for all her caring, there'd be any way she could really help the girl. It all depended on Eric Thorpe...and he was a completely unknown quantity.

WHEN BROOK PULLED onto the private road that led to the sprawling mansion built high on the bluff overlooking the ocean, Aurora felt a shiver run down her spine. Her only look at the Thorpe house had been an aerial view she'd caught on the television news. According to reporters, the secluded home had been designed by Katie's multitalented mother. She shuddered. It was no place for the widower or the bereaved child to return to after the interment.

"The three of us used to hang glide off this cliff," Brook pointed out a few minutes later, as they stood admiring the view from the bluff, passing time while they waited for the others to arrive. "Stacia was fearless."

"You've known the Thorpes for a long time," Aurora commented, trying to establish in her mind the relationship between the short, stocky schoolmaster and the striking, renowned playwright.

Brook nodded. "Ric and I roomed together in college. I went on to grad school when he headed for New York, where he met Stacia. His writing career took off like a rocket."

"He's prolific, isn't he?" Aurora remarked.

"Was," Brook amended, turning to look out over the wide expanse of rippling sea. "I'm worried, and I know he is, too. He hasn't written anything for the past year."

Before Aurora could voice any of her several unanswered questions, the crunch of tires sounded on the private gravel road far below. She and Brook turned to walk back to the front of the house. But the sedan that entered the circular drive wasn't the hired limousine.

"Good afternoon, Mr. Oliver," a stout woman called out after she'd shut the passenger door and the car had disappeared around the back.

"Hi there, Bridey," Brook answered, taking Aurora's arm and leading her toward the red-tiled patio that fronted the low facade of the white stucco house. "This is Dr. Duvall, Katie's pediatrician. Bridey is the woman who keeps this place running," he added to Aurora with a fond grin at the housekeeper.

"Pleased to meet you," Bridey said, extending her black gloved hand. "Now I understand Katie's sudden notion that she's going to be a doctor. Come right in," she added as she walked across the patio to unlock the front door. "I'll have a nice cold lunch ready soon. I expect people will be stopping by."

"May I help?" Aurora offered, stepping into the airy entryway.

The middle-aged woman shook her head. "No need. My old man, Mac, will give me a hand. You two just make yourselves comfortable." She moved off down the hall.

Following Brook's lead, Aurora stepped down from the foyer into a room that ran the length of the main wing. Glass panels, stretching from the hand-glazed Mexican tile floor to the high ceiling, opened onto an oceanfront patio, invitingly furnished with brilliantly upholstered couches and matching umbrellas. But the room that was meant to be spacious was so cluttered with furniture that Aurora had to weave her way to the patio doors.

"Stacia had an obsession for buying," Brook explained uneasily, as they looked back from the patio into the room's unbelievable jumble. "Some of that stuff still has the price tags on it."

With the eye of a practiced shopper at second-hand stores, Aurora could see that the individual pieces were of very high quality. Massive canvases covered the stark white walls. At one time their vivid, expressionistic beauty must have been the focal point of the room, but now they were eclipsed by the warehouse furniture showroom quality of their surroundings. An obsession for buying? That was hardly the term for it.

"I suspect Eric may sell this place and most of what's in it...."

"And a good thing that will be," Bridey remarked, appearing around the corner of the patio with a chilled bottle of wine and two glasses, which she put down on a table beside them. "This place is too big for the two of them. They need something smaller...in town would be best so that Katie could run around with her friends. Now, I hope this will hold you until the folks get back."

After thanking the housekeeper, Brook filled their glasses with the cooled beverage. But before Aurora could raise hers to her lips, the doorbell rang and the first group of visitors arrived.

"MY GOODNESS!" Carla exclaimed, crossing her shapely legs at the knee. "The audacity of those reporters snappin' pictures of all of us like that!"

"We should just be grateful, darlin', that they waited until the service was over and most of the people were gone," her husband put in mildly.

Ignoring his comment, she added, "I can't imagine what you were thinkin', Eric, to suggest that we go in your car. If we weren't behind this nice dark glass, they'd still be chasin' us."

"You were right about the limo," Eric agreed tersely, though he knew exactly what he'd been thinking. If he'd driven his own car, at least he'd be speeding along and in control, instead of sitting in a confined space with two people he hardly knew, and a daughter he understood even less.

"The flowers we sent for the casket were beautiful, weren't they, Tom?" Carla asked.

"Yes, darlin', they were."

Carla hadn't approved of Eric's decision to have the local florists take the flowers that were sent for Stacia to hospitals and nursing homes where they could be appreciated and enjoyed, rather than to the grave site where they'd have quickly withered away. Realizing that his sister-in-law was subtly needling him, Eric refused to rise to the bait. He had far more important things on his mind.

Katie hadn't spoken a word to him since her outburst before the service. A glance her way told him that his daughter's face was stubbornly turned toward the opposite window. He groaned inwardly. Lord, when had the little girl who'd liked nothing better than to spend her time with him flying kites off the cliff or listening to stories he'd written just for her, been replaced by this graceful child-woman who had told him only this morning that they "just didn't communicate"?

Well, she was right. They didn't. Maybe it had been a mistake to send her off to Seahurst to board as a little fourth grader, but he'd done it for her. He'd wanted to shield his precious daughter from a complete awareness of the awful truth of his and Stacia's life. He'd hoped by limiting the time Katie spent at home that he could create an illusion for her to keep reality at bay. But he could see now that he had only confused her. He'd been far less successful in spinning a captivating web of fantasy to lighten his daughter's heart, than he had been in pulling audiences into his fictional scenarios.

And as a result he was afraid he'd lost everything. Just managing to stifle a sob, he tried to focus his mind on what he could do to make amends for his mistakes. He wanted to reach out to Katie, to hold her hand . . . but, fearing her reaction, he didn't dare. He couldn't expect her to understand.

At the funeral he'd planned to hold her close . . . to somehow convey to her that despite everything that had gone wrong in her short life, the two of them still had each other.

But Carla's tactless remark that she wanted to take Stacia's place had set into motion a heated argument. The timing couldn't have been worse. He'd been forced to tell his daughter that he was considering sending her home with her aunt and uncle. There'd been no opportunity for further explanation, and Katie's rage had made the possibility of his holding her or comforting her unthinkable.

"Katie, dear, who was that woman you went tearin' off to? Was she a friend of your mother's?" Carla asked, picking a tiny speck of lint off her skirt.

"No...she's my friend," Katie answered after a deliberate pause.

"Is she a friend of the family, Eric?" Carla persisted.

He shook his head. "Brook said she's the school doctor."

"Can she be trusted?" Carla asked, her eyes narrowing.

"What do you mean 'can she be trusted'!" Katie spat out. "She's my friend. In fact, she's the only one who cares about me. She's going to help me. She promised she would."

"Your aunt is just worried about people carryin' tales, sugar," Tom soothed, "to the newspapers, and all. But if she's your doctor, there won't be any problem. Professional ethics, you know."

Although Eric would never admit it, he'd been upset and shaken when Katie had spotted the woman who'd come with Brook and gone running to her. For just an instant he'd worried that she might be some sort of publicity seeker. But he'd realized just as quickly, that if she were with Brook she had to be all right. And he still had no idea how he'd ever have managed to calm Katie down if the woman hadn't come when she had.

Yet afterward, the woman's presence had made him uncomfortable. He'd sensed her watching him, trying to size him up in light of Katie's accusations. He knew she had to be wondering what kind of father would send his daughter away and turn her over to the care of an aunt and uncle, right after she'd lost her mother. Well, he could answer that one. A desperate father. One who couldn't bear to see his child hurt by the vicious rumors he feared would run rampant in Seahurst and in the entire entertainment industry for months. One who wanted his daughter to live in the security and protection an insular community in East Texas could provide.

"Eric?" Carla's distinctive twang cut through his thoughts, as the limo made the turn to start up toward the house.

"I'm sorry, did you say something?" he asked.

"I was just wonderin' if you have reached a decision?"

He sighed. "Carla, Katie and I—"

"Daddy," Katie turned to face him, her blue eyes ablaze with barely concealed fury. "Dr. Duvall promised she'd talk to you about me. And if you don't listen to her before you give Aunt Carla an answer, I swear I'll never speak to you again in my life."

"Really!" Carla protested. "Are you goin' to let her sit there and talk to you like that? She's just a child. She doesn't know what she's sayin'. This is just more proof that she needs a mother's guidance."

"Who are all those people?" Katie shrieked as the limousine made its way through an assortment of cars that were parked in front of the house. "Daddy, there's Uncle Brook's Jeep, so Dr. Duvall must be here. You've got to see her before you decide."

Feeling the tension that had been building in the back of his head all afternoon tighten into a viselike headache, Eric responded wearily, "Honey, I will. Just as soon as I can."

LISTENING FOR SOUNDS of Katie's arrival, Aurora separated herself from the somber group on the patio. When the Thorpes finally appeared, knowing Eric Thorpe would have to greet the friends and acquaintances who had come to pay their respects, she quickly hurried through the living room and made her way to Katie's side. The girl looked frantic.

"Come on, sweetie," Aurora urged, "let's go to your room. You can sponge off your face and rest a bit." The strong nurturing impulse surged through her once again, shaking her composure. Ordinarily she was able to suppress such feelings, but this afternoon with Katie she was helpless to stem their flow.

"Daddy?"

Eric Thorpe stopped his progress toward the patio and turned. "Yes, Katie?"

"Remember what you promised?"

"Yes, of course." Directing his attention to Aurora, he said, "We need to talk. Would you mind staying until after my other guests have gone?"

Unable to read anything except urgency in his tone or eyes, Aurora agreed. "Not at all."

"My room's downstairs," Katie said, taking Aurora's hand and leading her to a wide, spiraling staircase.

Once they reached the lower floor, Katie's air of bravado evaporated, and she leaned against Aurora for support as they walked along a curving hallway to her bedroom.

After Katie swung open the door to her suite of rooms, she threw herself on the huge bed, wrapped her arms around the comforting softness of a worn and faded panda bear, and broke into sobs.

Sitting down beside her, Aurora gently rubbed her back, not wanting to interfere with the therapeutic tears. When the sobs had subsided to sniffles, she handed Katie a tissue from the box on the bedside table. "Feeling any better?" she inquired quietly.

"No, no! I told you, he wants to get rid of me!" Pulling herself up, Katie allowed Aurora to prop pillows against the padded, pale blue headboard. Settling back against them, she calmed herself enough to explain, "My Aunt Carla says I need a family life. She says she wants to be my muh-uh-ther." Fresh sobs racked her slender frame.

"Cry all you want, honey," Aurora whispered against the girl's fine hair. "It will do you good. But don't you worry. Nobody can take you away without your father's consent."

"That's just it! He's just about ready to agree!" Katie blubbered, her breath catching in her throat. "I told you, he wants to get rid of me!"

"Oh, I'm sure you're wrong," Aurora said, experiencing a sinking sensation in the pit of her stomach. After losing one parent, Katie shouldn't be rejected by the other.

"No, I'm not!" the girl shouted. "He thinks I'm crazy!"

"Why would you think a thing like that?" Aurora asked, seriously alarmed.

"Because I'm just like my mother and she was crazy!"

"Katie, honey," Aurora murmured, feeling as though her heart would break, "not everyone who takes her own life is crazy. Most of them are just upset—"

"Not my mother," Katie said with cold emphasis. "She was crazy."

"Sweetie, we're going to have to talk about this a lot more," Aurora said, wondering if there could be any truth to Katie's conviction, but remembering, too, that the first stage of grief is anger. Katie was most likely furious with her mother for having died and left her, and that fury was understandably compounded by the fact that Stacia Thorpe had committed suicide. "Right now, I want you to settle down and quit thinking about it all."

"I can't! Please, don't let Daddy decide I have to go. They're leaving tomorrow morning and they want to take me with them!" Her voice rose to a near shriek of panic. "You have to talk to him!"

"I will," Aurora promised, thinking with dread of discussing such personal issues with a man she had yet to formally meet. "Now, let me go upstairs and get you something to eat and drink."

"You'll come right back?" Katie asked, lying back among her pillows, her delicate chin quivering.

"I'll come right back and stay with you for as long as you want me to."

"I want you to spend the night," Katie stated plaintively. "I don't want to be alone, and I don't want you to go until my aunt and uncle are on their way back to their ranch."

"We'll see," Aurora soothed.

"No!" Katie insisted, sitting up again. "Promise me you'll stay!"

Seeing the girl's desperation, Aurora nodded her head in agreement, thinking that she'd have to arrange with her associate to cover her calls. "I promise. Now you settle down until I get back."

"All right," Katie agreed with an exhausted sigh, sinking back against her pillows again.

As Aurora slowly mounted the spiral staircase she wondered how Eric Thorpe would take the news that a stranger would be spending the night in his house.

Chapter Two

Carla was standing at the top of the plushly carpeted stairs, speaking on the phone. "Please, don't call in any more telegrams," she said crisply. "Print them up and send them to the house.... Thank you."

After placing the receiver in its cradle, she adjusted her pearl stud before turning toward Aurora. "Oh, Doctor..."

"Duvall," Aurora supplied.

"Yes, Duvall," Carla acknowledged with a nod, still looking impeccably fresh in black linen and a single strand of pearls. "How is Katie? Is she coming up?"

"I don't think she'll be able to handle it," Aurora said slowly. "She's very upset."

"Teenagers are so emotional," Katie's aunt responded with a brittle laugh, effectively ending the conversation.

Awkwardly feeling every inch of her five-foot, ten-inch height, Aurora followed the petite woman's adroit lead through the conglomeration of furniture in the main room. She knew it was ridiculous to make a snap judgment about a person, but she couldn't help feeling she had to protect Katie from this seemingly superficial woman.

Fifty or more people were quietly talking in small groups on the terraced patio overlooking the sea. A magnificent sunset lit the western sky with gorgeous hues of reds, golds and purples. Mac, Bridey's "old man," in a white jacket and bow tie was busily dispensing drinks from a portable bar. If it hadn't been for the subdued tone of the well-modulated voices and the marked absence of laughter, Aurora would have thought a cocktail party was in progress.

Quickly searching the room for a familiar face, she located Brook leaning against the wrought iron railing and made her way to his side. After excusing himself he motioned her to a secluded corner of the patio and asked, "How's our girl? Get her calmed down yet?"

"I'm working on it, but she's still afraid her aunt and uncle may abduct her before morning."

"Carla's not that spontaneous, so she doesn't have anything to worry about on that score," Brook remarked. "I know she and Tom are planning to stay at a hotel tonight. Katie's right about one thing, though. I talked with Ric and he is thinking of sending her home with them. Possibly as soon as tomorrow."

"Why would he do that?" Aurora demanded. "Katie already feels like her whole world is crumbling. Why would he want to make things worse for her than they already are?"

"He'd never deliberately do anything to hurt her. He adores that kid. He just isn't thinking straight."

Aurora let out a heavy sigh. "Katie's insisting that I spend the night. She's afraid to be alone. And frankly, I don't want to leave her in this condition. She's come to mean a lot to me. But what do you think? How will her father take my interfering?"

"You're not interfering," Brook assured her. "Katie needs you. Ric may be doing the wrong things for Katie, but he's doing them for all the right reasons. He's trying to protect her. Remember, he has agreed to talk to you. And better you than me. He needs to hear it from someone he believes has a little emotional objectivity. How about I run you home so you can grab some fresh clothes and toilet articles?''

Aurora shook her head. "No, thanks. I'm sure I can manage for the night, but I do want my black bag from your car. Katie's so overwrought I may have to give her a mild sedative later. Right now I'm going to try to get her to eat something.''

"Let's grab a couple of plates," Brook suggested, "and load them up with goodies to tempt her. There must be something here she'd like.''

"Did Bridey do all this?" Aurora asked in amazement, looking at the lavish array spread out over two linen-covered buffet tables.

"Yes, she's been in the kitchen ever since it happened. She says cooking takes her mind off her worries. Ric and Stacia never ate much, but I've sure had more than my share of great meals here.''

A moment later, feeling that someone was looking at her, Aurora glanced up from the table directly into Eric Thorpe's hooded black eyes. She held his gaze briefly before he turned his head away to respond to a remark made by the white-haired man to his left. Caught off guard by the impact of his gaze, Aurora's pulse raced. She sensed again the aura of quiet power radiating from him that she'd been aware of earlier in the day. He would be the center of any group, she realized, the type of man other men sought out for his opinions... the type of man women watched.

"Hey, there," Brook said with a knowing chuckle, as he slid his hand under hers to steady the plate she had absent-mindedly let slip. "I've always wondered why I don't have Ric's impact on women.''

Irritated that Brook had witnessed her moment of fascination, Aurora said, "He doesn't look very concerned about his daughter.''

"You're wrong, Doc. He's worried sick about her. He's been circulating among his guests as quickly as he decently can. He's anxious to have this formality over and done with," Brook remarked, as they both looked to where Eric, his hand extended for handshakes, was extricating himself from the group of men surrounding him.

"I'd better get back to Katie," Aurora said. "Would you ask Mac to bring along a pitcher of ice water and a couple of glasses when he has a minute?"

"Sure will," Brook agreed, saluting her with his goblet. "And Aurora... thanks."

"I just hope I can help," she responded, getting a firm grasp on the filled plates before starting to make her way through the crowd.

Katie's father caught up with her before she reached the staircase. His voice was deep and resonant, and a smile crinkled the corners of his intelligent eyes as he introduced himself. "Dr. Duvall, I'm Eric Thorpe."

She nodded. "Aurora Duvall."

"I appreciate your help with Katie at the cemetery. I have to tell you I was relieved to find you weren't an overly curious mother of one of Katie's school friends who'd tagged along with Brook to get a little more grist for the rumor mill."

When she didn't respond, he asked, "Does my cynicism shock you? I'm sorry, but I thought it best if we were frank with each other...."

"Of course," Aurora stiffly assured him. "I'm sure you've had reason."

"I have. In my business, a man and his family are the subject of close scrutiny and undesirable publicity even when there is no scandal. And as it is—" His voice broke off, and for a fleeting moment she could see past the guarded look in his eyes to the stark pain in his soul. But he recovered quickly and a veil of civility dropped over his dark eyes. "Of course I should have known that wasn't possible."

"What wasn't possible?" Aurora asked, confused.

"That you could be one of Katie's classmate's mothers. Now that I see you up close, you're far too young."

"You flatter me," Aurora stated evenly, uncomfortable with the direction their conversation had taken. Though she was nine years younger than Stacia had been, she was still old enough to have been Katie's mother. "If you'll excuse me," she said quickly, pushing aside the disturbing memories that train of thought aroused.

"Pardon me for letting you stand there like that," he said, offering a tray he'd been holding at his side for her to put the plates on. "I intercepted Bridey, who was bringing this to you." When Aurora had placed the plates on it and moved to take it from him, he said, "I'll carry it down," and waited for her to precede him.

Aurora was suddenly acutely conscious of her appearance. She hadn't taken time to even glance in the mirror since the funeral. Life-and-death struggles in crowded emergency rooms during her medical school and residency had taught her that there were many things vastly more important than the way she looked. Still, since going into private pediatric practice, she'd been relearning to take an interest in her wardrobe, her makeup and her hair. Her hair! Her hand reached up involuntarily to touch it. Ordinarily she was pleased that she'd been able to let it grow a little longer than shoulder length and that she'd been outdoors enough for its light brown color to become streaked with blond by the California sun. But at the moment she wished it was still in the ultrashort style she'd adopted while in med school. At least then it had stayed in place twenty-four hours a day!

As she reached the lower level, she wondered why she was letting Eric Thorpe affect her this way. Oh, he was charming, she had to give him that, but she sensed his charm was too polished. It seemed slightly calculated...as though he had something to hide.

"Has Katie mentioned me to you?" Aurora deliberately turned to face him as he descended, hoping to get some inkling of how he really felt about his child.

His smile faded. "Not until today, when we were on our way back here." He looked distressed. "I haven't had time...in too long...for a meaningful talk with my daughter."

"I hope that will change in the near future." Aurora turned to lead the way down the long hall, loathing the imperious statement as soon as it left her lips.

"So do I, Doctor," he answered, his tone matching hers. Was he mocking her? she wondered, glancing quickly to check. But his expression was again pleasant and bland, completely unreadable.

When they entered Katie's bedroom, he suddenly seemed ill at ease. After a moment's hesitation he walked over to the bed, set the tray down and lowered himself to sit beside his daughter. "How are you doing?"

Katie rolled her head to the side on the ruffled, eyelet pillow so that he couldn't look into her eyes. "Have you decided what you're going to do with me yet?" she asked. Despite her effort to keep her voice even, the terrible strain she was under was apparent in her tone.

"Katie, don't put it like that," he said miserably. "I've got to take into consideration what's best for you...."

"Have you talked with Dr. Duvall yet?" Turning toward him, her face was a stony white mask.

"Your father and I will talk later," Aurora interjected, hoping to forestall an argument. She smiled reassuringly. "Right now I want you to try to eat something."

Eric rose from the bed as if he didn't quite know what to do. Seeing his indecisiveness, Aurora said, "I know you have to go back up to your guests. We'll have time later. I'm spending the night."

When one well-defined eyebrow raised above his deep-set eyes, Aurora added somewhat lamely, "With Katie." To hide the deep flush she could feel rising beneath her tan, she busied herself rearranging the contents of the tray.

After Eric had excused himself and hastily left the room, Aurora returned to Katie's side.

"I hate him because he hates me," Katie said in a small, cold voice. "And I hate my mother, too," she added, trembling with anger. She flung herself over to the far side of the bed, picked up a silver-framed photograph from the bedside table and threw it against the far wall. The glass shattered and the frame fell to the floor.

When Katie's furious outburst was followed by dead silence Aurora decided to ignore it. "Your dad didn't look as if he hated you," she said quietly. And it was true, she realized. Eric Thorpe had behaved toward his daughter the way most men did who occupied themselves so thoroughly with their profession that they left the raising of their children to their wives—bewildered, but honestly solicitous.

"I don't care if he does hate me, he doesn't have to send me away. I just want to stay at school with my friends. I want to go to summer enrichment like I always do. I won't bother him."

At this, Aurora's heart broke. Kneeling beside the bed she coaxed the blue-eyed child in her arms. "Katie, dear, he loves you. Who could help but love a wonderful person like you? Right now your father is going through a terrible ordeal, just like you are, honey. Think about it. Are you acting like yourself?''

When Katie slowly shook her head, Aurora said gently, ''No one expects you to, and I'm sure your daddy isn't, either. I'll do everything in my power to keep you right here where you belong so you and your dad can work things out.''

''Oh, Dr. Duvall, I want him to love me,'' Katie sobbed, tears streaming down her cheeks. ''I just wish I could believe you.''

''You can, dear, you can,'' Aurora assured her over and over as they gently rocked back and forth together.

LATER THAT NIGHT Aurora waited to be sure Katie had fallen into an exhausted sleep before she picked up the framed photograph and carefully disposed of the broken glass. As she examined the unharmed picture, she suspected from the pose that it was an engagement photo of Katie's parents. A younger Eric and a woman, who could be none other than Stacia Thorpe, were captured in soft focus with her hand over his as they looked adoringly into each other's eyes. Aurora could see that Katie had inherited from Stacia her incredibly delicate coloring and startling blue eyes. There was not a trace of the brittle sharpness so apparent in Carla's features. Katie closely resembled the youthful Stacia's gentle beauty. Though she had taken her slight, willowy frame from her mother, it was also clear that Katie's height was from her father.

Aurora spent a long time staring at the photo. It seemed to hold such promise. What chain of events had caused the Thorpes' love to end in such stark tragedy? And what had gone so dreadfully wrong, she wondered, that it had robbed Katie of what should have been her birthright... having a mother to love and raise her?

Her heart was heavy as she placed the photograph face-down in the bottom of a drawer in the huge bathroom vanity for safekeeping. There was no use in speculating. Sighing, she went into the TV and game room that formed the rest of Katie's beautifully decorated suite to call her associate, Paula Sumner.

After explaining that she was at the Thorpe house, Aurora asked, "Have there been any emergencies?"

"Chris Peterson fell off his new bike and broke his arm," Paula said. "But don't worry, I called Lance Jorgensen in to set it. He says it's a simple fracture. Other than that and a couple of earaches, it's been quiet. How are things there?"

"Interesting," Aurora replied cautiously. "Had you heard any rumors about the Thorpes before Stacia's suicide?" Even as she asked, Aurora knew how futile her question was. Paula had been in Seahurst only a few months longer than she, and unmarried professional women, being somewhat isolated, were the last to get in on the gossip that swirled around them.

"Not really," Paula said after a pause. "I knew he was a famous screenwriter. Do you mean something more specific or personal?"

"Yes."

"Everything I've heard has been since then. Just the same speculation you've heard on why a wealthy pregnant woman who seemed to have the world by the tail would kill herself. What's Katie's dad like?" Paula asked.

"I don't know yet," Aurora admitted, unable to merge her varied impressions of the attractive man into an opinion. "He definitely is the type of man who's used to calling the shots, but on the other hand he doesn't seem to know how to handle his thirteen-year-old daughter. Something's really messed up in their relationship. And Brook's so emotionally involved in all this that he won't tell me anything.

But I can't help feeling there's a lot more going on here than meets the eye.''

The two talked a few minutes more, and Paula readily agreed to continue covering Aurora's calls for the rest of the night.

Though she looked longingly at the shower and the commodious robe Bridey had considerately supplied, Aurora knew she couldn't afford the psychological disadvantage of not being fully clothed when confronting Katie's imposing father. After settling for freshening up her makeup and running a comb through her hair, she went in search of Eric Thorpe.

The quiet drone of male voices drew her to the patio, lit by dozens of small lights artfully concealed in the lush landscaping.

"Are you expecting anyone else tonight?" she asked.

"I'll have Mac bar the door," Eric offered, his face in shadows.

"Not until I'm on the other side of it, if you don't mind," Brook said, stifling a yawn as he rose. "I've got to hit the road while my eyes are still open enough to see it."

"I'll walk you to the door," said Eric, rising. "If you'll excuse me for a moment, Dr. Duvall?"

"Certainly. Good night, Brook."

"Would you like me to come by for you in the morning?" Brook asked from the doorway.

She shook her head. "Thanks, but I'll just call a cab."

"Then good night."

Alone on the patio, Aurora took a few deep breaths of the glorious evening air. The distant muffled roar of surf pounding against the rocks at the bottom of the cliff added a dull pulsating rhythm to the star-studded night. She was tired, but she couldn't let herself relax just yet. Not until she was sure Katie was safe.

Eric returned. Not sure how to approach him, Aurora decided to let him set the tone for their discussion. They sat in silence for several minutes.

Finally he spoke. "I'm grateful to you, Dr. Duvall, for staying with Katie tonight. If she were still a little girl, I'd take her in my bed like I used to when she had bad dreams, but . . . she's gotten a little old for that."

"It's no problem. I'm glad to do it, and besides, I promised Katie that you and I would talk, and there's been no time before now." Feeling her confidence slip at the prospect of digging into Eric's private life, Aurora hesitated briefly. "She seems to think you're close to deciding to send her to Texas."

"I'm considering it," he admitted.

"Surely not too seriously," Aurora said with more emphasis than she'd intended.

"Why not?"

Don't you know how much she needs to believe that you love her? Aurora wanted to scream at him. But she kept her tone low and even, when she spoke. "If you want my professional opinion, it would be the worst mistake you could make. She's too old to be shipped off to her aunt's against her wishes."

"I'm only thinking about the summer right now," he explained. "Carla and Tom want her. They've never had children. I know it would take some adjusting on all their parts, but Carla wants the chance to become close to Katie. And it might work out fine. Katie'd have a horse of her own, something she's wanted for a long time. And there are other kids nearby for her to be with . . . shirttail cousins on Tom's side. By the time she came back, I might have some idea of what I'll be doing with my life."

"By that time you would also have put your entire future relationship with your daughter in jeopardy," Aurora said bluntly.

"Would it really make that much difference? I'm probably going to be selling this house—making a lot of important changes in my life, and possibly in Katie's. I can't see how involving her in all that uncertainty and upheaval would help her."

"But not involving her will alienate her. You can't sell her home out from under her and expect her to just accept your actions. Not unless she's part of the decision making. If you take this course, you'll be well on your way toward making her feel like a complete orphan!"

Eric got to his feet and walked to the railing. For a long moment he silently looked out over the moonlit sea. Aurora held her breath. Had she gone too far? she wondered, looking at his proud stance. If there was any chance of getting this man to let her really help Katie, she had to get close to him...to reach him. But if he asked her to leave now, she knew she'd have to do as he asked. She let out a silent sigh of relief when at last his shoulders drooped as he bowed his head and reached up to the railing as if for support. At least the decision she was almost certain he'd reached earlier wasn't yet absolutely firm.

"I don't know if I can cope with a teenage daughter right now," he said in a choked voice.

"You and Katie need each other," Aurora responded quietly, "more than you know." Aware of Eric's sudden vulnerability, her emotions did a flip-flop, and she just managed to stifle an impulse to comfort him. "Keeping her with you now is so important. Neither of you will have to bear your grief alone. You and she can share it, and it won't be as hard for either of you."

"We don't know how to talk to each other anymore," he confessed. He fell silent for a few moments as if lost in memories, then cleared his throat before continuing. "I don't know if we ever will again."

"It'll take time. And I'll help you, any way that I can. But right now Katie needs all the stability you can give her. She needs to feel wanted and loved...by you. She's a desperate little girl...far more frightened than she wants you to know. And she's angry about what's happened...furious. Sending her away, even for the summer, isn't the answer. You and she have to face this head-on. There'll be no true healing until you do."

Seeing the luster of tears on Eric's cheeks, Aurora realized he was on the verge of breaking down. "I can imagine how difficult this must be for you. But please believe me, it would be a mistake to make a hasty decision to send Katie away right now. You should sleep on it," she said softly, as she stood. "If you'd like, I could give you a sedative."

"No, thank you," he answered distantly. "I'm not ready to sleep just yet. But don't let me keep you up."

"I'll say good night then," she replied softly, rising to her feet.

"Good night," he answered, before turning to gaze again out over the silvered sea.

Chapter Three

Eric stayed on the patio long after Aurora Duvall had gone to bed, considering everything they'd said. Though he was certain the doctor was well-meaning and that her concern for his daughter's welfare was genuine, he knew she couldn't begin to understand how little time he would have for Katie in the coming months. His life was a tangle of unresolved questions that loomed large in his bone-weary state. He felt a nearly relentless pull toward oblivion, escape. Was this depression? he wondered in alarm.

He wasn't emotionally ill, he assured himself, only heartsick, and surely that was to be expected. He could fight this dull, heavy lethargy with hard work as he'd done in the past. Even his not being able to write wasn't a problem for the time being. He had too many other things to do to consider sitting down in front of his computer screen, even if the ideas that had always flowed faster than he could get them down weren't blocked behind the invisible barrier that he now feared was permanently in place in his mind.

Besides taking on the monumental task of breaking up the household, he would have to find a suitable situation for Bridey and Mac. The sprightly pair didn't look it, nor wish to be reminded of it, but they were both approaching retirement age. The catch was that it would still be a few years before they'd be old enough to draw Social Security. He knew that, even though they'd been the first to urge him to make a move, they had believed this would be their last position. They had to be worried about their future. And they were much more than employees to him. He had a responsibility to them he couldn't shirk.

Then there was the matter of that damn play he'd agreed to put on as a benefit for Seahurst Academy. When he'd agreed to produce and direct *Marcie, I Love You*, he'd thought it might amuse Stacia to see a production of the story he'd written as a tribute to their first wonderful years together. He'd even hoped that she might be drawn into helping with the props or costumes. He'd deluded himself. And now that she was gone…he wasn't sure he could carry through with the plan. Brook had said he'd understand if he decided to bag it, but Eric knew it wasn't as simple as that. Katie's school had already budgeted the projected funds the theater-in-the-round production would generate into its next year's operating expenses.

Running his fingers through his thick, short hair, he walked down the terraced steps to the lawn. Striding briskly across the damp grass, he reached the edge, where the cliff dropped off steeply to the sea. Warm air from the land, rushing toward the coolness of the water caused an updraft that whipped the ends of his dark silk tie. Breathing in deep gulps of the faintly salt-tanged air, he suddenly felt stifled by the constraint of his tie and stiff collar. Reaching up, he roughly loosened the knot that seemed now to be nearly choking him. After yanking the tie from his neck, he flung it into the air where it rose and fluttered, twisting like a black snake, before it slithered down toward the sea.

Tomorrow, when the sun came up, would be a perfect day to hang glide, he thought with a sigh that caught in his tense throat and came out as a sob.

In that moment, with a vision playing in his mind of Stacia's body soaring free as a white-winged gull above the deep sea she loved so much, he suddenly understood. He'd been tormented, speculating on the reason she'd chosen to jump to her death. He'd feared that in a lucid moment she'd chosen that method of ending her life as self-punishment. But now he was certain that in a flight of mania Stacia had believed she could fly away, far away from all the ills of the world.

Letting tears run freely down his cheeks, he allowed himself to remember the long ago days when Stacia had been his happiness, his inspiration, and he allowed himself to grieve for the love that had long since become only a memory. A healing sense of bittersweet relief began to mingle with his pain. *Thank you for leaving a part of yourself behind in Katie. Whatever it takes I...I won't lose her, too,* he vowed to his lost love.

IT WAS EIGHT-THIRTY when Aurora managed to open her eyes. It had been after two before she'd been able to get any rest on Katie's chaise lounge. And even then, she'd only slept sporadically until the early morning light had streamed through the windows, chasing away the shadows and giving her enough peace of mind to fall into a deeper sleep.

Glancing at the still-sleeping child, Aurora groggily made her way to the shower. The cold water streaming down her body effectively awakened her, bringing back to focus the reason she'd spent the night in the Thorpe house.

Toweling herself off, she wondered what her next step should be. Until she learned Eric Thorpe's decision, she had no answers for Katie. Quickly slipping on the bra and pantyhose she'd washed the night before, she tiptoed back into the bedroom.

As Aurora was pulling the black dress she'd worn to the funeral over her head, Katie sat up in bed. "Dr. Duvall? Where are you going?"

"Nowhere yet," Aurora assured her, smoothing the sheath down over her hips. "How are you feeling?"

"Okay, I guess," the girl said gloomily. "Is Aunt Carla here?"

"I don't know."

"Do I have to go to Texas?"

"I don't know that yet, either," Aurora admitted in a worried tone. It wasn't natural for a child to have to be so concerned about her future at a time when she should be free to focus totally on her loss. Anger at Eric Thorpe rose within her. He'd had no right to add this extra burden that was interfering with the normal progress of Katie's grief. "Why don't you shower and dress, and we'll go up together to see what we can find out."

"Did you talk to my father?" Katie persisted hoarsely.

"Yes, dear, I did," Aurora assured her softly, remembering with a pang the tear-streaked face of the man she'd confronted the night before. "And I'm sure he's trying to do what he feels is best for you," she added, reaching out to caress the child's smooth cheek.

Katie shot Aurora an anxious glance before heading for the bathroom, adding, "I don't think he knows what that is."

"Out of the mouths of babes..." Aurora murmured under her breath.

While waiting for Katie, Aurora called Paula.

"Everything's fine," Paula assured her. "I even got to sleep for six whole hours! Your patients all behaved their little selves, and mine were totally cooperative, too. No colic and not a labor pain on the scene! How are things with you?"

"I'm in a bind," Aurora admitted. "I have to check on my two hospital patients before I go home, but I can't leave Katie here alone. I'm really worried about her. She just isn't dealing with her mother's death."

"I'm going over to your place in a little while to run my dogs on the beach. Bring her down and I can watch her for you. But where's her father?"

Hearing the shower stop, Aurora lowered her voice. "I'm sure he's here. But... well, there are problems I can't discuss right now. I'll get home as soon as I can."

Aurora made Katie's bed and folded up the light comforter she'd used as a cover. She could hear the girl moving around in the huge walk-in closet that opened off the bathroom. Katie soon appeared in a pair of white shorts and a bright pink tanktop, scuffing her feet into a pair of leather thongs. She slipped past Aurora shouting, "I just can't wait any longer to find out what's going to happen to me!"

Aurora grabbed up her purse and black bag before following Katie down the hall.

"Daddy, Daddy," Katie shouted, pounding on the door closest to the stairwell. Getting no answer, she bounded up the staircase, taking the steps two at a time, still calling for her father.

By the time Aurora reached the top of the stairs, she heard Eric Thorpe's voice coming from the direction of the patio. "I'm here, Katie."

At first Aurora feared that he'd spent the night on the patio. But as he hurried across the crowded living room, she could see he was dressed in shorts and a sport shirt, and his strong-boned cheeks were clean shaven. Hopefully he'd had at least a little rest during the night and had awakened with a clear head that would allow him to make the right decision.

Father and daughter met at the edge of the wide front hall where Aurora stood.

"Where's Aunt Carla?" Katie demanded.

He glanced at his watch. "Probably somewhere over Arizona . . . on her way to Texas," he answered, opening his arms to Katie, meeting Aurora's approving gaze over his daughter's head.

So, she thought with relief, he'd changed his mind.

"How do you know?" Katie asked, holding back, her tone openly skeptical.

"I called her at the hotel early this morning . . ."

"What did you say?" Katie interrupted.

"I told her that maybe we would both come for a visit later this summer."

"She's really gone? And I'm staying here . . . with you?" Sliding her arms around her father's trim waist, she warily searched his face.

"Cross my heart, till death do us part," Eric Thorpe quipped. A horrified expression distorted his features as he suddenly realized the inappropriateness of the lighthearted vow he and his daughter had always carelessly bantered between them.

"That's not funny anymore, is it?" the young girl said, burying her face in his chest and tightening her arms around him.

"Sorry, sweetie," he murmured, resting his cheek on her dark brown hair. "A lot of things aren't funny anymore. We probably have some rocky times ahead of us, but we're just going to have to help each other through them.

"Meanwhile, how would you two like to go out for breakfast?" he asked. "I gave Bridey and Mac the day off. They need some rest after all they've done the last couple of days."

"Thank you," Aurora answered, suddenly wishing she didn't have to leave the two of them alone, "but I have to go to the hospital to make my morning rounds. I'll just call a taxi."

"No, don't do that," Katie objected, a determined spark in her blue eyes. "Please have breakfast with us. We can take you to the hospital first, can't we, Daddy?"

"Certainly. I was going to suggest the same thing." Smiling, Eric put his hand in his shorts pocket and brought out a leather key case.

Looking closely at him, Aurora could see dark circles beneath his deep-set eyes, but the haunted, almost lost look they had held the night before was gone. She warmed to him, thinking he'd given far more thought to what was in his daughter's best interests than she'd feared he would. And both of them seemed relieved at the thought she'd be with them.

"Well," she said, "I don't want to trouble you..."

"It's no trouble," Eric put in quickly. There was an urgency in his voice that he didn't try to hide. "Katie and I can wait until you're through, and then we can all enjoy a leisurely breakfast together."

"I really won't be long," Aurora conceded with a smile. "I only have a couple of little guys on the ward. One's recuperating from an appendectomy, and the other one is going to be just fine, but he'll probably think a long time before he tries to use his big brother's skateboard again."

When Eric let out a chuckle, Katie offered, "Dr. Duvall knows what to do about everything, Daddy. You should see the kinds of problems she takes care of in our infirmary, and we're all girls!"

"You girls are so active, I don't think two hundred boys could give me any more trouble." Aurora grinned, starting toward the door with the two Thorpes in tow. "While you're waiting for me you can get a cup of coffee or some juice at the cafeteria. There's a nice outside deck area where you can sit. After I'm finished, we can go to my place and I'll cook breakfast."

KATIE QUICKLY HOPPED into the back seat of the convertible in the circular drive, insisting that Dr. Duvall sit in the front, next to her dad. She knew it was stupid, but she'd like anyone who saw them to think that the three of them were a normal family, going out to Sunday brunch…like it wasn't any big deal. She couldn't remember having a real family meal with her parents when everything hadn't been spoiled before it was over. It had been a long time since they'd even tried. But with Dr. Duvall she knew it would be different.

Her dad and Dr. Duvall made a great-looking couple, she thought with approval. She knew her dad was handsome, even the older girls at school said so whenever he came to pick her up. She supposed he was, for being forty and all. And Dr. Duvall was beautiful. If only she wasn't wearing that awful black dress she'd worn for the funeral. Katie planned to burn the white dress Aunt Carla had made her wear yesterday, as soon as she could sneak it down to the incinerator without Mac catching her. She didn't want anything around to remind her of what her crazy mother had done.

"Dr. Duvall…" Katie's father's voice broke into her thoughts.

"Please, call me Aurora," the doctor interjected as she put on a pair of oversize sunglasses that Katie thought made her look just like a model.

"Can I call you that, too?" Katie asked, leaning up to rest her chin on the passenger headrest, enjoying the feel of the doctor's soft sun-streaked hair blowing against her cheeks. "It's so hard saying Dr. Duvall all the time. Besides," she added, suddenly feeling a little shy, "you're kinda like getting to be my best friend."

"Of course, you may," Aurora answered warmly, turning to give her a terrific smile.

"Then I expect you to call me Eric," her father said to Aurora.

Here was her chance. Her roommate, Jenni, called her parents by their first names. Just maybe he'd go for it. "Oh, can I call you—"

"Definitely not, young lady," he interjected with a chuckle.

What was so funny about that? she'd like to know, slumping back into her seat. It was what she should have expected from her dad, though. He still thought she was a little kid.

"I'm still Daddy to you . . . unless, of course, you'd like to call me Fah-ther."

"Really, Daddy," Katie said indignantly, her cheeks flaming. Didn't he have any idea how embarrassing he could be? And didn't he have any idea how much easier it would be for both of them if he quit pretending that he liked being her father, and let her call him Eric?

She knew he wasn't keeping her here because he wanted to. If it had been up to him, she'd be on her way to Texas. But Dr. Duvall had probably convinced him that it wouldn't look good for him to send his daughter away right now. More than once during the last year she'd overheard him say something to Bridey or Uncle Brook about "keeping up appearances." That was all he ever did.

She didn't even know what he was really like anymore. Maybe she never had. Maybe all those times he'd played games with her and told her stories, before he'd sent her away to school, he'd just been "keeping up appearances,"

too. How would she know? He never told her anything . . . except lies.

And, she thought, fighting down tears that stung behind
her eyelids, she wasn't sure she cared anymore. If she was
really lucky, and she tried hard enough, she might convince
Dr. Duvall to adopt her. Then he wouldn't ever have to
worry about her again.

"You were going to say something to me, Eric?" Aurora
asked.

"Yes," he said, glancing significantly over his shoulder
at Katie, "but it can wait until later."

It figured. He'd wait until she wasn't around to talk about
anything really important. Well, he could take his stupid lies
and secrets, and stuff them! But he wasn't going to take Dr.
Duvall away from her!

PAULA'S STATION WAGON was parked behind Aurora's beach
house when they pulled into the gravel driveway after a
quick stop at the hospital. Hearing the barking of the rottweilers at play, she knew Paula was waiting for her and Katie.

Aurora urged Katie and Eric around to join Paula on the
beach side of the house and went inside to put on a rasher
of bacon to fry while she changed into linen shorts and a
soft, peach-colored shirt.

She hurriedly set the table in front of a side window,
mixed up the orange juice and took some Danish rolls from
her freezer. When the bacon was crisp she drained it and
went to the deck to ask Eric and Katie how they wanted their
eggs.

Katie came running over. "I'm not hungry. That milk-
shake I drank while we were waiting for you filled me up.
Dr. Sumner says it's all right with her if I come along to run

the dogs. She says we'll be back in about an hour. Can I go?''

"It's up to your dad," Aurora replied with a smile.

"It's fine with me," Eric Thorpe said, joining Aurora on the porch. "I'm sure Katie will enjoy the exercise."

His gaze followed the willowy child as she kicked off her shoes and ran toward the impatiently waiting dogs. Then abruptly he turned and Aurora felt the full force of his piercing gaze upon her face. For a long moment she stood, pinned by his searching scrutiny.

As though satisfied by what he saw, a slow smile lifted the corners of his mouth, releasing her from her near trance.

A chill ran down her spine as the rational implications of what she'd done by impulsively thrusting herself into Katie's and Eric's lives gripped her. How could she have been so hasty?

She'd sealed herself off from family commitments for years…ever since she was eighteen. She'd never planned to raise a child . . . had never felt she had the right to.

Now Eric Thorpe was opening her screen door for her saying, "I need to talk to you about Katie."

Aurora hesitated. For a fleeting moment she considered bolting down the beach toward the distant figures on the strand. But she couldn't do it. Still, somehow she felt certain that by going through that door with Eric Thorpe, she was altering the entire direction of her own life.

Chapter Four

"Are scrambled eggs okay?" Aurora asked, recovering her composure.

"My favorite kind," Eric answered. "I'm really hungry...for the first time in several days."

"Then you can eat yours and Katie's shares." She stepped behind the cooking island separating the kitchen from the rest of the large room. "This will only take a minute. If you'd like, go ahead and sit down at the table," she said, pouring the mixture into the heated frying pan.

But he waited, tall and impressively handsome, taking in the room, his gaze resting here or there on some "treasure" she'd unearthed in her rummaging through secondhand stores. Seeing her furnishings through his cosmopolitan eyes, she realized that her home was filled with objects that previous owners had discarded. The entire lot wouldn't bring as much at an auction as any one of several good pieces she'd seen in his living room.

She watched, spatula poised above the skillet, as he walked over to an overstuffed chair and fingered the crocheted doily spread over the back cushion.

"My mother used to make these," he said pensively. "We had them all over the house. I'd forgotten how pretty they were."

"Are you a native Californian?" she asked, frantically stirring the neglected eggs.

"No, a transplanted one, like most of us seem to be. My father was a history professor at Indiana University, in Bloomington. He was a crusty old bachelor, almost fifty, when he married my mother who was a campus librarian. She was past forty, and I think my coming along was a surprise that they never really quite got used to. They were very relieved when they could ship me off to college," he said with an amused smile, "and they could retire to Mexico."

Fortunately the eggs were ready, and she busied herself serving the warmed plates. Although she was interested in hearing more of his background, she didn't want to ask questions and risk having him ask about her past.

She carried the plates to the gate-legged table that she'd lovingly refinished, and he pulled out a high-back, caned chair for her. It was another product of her restoration skills. After seating himself, he poured orange juice for them both into striped glasses that matched the plates.

"My Lord," he exclaimed, "Fiestaware. I haven't seen this for years. My grandmother gave my mother a set when she married. We always used it. I remember I fed my dog off a saucer once. I'll tell you I never heard the end of it."

"I can relate to that," Aurora said with a laugh. "It's taken me a long time to collect my set, and I don't think I'd like to see a piece of it on the floor, either."

During the meal she relaxed, watching Eric. As they talked, some of the lines of anxiety that had seemed permanently etched on his face faded, making him appear younger and more carefree than she'd ever seen him. He seemed caught up in fond memories. She was glad she'd invited him here if it reminded him of a happier time. Sipping her juice, she watched him eat. He was hungry.

"But you're not eating," he remarked, after he'd poured them each a mug of coffee from the insulated carafe she'd set at his elbow.

"I don't usually eat much in the morning." She hedged to cover the fact that her normally healthy appetite had deserted her in his presence. Her stomach was in as much turmoil as her brain. He hadn't yet mentioned anything about Katie, and for a moment she found herself wishing he were here under different circumstances. He had to be a fascinating, witty man to have written the screenplays that had earned him his reputation as a trendsetting playwright. He was the sort of man she'd never dreamed of having touch her world, other than peripherally. Yet here he was, sitting in her home only hours after their first meeting.

He was an alluring man, made all the more so by the air of secrecy that seemed to surround him, sensual and exciting even in the morning light. Yet his appearance did not fit the madcap brand of humor that was his trademark. If she'd had to guess, she would have picked deep, compelling drama as being his forte. Had he stayed exclusively with comedy as an escape from the realities of his own existence? His wife's suicide hadn't come out of the blue, she was sure of it. He was hiding something...she suspected he'd been doing it for a very long time.

"Breakfast was delicious, thank you," he said a few minutes later with a disarming smile. "I feel very comfortable here. Would you like help with the dishes?"

"Let's just leave them." Aurora rose, forcing a smile to cover her nervousness. "Shall we take our coffee outside? I look forward all week to relaxing on the deck on Sundays."

Following with the coffeepot in hand, Eric joined her, stretching out his length on the chaise lounge next to hers.

Willing herself to not be distracted by the sight of his lean, muscular torso and long, muscled legs, she commented,

"Paula has as much energy as her dogs. It will probably be an hour or more before she and Katie start back this way." Hopefully he would take this as a cue to begin revealing whatever was on his mind.

Instead he asked, "More coffee?"

"About a half a cup," she replied, holding out her mug. After he'd refilled his own, too, he settled back, staring out over the water. She followed his aimless gaze. The June day was cloudlessly perfect, and heat was already starting to shimmer up from the beach. The only sounds were the gentle splash of waves and the cries of the circling gulls.

"Do you own this place?" Eric asked.

"No," Aurora replied ruefully. "I wish I did. It's ideal for me, but the owner intends to retire here himself in a few years. In the meantime, I plan to enjoy it. This will be my first summer here."

"So you haven't been in Seahurst long."

"No, I came a few weeks before the second semester started at the academy. Paula told me that Dr. Noble wanted to retire, so I bought his practice. He suggested that I might want to take over at Seahurst, too, and I have to admit that I'm enjoying it."

"Brook told me yesterday that he'd asked you to take Katie under your wing. Thank you, for everything you've done for her."

"I haven't done anything," Aurora protested. "Katie was one of my infirmary assistants. I ate lunch with her as often as I could in addition to letting her help me whenever I was there. We talked, that's all."

"She seems very close to you." Eric's voice took on a wistful note.

"I'm very fond of her," Aurora admitted, "but..."

When she didn't continue he abruptly turned to look at her. "But what?" he demanded.

Putting her now empty mug down on the table between them and looking him straight in the eyes, she said, "I'm pretty darn frustrated. I want to help you with Katie, but I feel something more than her mother's death is bothering her. And since I can only guess what that might be, I'm really handicapped. In light of what's happened, I wish when Brook asked me to befriend Katie he'd told me more about her."

"You mean, more about her parents," Eric said flatly, meeting her steady gaze.

"I suppose that's what I do mean." Aurora lifted her chin a little. "I didn't even know that you lived in Seahurst. When I discovered she was your daughter, I assumed you and your wife lived nearer Hollywood, since the local girls are mostly day students. And the funny thing is, Katie never told me."

"Maybe it bothered her for people at school to know," Eric said. The haunted expression returned to his deep-set eyes.

"To know what?" she almost whispered.

"That her mother was . . . ill." He looked away.

"Katie hasn't talked about her mother at all," Aurora said tentatively, afraid of pushing too hard. "Before . . . or since, except to say that her mother was—" Again Aurora stopped. She couldn't say the word *crazy* to the troubled man.

Propping his elbow on the arm of his chair, he rested his chin on his fist. "I know," he said, nodding his head, "crazy."

"I'm sorry," she apologized. "I didn't mean to . . ."

"It's all right," he said wearily, shutting his eyes. "Katie has screamed it many times, after witnessing one of her mother's irrational acts. She's just not mature enough to be able to distinguish between an ill person and an insane one."

There was a sudden haggardness to his chiseled good looks. "Someday I hope she'll understand."

Aurora straightened to a sitting position. Had anyone tried to explain the difference to the girl? she wondered. It almost seemed as though Eric was protecting his wife from attack by their child... almost as if he blamed Katie for something. Katie was right about one thing; her father did think she was still a child. But Aurora was not a child. If Eric Thorpe wasn't going to level with her about the nature of Stacia's illness, they were wasting each other's time.

"I'm sure Katie can understand more than you think," she began. "But in any case I'm not Katie. I'm a physician and I'm trained to diagnose patients. I know that most female suicides don't choose a violent means of destroying themselves. Only an extremely disturbed woman would throw herself from a bridge." She waited breathlessly, wondering what effect her blunt statement would have.

Eric raised a knuckle to his mouth, absently biting at it. "Stacia was an extremely disturbed person," he said hollowly. After a long pause, during which he swallowed several times as though fighting back tears, he added, "And a very wonderful person, too."

"Why don't you tell me about her," Aurora prompted quietly, turning and tucking her feet under her.

Letting out a ragged sigh, he began, "It's hard, you know, to let go of thirteen years of pretense and lies. Except for the professionals I consulted and, of course, Bridey and Mac, in all that time I haven't talked about her with anyone except Brook." He looked at Aurora for a moment, as though to see how this disclosure would affect her, but she kept her face a serene mask of encouragement.

"When Stacia and I were married everyone thought we were the perfect couple. I suppose we were. We were madly in love and had so many things in common . . . our careers, our favorite sports, our tastes.

"When we moved out here, Stacia designed and supervised every detail in the construction of our home. And after it was finished she entertained constantly. She was a fabulous hostess. Friends from Hollywood would fly up just for the evening. She was so full of vitality and life. Everyone loved her." He shifted his gaze from her face.

"But something went wrong, didn't it?" she suggested in a husky whisper.

He nodded. "After Katie was born, Stacia went into severe postpartum depression. The doctors said to give her time, but as the weeks passed she just seemed to sink deeper. She wasn't even interested in the baby."

Shocked at his words, Aurora hugged her arms across her breasts. As a physician she knew some unfortunate women had that response to giving birth, but to associate that sad beginning to life with Katie was almost more than she could stand.

Her voice shook as she asked, "What happened to Katie during that time?"

"I adored her from the moment she was born," he said simply. "I took care of her most of the time, myself. Stacia was filled with so much anger that she could hardly stand the sight of either of us."

The haunting bleakness in his eyes suddenly seemed to pierce her very soul, drawing her into the magnitude of his loss. He'd had it all: early professional success, a beautiful, talented wife, a love-filled marriage, and an adorable child. But now she knew that everything that should have embodied his happiness had turned to ashes. She had experienced similar devastation. Her relationship with her parents had been shattered and she'd lost the only child she'd ever have. It had taken a long time to rebuild her life on new premises.

Empathy for the proud but hurt man flooded over her. Blinking away sudden tears, she sat quietly as he was lost in a contemplative moment. A surge of tenderness flowed through her and she had to fight down the impulse to take his hand. Finally she asked, "What did you do?"

"I didn't know what to do. After a few months, when Stacia didn't snap out of it, her doctor suggested a complete change of scenery. I'd had a part-time nurse to help me with Katie right from the start, and she agreed to stay on full-time. I hated to leave the baby, but Stacia'd always said she wanted to go to Australia. So I booked a cruise for the two of us."

"Did that help?"

"At first it seemed to. Stacia acted like her old self again. She enjoyed the islands we visited, and I began to hope that everything would be all right." His eyes clouded in pain, and his deep voice dropped even lower. "But the good times began to alternate with bad, so bad that when we got to Sydney there was nothing left for me to do but to get her on the next plane home. I took her from the airport to a special clinic for evaluation." He stopped. A muscle worked in the side of his jaw.

After waiting for him to go on until she was afraid that he might not, Aurora prompted, "The diagnosis?"

As if coming out of a deep reverie, Eric repeated her words, "The diagnosis? Manic-depressive." His voice was lifeless.

"But, Eric, with medication the disease can be regulated," she said, her body stiff with tension.

"To a certain degree, I suppose, and in some cases better than others. Things went along pretty well for the next several years. The medication seemed to help... as long as Stacia took it. But either the drug or the knowledge of her disease did something to her spirit. When she was feeling well, she'd refuse to take it. Then she'd have a relapse.''

"That's a typical pattern with many manic-depressives," Aurora interjected, knowing how many times he must have heard that from the medical establishment and also knowing how little comfort she offered with the cold statement of fact.

"There were times when Stacia'd first go off her medication," Eric continued as if he hadn't heard her, "that she'd act so well and high-spirited it was hard to believe anything was wrong with her. But her highs would spiral up until she'd lose control, then she'd crash down into depression."

"That's why you put Katie in Seahurst the first year they'd take her as a boarder," Aurora said. It wasn't a question.

Eric nodded. "She was getting old enough to realize that something was wrong. I thought if I could limit the amount of time she was home, I could keep her from knowing the truth." He looked at Aurora for understanding, his face twisted with anguish. "But it didn't work out that way.

"Many times I'd have to call and cancel out on a weekend visit or have Mac take Katie back to school early because Stacia would be hit with a wild mood swing. She could be just fine and the next thing you'd know, she'd be talking a mile a minute, making all sorts of impossible plans, gesturing wildly or holding Katie to her in a viselike grip, telling her all the wonderful things they were going to do together. And the next, she'd be weeping uncontrollably, pushing Katie away, saying she wanted her out of her sight."

"I'm so sorry," Aurora put in, thinking how terrible it must have been for all of them.

He drew a ragged breath. "It was more than I could handle... I'll admit it. Since I felt I couldn't explain to Katie what was wrong, without confirming her suspicions that her mother really was crazy, I know she blamed me. I'm not proud of it, but not only did I hold back the truth, but I started to deliberately try to deceive her. I knew I had to give her some explanation, so I got to the point where I began implying that her mother was an alcoholic.''

Aurora let out a small gasp. How terribly lonely and afraid he must have been all those years, trying to come up with solutions to such overwhelming problems. Small wonder he'd considered sending Katie away for what he hoped would be a fresh start. Their lives had become so hopelessly muddled that she was sure he no longer felt the past could have any resolution.

''And that's when our relationship, that I'd worked so hard on all the years Katie was little, began to fall apart. She thought that I should get her mother treatment, but what she couldn't know was that I'd taken Stacia everywhere and that I'd gotten her every sort of treatment available. I know now that Katie felt terribly rejected and left out of our lives, but that was the last thing I'd intended. Looking back, I can't defend my decisions, but at the time I didn't know what else to do. I wanted to be there for Katie, but I felt my first obligation was to try to get her mother healthy and stabilized in the hope that everything else would fall into place.''

With a relentless ache of regret, Aurora realized Katie had been dealing with a deep sorrow all the time that they'd lightheartedly chatted together. If she, herself, felt such pain knowing how she had failed the young girl, what must Eric be feeling? She wanted to offer him a consoling hug, as she often did for parents during the dark hours of a child's illness while they waited for the time of crisis, but something in her unfolding relationship with Eric Thorpe held her back. Oddly, in less than twenty-four hours this man had affected her life more profoundly than anyone had since her childhood. The simple gesture of holding him close would take on a significance for her that she wasn't sure she was ready to accept.

"It was my fault, you know," he said, his face ashen beneath his tan.

"What was?" she asked softly.

"I wanted children. If Stacia hadn't become pregnant, she would never have gotten sick."

"You can't know that," Aurora protested, wondering why in the world he'd let his wife get pregnant again if he felt this way. Had someone, among all the experts he'd consulted, said something that he'd misinterpreted to mean that another pregnancy might reverse the progress of Stacia's disease? It was always possible. "Her pregnancy was just the trigger," she explained gently. "Stacia's tendency toward manic-depression had to already be there. Something else could have set it off at any time."

"You don't know that," he countered with a grim set of his jaw.

"Not for certain," she admitted, "but there's a good chance." She let out a ragged sigh. "So, you blame yourself..." Gathering up her courage she whispered a question that she wasn't sure she wanted to hear the answer to, but it was one she knew had to be asked. "How about Katie? Do you blame her, too?"

He leaned forward, resting his chin on his chest, letting out an explosive sigh. "You have to know I've asked myself that question many, many times. And I can tell you," he lifted his head and turned toward her with a look in his eyes that left absolutely no doubt as to his sincerity, "I don't. I never have. Katie was as much a victim of all this as her mother was.

"I don't know if you can understand what I'm going to say... and I'm not even sure it makes sense. But for me, in the hundreds of sleepless hours I've spent over the years, the question has been what I would have done if I'd had the choice. It may sound illogical to you, because it's all been after the fact, but for me it has been very real... very painful. You see, it comes down to this—had I been able to see the future, would I have chosen for Stacia to be well and for there to have been no Katie? Or for there to have been Katie, and for Stacia's life to have been destroyed?"

Suddenly, his pain became hers. How many wakeful hours had she spent agonizing over a similar question? She could understand his despair only too well. Rising to her feet, her tears flowing freely, Aurora sat on the arm of his chair and cradled his head to her breast, stroking his hair. He reached up to take her hand from his shoulder and tuck it under his chin. "Oh, Eric. I wish there was something I could do or say. It's natural for you to be troubled by that question. I don't have the answer for you. No one does. All I know is that you have to try to believe that things turn out the way they were meant to be, no matter how difficult that is to accept. But sometimes I wish we could know the reason why.

"It might help to remember that Stacia nurtured that little girl for nine months... and gave birth to her. I just can't help but believe that if she were alive and rational, she'd tell you to focus on Katie. She'd want you to be the best father you could be."

Eric let go of her hand and she straightened, taking her arm away from his shoulder and putting her hands in her lap, as he wiped the tears from his face.

"You're right. I know you are. Stacia was a very loving person. Last night, after you went in, I gave a lot of thought to her suicide. I've come to terms with it," he revealed hoarsely, "but to tell you the truth, I think I did my true grieving for her long ago, when I was forced to accept the fact that I'd lost her to an illness that both of us were powerless to control. After that, as hard as I tried to deny it even to myself, I became a caretaker to a stranger."

He lifted his head to meet her eyes. "What I feel most strongly now is relief. And maybe it's terrible, but I don't feel guilty about it."

"You shouldn't. You have a right to your feelings."

"I've decided that Katie and I deserve a second chance for happiness. I'm counting on your help in putting the past behind us and learning to get on with our lives."

"You've got it. But I can't promise it'll be easy," Aurora said tenderly, slowly shaking her head, thinking of the stony faces of the father and daughter as they'd stood separately at the grave site. "You and Katie have a lot to work out between you.

"Her actions make so much more sense to me now. I'm afraid the years of Stacia's illness have left the two of you with an estranging legacy of confusion, anger and resentment. You may have come to terms with Stacia's loss, but Katie hasn't. And neither one of you seems to have the slightest idea what the other thinks or feels. Katie's sure she's lost you, too."

He shook his head and let out a deep, puzzled sigh. "I just can't believe she really feels that way."

"Well, she does," Aurora affirmed. "But you've got the strength to deal with it. It took a great deal of courage... and love... for you to decide to keep her here. Kids Katie's age are difficult at best. But we'll work through it together."

"If you can help us," he said, his dark gaze searching hers, "I'll be acquiring a debt I can never repay."

"No," Aurora said, remembering her own old wounds and wiping the remnants of tears from her cheeks, "you'll owe me nothing. By allowing me to help Katie and you, you'll be letting me repay part of a debt I've owed for a long time."

She stood and pulled him to his feet. "Let's go for a walk," she suggested.

Bonded by their common hope they walked together, two humans comforting each other against the backdrop of the timeless sea.

Chapter Five

Dangling their shoes from their fingertips, Aurora and Eric walked on the warm sand until they met up with Katie and Paula who were returning to the beach house. The rottweilers, Gretchen and Gretel, greeted them first, circling around them, making false rushes at their feet before dashing off. Though amused by their antics, Eric's attention was caught by the flushed glow on Katie's happy face. Maybe everything could work out, he thought, allowing himself the joy of hope. Since confiding in Aurora he felt that the weight of the world had been lifted from his shoulders.

"Race you back," he impulsively challenged his daughter.

Katie paused for an instant, checking his expression to see if he was serious, before she took off with her hair streaming behind her. Flashing Aurora a quick smile, he started out. Running behind Katie, with fatherly pride he watched her legs extend, gracefully driving her across the loose sand. He felt an overpowering sense of protectiveness for the child he'd neglected far too long.

He wanted to scoop his little girl up in his arms and hug her close. To tell her how much he loved and cherished her. To beg her forgiveness for all the lies he'd told her and all the times he'd disappointed her. But more than that, to tell her that from now on he would always be there for her.

But Aurora had cautioned him to take it easy, he reminded himself, as he regulated his breathing to match his steady pace. It would be a mistake to overwhelm the child with lavish attention motivated by his guilt-ridden conscience. She didn't know where he stood. Only the day before he'd misguidedly planned to send her away, and she knew it. She wasn't going to forget or forgive that final blunder for a while. If only Brook had introduced him to Aurora when he'd first asked her to watch over Katie, he might have turned to her for advice earlier.

Eric snorted, mentally pulling himself up short in self-derision. Who was he kidding? As long as Stacia was alive he would never have opened up to an outsider about her condition or have confided his feelings about it. And, he realized now, that had been his greatest mistake.

He should have listened to the host of doctors who had subtly suggested that he seek counseling for himself and Katie. But he'd refused to even consider it. He'd thought Katie was too young to understand, and he hadn't wanted to do anything that might endanger the illusion he'd tried to create for her. Besides, counseling had been for some other guy, some weakling. He'd been a proud, egotistical fool, who'd convinced himself that he could make it on his own. Well, he'd made it all right, he'd made a botch of it, and unfortunately Katie was paying the price.

He had to face facts. It wasn't going to be easy to regain the innocent trust she'd once given him without reservation. Katie was wary now, and, he conceded, she had every right to be. She was like a wounded little animal, who would have to learn to trust again. It wouldn't happen overnight. In fact, he sighed, as doubt began to darken his hopes, was it realistic to believe that she'd ever trust him again after all the damage he'd unwittingly caused in her young life?

Catching up with her in a few long strides, he ran by her side until they reached Aurora's porch. Panting, they dropped down together on the sun-heated sand.

"You're very precious, you know," he said softly, reaching out to smooth back her thick hair.

She shot him a look of surprise before the dogs were on them, rolling Katie over and pouncing playfully on his back.

"Gretch! Gret! Heel!" Paula called as she and Aurora jogged toward them. Immediately the large animals galloped off to obey. Standing, he gave Katie a hand up, then looked to Aurora for approval.

Watching the long-legged woman lightly running toward him, he felt a constriction in his chest. Aurora Duvall was beautiful, much more so than he'd realized. Far from being painstakingly dressed and made up, she hadn't taken time to do anything other than to slip on fresh clothes before preparing breakfast. Yet her well-proportioned figure, with its high firm breasts and slender waist leading down to narrow but curvaceous hips that moved fluidly above her shapely legs, was as effortlessly lovely as any female form he'd ever seen captured on film.

As they'd talked, he'd been captivated by her kindness and her intelligence, and had come to appreciate her inner beauty. But all the while, even as she'd held him to her breast, he'd been oblivious to her alluring femininity. How had its impact escaped him until now? Had he been so wrapped up in himself and his problems that his senses had been dulled? His mind quickly answered that question. It had been a long time since he'd allowed himself to be emotionally touched by any woman. But he was certain that neither in the carefree days of his youth, nor in later times when he'd deliberately forced a rigid emotional detachment on himself, had he ever experienced such an instant reaction to a woman . . . not even to Stacia.

Entranced, he could only stand and stare.

"Now sit," Paula commanded the dogs. The chorus of feminine laughter evoked by the sight of the two rottweilers promptly plumping their backsides at her feet, their long red tongues lolling out of their mouths, broke his dazed absorption.

"I'll take you in for a swim as soon as I change into my suit," the short, freckled woman promised her obedient pets in a fond voice. As though understanding every word she spoke, the dogs followed her onto the deck and plopped down beside the door.

"I think it's time Katie and I got on our way," Eric said to Aurora, finding to his surprise that he had perfect control over his voice. "I can't tell you how much I appreciated our talk."

"Do you have to leave now?" Aurora asked. The slender gold chain encircling her tanned wrist sparkled in the sun when she offered her hand.

Nodding, he took it into his, enjoying the touch of her firm, fine-boned palm and long fingers.

"Where are we going?" Katie demanded, a frown replacing her smile. The rapport they'd enjoyed during their run vanished.

"I thought we'd visit Uncle Brook for a while," he said, keeping his voice pleasant.

"I don't want to go there," Katie retorted. "I want to stay here with Aurora . . . and the dogs!"

Katie was obviously panicked by the idea of losing her protector. Eric looked helplessly at Aurora, no longer sure it was fair to expect her to be an arbitrator between him and his daughter. Even though she'd made the offer to help him with Katie, he suddenly felt ridiculously presumptuous for having taken her up on it. The beautiful, accomplished woman surely had less taxing ways to spend her time.

"I know you must have many things to do," Aurora said with an unconsciously disarming smile, unwittingly echoing his unvoiced concerns about her.

"Yes, I do," he agreed slowly, thinking of Brook and the talk he needed to have with his friend.

"Then why don't you go and let Katie stay here with us for the afternoon. She seems to have fallen in love with Paula's dogs." Aurora searched for the right words to heal this new breach between father and daughter.

"If you don't mind . . ." Eric said lamely, inwardly kicking himself for the sense of relief he felt.

"I want her to stay," Aurora assured him, catching Katie's hand and drawing the now smiling child to her side. "We'll be fine."

There was no way around it, he thought as he walked back to his car, he was terrified of being alone with his thirteen-year-old daughter for longer than a few minutes. What the hell was he going to do? For one preposterous moment he considered turning back to go down on his knees before the gorgeous doctor to ask her to marry him, promising her all of his worldly goods—and only as much of his company as she wanted to put up with—if only she would become his daughter's mother. The moment passed as quickly as it had come, and as he climbed into his car he gave silent thanks for the shred of reason that had kept him from making an even more complete fool of himself.

DRIVING THE SHORE ROAD toward Brook's house, Eric let out a guilty sigh. He still felt as though he was making an escape, but it was just as well that Katie wasn't with him. After all, what he had to say to Brook couldn't be said in front of her.

And, he admitted candidly, he needed time alone to distance himself from Aurora Duvall, until he could get a perspective on the physical attraction she'd aroused in him.

Turning into the lane that led to Brook's modest A-frame chalet on a bluff not far from his own, Eric shifted down to maneuver the rutted road. As usual, the winter rains had taken their toll on its steep, graveled surface, and on a schoolmaster's salary, Brook couldn't afford the necessary monthly maintenance. Later in the summer, when Brook rented a bulldozer to do the work himself as he did each year, he would come over to help him. Eric found himself looking forward to it. He felt the need for some strenuous exercise.

"Hi, buddy," Eric called after he'd let himself into the house.

"Out on the deck," Brook answered. "Where've you been?" he asked, as soon as Eric joined him. "I've been calling your place, but I couldn't get an answer."

"Bridey and Mac have the day off, and Katie and I have been at Aurora's . . . I mean, Dr. Duvall's." He was startled to realize how quickly he'd stopped thinking of the lovely woman by her professional name.

"Hey, buddy, I'm glad it's 'Aurora,'" Brook said with a laugh. "She's okay. It was a lucky day for Seahurst Academy when she took over the dispensary. The girls used to be embarrassed to go to old Dr. Noble." He chuckled. "If they got sick, they'd hide their symptoms until they either got better or they couldn't get out of bed! Actually, I'm kidding. It wasn't that bad. But they do enjoy having a woman doctor to talk to. They line up at Aurora's office door on her visiting days."

"She's certainly won over my daughter," Eric agreed, wondering how he was ever going to pry Katie away from her.

"Have you decided what you're going to do with Katie this summer?" Brook asked, a worried look quickly replacing his broad grin.

"I'm keeping her here with me," Eric answered with a cheerfulness he didn't feel.

"That's a good decision," Brook said gravely, "for both of you. I didn't put my two cents worth in yesterday when I heard Carla's plan, because I figured that you'd make the right choice yourself."

"I almost sent her off." Eric shuddered, sitting down on a cushioned rattan chair. "But Aurora convinced me that I'd lose her if I did."

Seating himself, Brook leaned forward. "I've been afraid of that happening for the past couple of years. I never mentioned the steady withdrawal I could see Katie making from you, because I didn't want to add to your troubles with . . . Stacia." He said the name hesitantly and carefully as though he were touching it gingerly to see how much pain it would cause him.

"Yeah." Eric absently drummed his fingers on the chair arm. "I knew it was happening, too, but I didn't know how to stop it. And the worst part is I still don't. But Aurora has offered to help."

"That's what you need." Brook looked at Eric for a long moment as though he might have something more to say on the subject, but instead he forced a smile and said, "Hey, look here." He picked up a shoe box from a small rattan table next to his chair. Opening it, he pulled out a pair of running shoes.

"You?" Eric had to laugh. "Taking up running?"

The blond man grimaced. "Don't rub it in. I tried to get into last summer's shorts this morning. As usual they were a size too small. That's been happening regularly for the past few years," he said ruefully, glancing down at his bulging waistline, "and the department stores are running out of sizes. So I stopped by the sporting goods shop and picked these up so I could keep you company on your morning runs."

"I'll be darned," Eric said with affection, seeing right through his friend's gesture. Brook was offering to make the supreme sacrifice just to keep him company. "Well, put them on, then, and let's get started. We're going to have to break you in easy."

"Right now?" Brook asked, his face crumpling in anticipation of the punishment to come.

"Now," Eric insisted with a grin. "We'll take the trails to my house. And," he added, seeing he was going to have to throw in a little added incentive for all Brook's good intentions, "we can cool off afterward in the pool." The little under-two miles that separated their houses would be a good distance for Brook's initiation.

"But you only have on sneakers," Brook observed, a hopeful note in his tone.

"I'll keep up with you," Eric assured him.

"But what about your insteps?" Brook persisted, giving it the old college try.

"Not to worry," Eric said with a laugh. "The distance we're going, my insteps will be just fine."

Releasing a sigh that acknowledged he'd lost the verbal skirmish, Brook pulled a pair of new sweat socks from the box, and slid off his worn slippers.

After coaching his friend through some simple warm-up exercises, Eric led the way across the overgrown lawn and down the trail at an even walking pace.

"I thought we were going to run," Brook objected, catching up to walk beside him. "If we're going to do this thing, let's do it and get it over with."

"Have to learn to walk first."

"I've been doing that since I was a year old," Brook scoffed.

"Take it easy," Eric cautioned. "We'll have you running in a couple of weeks. Probably would be a good idea for you to see your doctor for a checkup first."

"Great idea!" Brook said with a chuckle.

Immediately the vision of Aurora's face invaded Eric's mind. "You aren't thinking of going to your house doctor, are you?" he teased.

Brook laughed. "I've been trying to catch a cold for the past five months without any luck. But, as much as the idea of going to her for a physical appeals to me, there's not a chance. Unfortunately she limits her practice to pediatrics."

"With that baby face of yours, you might swing it," Eric suggested drolly. "She is a beautiful woman," he added.

"She sure is," Brook agreed, "and, as far as I can make out, unattached."

"How do you know that?" Eric asked, trying hard not to sound too interested in the answer.

"I haven't seen her around town with anyone except her business associate, Paula Sumner, and Paula's boyfriend, that musclehead, Bill Brady." He wiped his perspiring forehead with his hand.

Eric slowly let out the breath he'd been unconsciously holding. If anyone would know about Aurora Duvall's social life, Brook would. Naturally gregarious and a highly respected leader in the community, Brook held honorary memberships in several clubs in the area. He went everywhere and knew everyone.

"Then how come you haven't made a play for her? She's a professional woman, and yet she's down-to-earth. Seems to me that she'd be someone you'd have a lot in common with."

"Isn't it obvious?" Brook asked breathlessly, slowing his pace as the steep grade took its toll.

"Isn't what obvious?" Eric asked, puzzled.

"Do I have to spell it out? Aurora Duvall is what they call statuesque. Look at me! In heels she's at least a head taller than I am."

"True love knows no physical limitations." Eric laughed uneasily. Aurora's height hadn't been the problem, and he knew it. As long as Stacia had been alive, Brook wouldn't have become interested in Aurora if she'd come made to order. Though they were both aware of the reason Brook hadn't been attracted to any of the lovely women his eager hostesses had thrust upon him over the years, it had always remained—known though unspoken—between them. But, Eric reminded himself, he'd come here today to bring it out in the open.

"Easy for you to say," Brook countered, glowering. "There's not much chance of your having to walk around with a woman who'd have to put her arm around your shoulders! Wait! Whenever I think I've come up with something original it turns out to be a line from one of your plays. Did you say that first?" he asked suspiciously.

"No," Eric said slowly. Then brightening for his friend's sake, he quipped, "But it's pretty good. I might use it . . . someday."

Unconsciously quickening his pace, Eric walked on, his long strides outdistancing Brook's shorter ones. He was several yards ahead when he broke from the underbrush onto his own extensive property. Stopping, he looked over the carefully landscaped grounds to the house in the distance. It had been a long time since it had been a home for him.

"I think I'll call a realtor tomorrow," he said, as Brook walked up to join him.

Brook sighed. "I was afraid that was coming. But don't you think you should talk to Katie about it first?" he asked, bracing himself with a hand on Eric's arm while he pulled off one of his new shoes.

Chagrined that he'd forgotten Aurora's advice so quickly, Eric answered in a chastened tone, "You're right."

Then looking at Brook's bare foot, he added, "Shoes bothering you?"

"A little," Brook admitted with a lopsided grin, wiggling his toes. "I think I may have trouble with my insteps."

"If you're really serious about running, we can get those fitted with some custom supports."

Brook grimaced at the thought as he pulled off the other shoe. "Give me a few days to think about it, and I'll let you know."

"Whatever." Eric nodded with an understanding smile. "I appreciate the gesture."

AFTER STRENUOUSLY swimming around the circular pool until he felt a soothing exhaustion replace his nervous tension, Eric pulled himself out and sat down next to Brook who was eating one of the platefuls of thick sandwiches Bridey had brought out to them. He'd been glad to see she and Mac had appeared somewhat refreshed after returning from the long drive they'd taken along the coast earlier in the afternoon.

For some time the two men sat together in companionable silence, each lost in his own thoughts. At last Brook spoke. "This place has known some great times. But with Stacia gone, I can see why you'd want to... sell it."

Eric didn't look at his friend. He knew from Brook's choked tone that he, too, needed time to recover from Stacia's death. Recalling the day he'd brought Stacia here as a young bride to meet his best friend, Eric remembered the almost worshipful look that had appeared on Brook's face when Stacia had impetuously announced that she wanted to live in Seahurst instead of L.A.

And it had been Brook in his off-hours, who'd helped with her plans for the house. They'd spent countless hours together on the project, while he had been busy commuting between his job in the movie colony and Seahurst.

Brook had shared the good times with them, but it had also been Brook who had suffered with him during Stacia's long illness. And he feared Brook was going to have as much trouble adjusting to the changes in his life now that Stacia was gone as he was.

Clearing his throat, Eric said, "We've never talked about this, and as I look back, I can see that for your sake we probably should have a long time ago. I know you were in love with Stacia and you continued to love her through it all."

"But I never..." Brook broke in, his pale blue eyes wide with surprise.

"I know that, buddy," Eric answered soothingly. "I trusted you, and you never betrayed that trust. But I also know that you never looked seriously at any other woman."

"None of them could compare to her," Brook declared vehemently. "And then, when she got sick, I thought she... I mean, both of you needed me more than ever."

"We did," Eric acknowledged frankly. "And I'll always be grateful to you for standing by us. But I shouldn't have let you. I think that if Stacia hadn't become ill, you would have found someone else long ago."

When Brook started to protest, Eric stopped him. "No, I mean it. As it was, you would have felt disloyal to her if you'd found happiness. I was so wrapped up in my own misery that I was incapable of acknowledging what was happening to you. But Stacia is gone now." He lowered his voice confidentially. "You and I both know she's been gone for a long time. You have to take your life off hold, and start doing what's best for you."

Brook slowly nodded his head. "In time . . . in time. It's just that I feel so empty. So vacant. It wouldn't be fair to anyone if I took up with them now. I'd just be using them to fill the void."

An uneasy thought spread in Eric's mind at the memory of Aurora Duvall's tanned face with its earnest hazel eyes, high perfect cheekbones, full almost pouty lips and softly determined jawline. Was he just using her? But before he could explore the distressing thought further, Brook went on.

"You're lucky you have Katie."

"I know." A remorseful stab of pain reminded him that right now he felt closer to his old friend than he did to his own daughter. A renewed determination to remedy that sad situation gripped him.

"And you have both of us," he declared, putting his hand on Brook's arm. "Now, come on, let's get you home. I have to pick up my car from your house and go get my daughter. We'll grab a couple of bicycles out of the garage."

"You sure know how to torture a guy." The thickset man got up stiffly with a mock groan. "You're not going to be happy until I ache in every muscle I've got!"

"SHE'S ADORABLE," Paula said, watching the exceptionally graceful child at play against the glowing colors of the evening sun.

"She's very special," Aurora agreed.

As if sensing their admiration, Katie came up to the deck, an arm around each of the large black dogs. "You know,

Aurora," she said in a deliberately offhanded way, "I don't think I'll go home tonight. I'll stay here with you."

"But I have to go to work tomorrow," Aurora protested gently. "And I think your father might have something to say about your plans."

"Oh, he'll only say that I shouldn't impose on you and all that kind of stuff, and that he wants me to come home. But he won't mean it," Katie said flippantly. Then sobering, she added, "I've thought about it a lot, and if I enroll in summer enrichment I'll have some place to go during the day while you're working and then I can spend the nights here with you."

"And when I'm on call and have to leave in the middle of the night, who'll take care of you?" Aurora asked, her heart heavy at this evidence of how easily Katie could dismiss her father's feelings.

"I'm old enough to stay home alone. And we could get some dogs like Paula's," the child suggested hopefully. "They'd take care of me if anyone came around."

"Honey, I'd love to have you," Aurora said tenderly. "I can't think of anything in the world nicer than having my own little girl." Her eyes stung with tears at the thought of the painful secret her heart harbored. "But sweetie, you're not my little girl. You're your father's child. He loves you and he wants you." Seeing the child's face set into an implacable mask, she added with a sigh, "We can ask about your staying tonight, but we'll have to work out arrangements with your father."

"Let's hose off the dogs," Paula said, quickly getting to her feet. "I can't take them home loaded with salt and sand. Lead them around to the back of the house for me, will you?" she asked Katie.

"You've got your hands full with her," Paula said, after the girl had disappeared around the side of the bungalow.

"She looks like a creampuff, but I suspect she can be tough."

"I know," Aurora admitted glumly, wondering again how she could have been so impulsive as to jump into the middle of such a potentially explosive emotional entanglement. It just wasn't like her to take on more than she was objectively qualified to handle. But for some reason she had no objectivity when it came to Katie . . . or, for that matter, Eric Thorpe.

AFTER THE THREE of them had merrily rinsed off the dogs, as well as themselves, Katie and Paula took the energetic pair for a walk on the back road. Aurora had declined to join them and was just finishing tidying up the kitchen when she heard Eric Thorpe drive up.

Looking out to see that he was dressed in white duck pants and a crisp cotton navy-blue sport shirt, Aurora grabbed up a beach towel. She hastily wrapped it about her shoulders to cover the brief bikini she still wore, before opening the back door to his knock.

"I passed the animals and the animal lovers on the road," he greeted her.

"They're drying off the dogs," Aurora answered, awkwardly grasping the towel as she held the door open for him.

"I came to take you and Katie out for dinner," he announced with a broad smile.

"Oh . . . fine," Aurora said quickly, wondering what Katie's response would be. "I have to change," she added, clutching the towel tighter.

"No hurry," he assured her. "I'll wait out front."

But Aurora did hurry through her shower. Then, after slipping on a white knit halter dress, she laced a pair of white espadrilles around her ankles. Taking a colorfully embroidered Spanish shawl from a drawer, she came out of her bedroom in time to hear Katie shrilly protesting, "No way! You're not going to get me in that car!"

"But, Katie," Eric was pleading when she joined them, "it's just for dinner. You have to eat."

"No, I don't," the girl retorted unreasonably. "If I go with you, you'll make me go home and Aurora said I could stay with her."

"I said you could stay if it was all right with your father," Aurora said, putting an arm around her.

"I'm not trying to abduct her," Eric said, almost apologetically. "I only want to feed her."

"We can just stay here and I'll fix something," Aurora offered soothingly.

"There's no need for that," Paula put in. "You're all dressed up and ready to go. Go some place nice where they don't want to be bothered with stinky little kids," she said in a teasing tone, diffusing the tension. "And let me take this stinky little kid home with me. I can put up with her a little longer. We'll pick up a hamburger on the way. Besides, I promised to lend her some books on dog care. You can pick her up there after you've had a pleasant meal."

Feeling as helpless as Eric looked, Aurora shrugged her shoulders as Katie took the dogs' leashes from Paula as though the matter were settled.

But the sense of helplessness remained with them as she and Eric drove to a waterfront lobster house on the other side of town. While they picked at their food, their dinner conversation centered on the child and her needs. They left early, mutually conscious of the importance of getting Katie to bed at a decent hour. Katie was emotionally exhausted, they assured each other, and it was only reasonable that she should still be exhibiting signs of extreme stress.

After Eric had given Katie a good-night hug and told Aurora goodnight, Aurora took the sleepy yet chattering girl into the guest room to lay out a nightshirt and things for her shower.

As she kissed the sun-flushed cheek of the young girl, she realized that she hadn't wanted to part with her. She'd wanted her to stay as much as Katie had wanted to.

Going into the main room, Aurora turned off the lights. When locking the front door, she was startled to see Eric stretched out on a lounge on the deck. Quietly opening the screen and stepping out, she softly called his name. Getting no response, she realized he was deeply asleep. Was this another Thorpe who didn't want to go home?

Bathed in pearly moonlight, his face in repose, he looked deceptively content. But only a few short hours ago, this same handsome face had been contorted by the tormenting worry that he'd irreparably harmed his beloved daughter. Unable to take her eyes from him, she stealthily sat down on a chair beside him, letting her senses absorb the appeal she knew she must take care to consciously suppress in the full light of day.

How ironic, she thought, suddenly bitter, that she had within her grasp the two things her lonely heart sought most: a lovable daughter and a sensitive man. Yet, neither of them were hers, nor was it likely they would ever be. Rare tears of self-pity welled up in her eyes. She let them course down her cheeks. There was no one to see them nor care if they fell.

For some time, waves of long-suppressed emotion washed over her heart. Relentlessly they scoured away the protective layers she'd carefully acquired over the years. When at last the pain of her darkest hour lay revealed, she raised her tear-stained face to the glittering stars, but found no solace in their impersonal distance.

Stumbling into the darkened house, she threw herself on the couch. Muffling her sobs in a pillow, she railed against a fate she seemed powerless to escape. How long she cried, she didn't know. Only when a cool breeze reached her uncovered back and arms, chilling her smooth skin into bumps, did she again remember the man on her deck.

Getting a blanket, she took it out and carefully draped it over his sleeping form. While tucking it around his neck, she allowed her lips to touch his forehead. The clean smell of his hair and skin tingled enticingly in her nostrils. Abruptly she fled for the lonely solitude of her own bed.

Chapter Six

The ringing of the bedside phone roused Aurora instantly.

"I need you," Paula said tersely. "Anna Parkins has gone into labor."

"She wasn't due for over a month, was she?"

"No, she wasn't."

"Be right there," Aurora answered, pushing back her hair to glance at the clock. Four o'clock, her mind registered as she hung up the phone and snapped on the light. She slipped into the clean jeans and top she kept in readiness for night calls. She'd shower and change into surgery gear at the hospital.

Then, remembering her sleep-over guests, she reached into the bedside table drawer for a pad of paper and pen. "Emergency—sorry," she wrote. "Don't know when I'll be back. Aurora."

Uncertain where to put the message, she finally decided to prop it up on the table in the main room. Then, in a moment of panic, she wondered if Eric had gone and if she'd be leaving Katie alone. A quick glance out the glass door at his still-sleeping figure settled her mind on that score, but did nothing to calm her racing pulse. A baby's life was on the line, and she knew that no matter how many times she answered them, calls like this would never become routine.

Silently letting herself out the back door, she got into her car and drove away through the gray light of the coming dawn.

"NO PROBLEMS YET," Paula greeted her calmly, her serene countenance masking the worry Aurora knew she was feeling. "The mother's fully dilated and the baby is low in the birth canal. I'm monitoring the baby's vital signs, and they seem to be fine so far."

Composing her own features, Aurora approached the writhing woman, propped up on a tilted delivery table. She was being solicitously, if ineffectively, attended by her green-swathed husband. She'd met both of them when they'd come in to talk with her a few weeks earlier about her being their expected baby's pediatrician. "Hang in there," she said encouragingly, taking Mrs. Parkins's hand. "You're doing fine. I'm here to take care of the baby when it comes. It shouldn't be much longer."

But the woman was in too much pain to hear or understand her. Only the frantic eyes of the helpless husband acknowledged her presence.

It was full morning before Aurora walked down the corridor to the maternity ward to place a healthy infant boy into the arms of the exhausted father. He'd collapsed limply in a chair at his dozing wife's bedside while they'd waited for the results of her extensive evaluation of the child.

"He's perfect," she said with a smile. "He'd have been a whopper if he'd gone full term."

Watching pure bliss transform the parents' exhausted faces into smiling studies in ecstasy as they gazed in rapture at their baby, Aurora experienced a stab of piercing envy. Unable to pull her eyes away from the compelling charm of the intimate scene, she thought how every woman who bore a child deserved to share this sublime moment with the father of her baby. But she knew with gut-wrenching surety that many never knew the fulfillment of the unique experience.

A few moments later, still shaken by witnessing the event, Aurora sank into a chair opposite Paula in the otherwise empty physicians' lounge.

"What's wrong?" Paula asked, searching Aurora's face as she pushed a cup of coffee across the table toward her.

"You'd think that after all these years I'd have gotten over it, wouldn't you?" Aurora wrapped her fingers around the hot mug and stared down into its steaming contents. "But this one really got to me."

Paula, perceptive as always, silently reached across and covered Aurora's hands with her own.

"The agony of that long, terrible delivery simply vanished when they looked at their son with such . . . such adoration." Aurora's voice broke on the word. "Lucky little kid," she added, attempting a smile while she pulled one hand out of Paula's to wipe a tear from her cheek.

"I think you're feeling this way because of Katie," Paula said, picking up her own mug.

"Maybe," Aurora admitted, refusing to meet Paula's gaze.

"I'm sure I'm right. I watched you with her yesterday. Your heart was in your eyes. It's not good for you to become too attached to her, Aurora. She's not your child, and it would be wrong for you and Katie both if you tried to use her as a substitute."

"I suppose so," Aurora said reluctantly, "but I can't seem to help myself. Katie is only a few months older than . . . mine. I buried all thoughts of her for so long. But even though I wouldn't give it up for anything, being around the Seahurst girls has been bittersweet. I can't help but wonder where my daughter is . . . what she's like . . ."

"It's tough," Paula said quietly, compassion in her clear blue eyes. "In some ways separation is tougher to deal with than death. And I wish I could tell you that you'll get over it some day, but I'm not sure you ever will. Still, getting yourself so involved with Katie is very likely just going to compound your loss."

"How?" Aurora asked, bewildered.

"Think about it. Is all the love and tenderness you're feeling now for Katie, really for Katie, or for her circumstances of being a motherless child? Or, even, could it be caused solely by your guilt over giving up the little girl you gave birth to?"

"I know what you're saying," Aurora answered after reflecting for some moments, "and it may all be mixed up together. But right now Katie Thorpe needs me. And whether I help her out of love for herself or out of love for another little girl, I don't think it matters. Besides," she added, straightening in her chair, "you know I've already promised Eric that I would help him with her."

"I just don't want to see you hurt." Paula stood and stretched wearily. "Time to get dressed for office hours."

Getting to her feet, Aurora followed her friend to the locker room, wishing she were as confident of the rightness of her decision to help Katie as she'd tried to appear.

"AURORA," Katie's agitated voice pleaded on the office phone. "I've got to see you. Right now. I won't stay here any longer."

"Where are you?"

"Home, but my dad said he would bring me into town."

"Well, how about lunch then?" Aurora suggested, looking at her watch. What, she wondered, had happened between the Thorpes to spark this much antipathy in so short a time? "In about an hour? Will that be soon enough? I have a couple more patients to see."

"I guess so," the child answered with reluctance. Before hanging up, she added on an ominous note, "Wait until I tell you what he said!"

"SO WHAT DID your father say to get you so upset?" Aurora asked as soon as she and Katie were seated in the small German café across the street from her office. She'd had a hard time concentrating in the hour since Katie had called. Her mind had run a gamut of possibilities, each worse than the one before. By the time an obviously angry Eric had wordlessly delivered his equally angry daughter to her door, Aurora had worked herself into a state of anxiety that was quite unlike her. She couldn't remember when her emotions had last taken such a roller-coaster ride.

"You know that big old empty beach house that we saw yesterday when we ran the dogs?"

Aurora nodded. She knew the place. A rarity among the ocean-front rental properties that were usually snapped up the minute they hit the market, it had been empty for the last three months.

"I just asked him to rent it and to get me a dog so that we could live near you, and he said it was—" Katie forced her voice lower in an attempt to mimic her father "—'absolutely out of the question!'" Her blue eyes darkened as she added, "He wouldn't even talk about it! So I told him that I'm moving back into the dorm right away. I'm not going to live with somebody who hates me!"

Dumbfounded, Aurora looked at the child's set face and flashing eyes. It must have been some scene, she thought, to have stirred up so much defiance. And, she worried, suppressing a sigh, Katie's childish demands had probably done nothing to diminish her father's conviction that she was too immature to have a say in things.

"Honey," she said soothingly, "refusing to rent the house you wanted doesn't mean that he doesn't love you and doesn't want you with him. I can understand why he wouldn't—"

"I don't care what you say," Katie declared loudly. "You don't want me at your place, so I'm going back to school. I don't care if the kids do talk about me behind my back. I can take it. I just can't take being around him! All we ever do is fight anyway!"

Aurora watched as the defiance drained from the young face, and a slight tremor shook the delicate chin. It was time someone leveled with Katie. It was cruel to leave the child floundering for a foothold in the morass caused by her mother's illness and death. But without Eric Thorpe's explicit consent, did she have the right to speak for him? Seeing the suffering on Katie's face, Aurora decided she had no choice.

"Let's eat and then take a walk in the park. We can talk there," Aurora suggested. The busy café was no place for a serious discussion. "I come here nearly every work day. The food's delicious. What kind of sausage do you like?" After signaling the waitress, they ordered the crispy crusted *brotchen* sandwiches the place was noted for.

Before they left, Aurora called her office to tell her receptionist that an emergency had come up and to reschedule the routine physicals that made up the afternoon's first hour of appointments.

A few minutes later, seated on a bench beside a rockbound pond, Aurora took the young girl's hand. She quietly asked, "What do you remember about your mother?"

"Nothing," Katie replied sulkily, slumping her narrow shoulders.

Taking a deep breath Aurora tried again. "You spent thirteen years with her—you must have some memories."

"She used to slap me." Katie tightly compressed her lips into a thin white line.

"Often?" Aurora asked. Putting her arm around the rigidly stiff young girl, she pulled her close and held her until she felt her tense muscles relax. "Tell me," she gently urged.

"I don't want to think about her," Katie whispered. "It's too awful. I wasn't making it up . . . she was crazy."

For a long moment Aurora stared unseeingly at the brilliant blue sky. How was she going to make this girl who'd had such a blighted childhood understand her mother's mental illness? It seemed hopeless, but she couldn't give up. Remembering her own desperate need as a teenager for the counsel and love of an understanding adult, she persisted.

"Your mother was sick, honey, she wasn't crazy. She couldn't help the things she did. She had a terrible disease that left her with no control over her mixed-up emotions. When she was abusive toward you, she didn't realize what she was doing."

"That sounds crazy to me," Katie insisted.

"There's a difference, sweetie, there really is."

"If she was sick, then why didn't my father put her in the hospital instead of sending me away?" Katie demanded furiously, jerking herself free.

"He did put her in hospitals many, many times. He didn't tell you because he didn't want you to worry about it. He kept hoping she would get better," Aurora answered, her heart nearly breaking for the child, "for your sake, as well as for hers. You've got to believe that, Katie, because it's the truth."

"He used to love me," Katie recalled softly, tears springing from her eyes, "when I was little. But," her voice became harsh, "she turned him against me."

"No, honey," Aurora said, putting her arm back around the miserable child, "your mother didn't try to do that. And no matter what, there's no one who could have. He's always loved you. He didn't want you to be hurt. He knew it was better for you to be at Seahurst than at home."

"Why didn't he tell me what was really wrong, instead of lying to me all the time?"

"He should have," Aurora admitted, "but he didn't think you were old enough to understand. He wanted you to have some happiness."

"Huh!" Katie said disbelievingly, pulling away and reaching down to break off a dandelion that had gone to seed.

"I'm going to tell you something that most people don't know about me," Aurora said, needing suddenly to show the child that they had some common ground. "I know more about how you feel than you'll probably believe. I know how hard it is to be at odds with your parents. My life hasn't always been a happy one, either. I wasn't that much older than you are when my mother caused some things to happen to me that I'm still having a very hard time trying to forgive. But the difference between you and me is that my mother knew what she was doing. And in a way, she did come between me and my father."

"Really?" Katie's eyes widened with interest.

Aurora nodded over the lump in her throat, realizing how much it all still hurt. "Really. So I know what I'm talking about. And I also know that your case is different from mine. You and your dad can find the closeness you had before. He wants that, and deep down inside you do, too. You see, under the circumstances there's nothing unusual about the problems you two are having. When one member of a family is mentally ill, it affects everyone else. One of the worst things that happens, if it goes on for a long time, is that the people who are well find they can't communicate with each other any more.''

Katie looked up at Aurora in surprise. ''This happens to other people?''

''Yes, dear, it does. And if they don't recognize it, and do something about what's happening to them, they can become estranged forever.''

''I don't think my father would care if we were estranged,'' Katie responded, dropping her head again. ''He even wanted to send me to live with my gross Aunt Carla. Away from all my friends.''

''Oh, honey, believe me, he wasn't trying to hurt you. And he proved that by deciding to let you stay here. It takes time to heal, Katie. Lots of time.'' She reached over gently to turn the child's face toward hers. ''There's so much to be talked out and understood, but in the meantime you still have to go on with your everyday lives. You know what I think?''

The girl shook her head and turned away, letting the frothy weed fall from her hand.

''I think it would be wrong for you to move into the dorm right now. Your father needs you, and you need him.''

When Katie did not answer Aurora took it as a good sign that she was thinking it over. ''I'll be here for you to talk to, and help you through this bad time,'' she promised, dropping a kiss on the girl's sweet-smelling head.

''Now, how would you like to spend the afternoon with me at the office? You can see what my day is like.''

She was encouraged by the tearful smile Katie gave her as they rose from the bench.

THAT NIGHT over dinner, Aurora listened sympathetically while Eric gave his version of the waterfront house scene. He ended by saying, ''Before I could get a word in, she demanded to move into the dorm. I just don't understand it. I thought she wanted to be with me.''

"She's trying to put down roots somewhere, trying to establish some continuity in her life,'' Aurora explained. "And unfortunately,'' her voice lowered, "she doesn't trust you to provide it for her.'' Aurora flinched at the pain that crossed his face.

"What can I do?'' he asked after a moment.

"Be patient and be there,'' she advised gently, wishing she could will all his troubles away. "That's all you *can* do right now. Unfortunately Katie's at a very difficult age. She's trying to define herself, just as they all are. Her behavior isn't unusual for a thirteen-year-old girl, but some of the problems she has to work out are. She'd be insecure even if her family life had been conventional. Her insecurity is intensified by everything that's happened, so it isn't surprising that her acting out is going to be intensified, too. The best thing you can do for her is to let her know where you stand, so she'll have some idea where she stands with you. Talk to her.''

He rolled his eyes and groaned softly.

"I know…she can be impossible,'' Aurora admitted with a smile. "But you've got to keep trying. Share your immediate plans for the future with her. She has to know that she'll be a part of them.''

He spread his hands and shook his head. "How can I talk to her about that when I don't even know what I'm doing myself?''

"What about the play you plan to produce and direct for the academy?''

"I haven't made up my mind about that yet. I still have to sell the house, and after that I don't even know where I'm going to live.''

"The beach house?'' she suggested.

One dark eyebrow lifted defensively before he realized she was being facetious and joined her in a laugh.

"Chances are your house won't sell immediately," she reasoned. "You'll probably be living in Seahurst at least for the summer. You could carry on with the play. I think it would be a good opportunity for you and Katie to be involved in something together."

He dropped his gaze to his plate and remained silent for some time. Aurora sat very still, surprised once more by the depth of feeling he stirred in her. No other man had ever awakened the tenderness she felt for him. It wasn't just for Katie's sake that she wanted Eric Thorpe made whole again, she realized uneasily.

But she truly believed the past controlled the future. Her own past still shadowed her present. How could she expect it to be any different for him? Perhaps she was drawn to him by the strange bond they shared in hiding the turbulence of their pasts from the world. Perhaps a part of her was even hoping that he might be the man who would understand the intensity of her own secret pain.

But if that were so, she warned her heart, it would be a mistake to allow herself to care too deeply. Once he got over the final trauma of Stacia's death, it was possible that he would want to put everything, including the person who had helped him through it, behind him, not wanting any reminders.

Unwilling to nurture such thoughts any longer, she spoke. "When is the play to open?"

When Eric lifted his gaze to her face she was surprised by the grin lifting his mouth and crinkling his eyes.

"You're not going to let up on me, are you?" he asked with a chuckle. "The end of July, to answer your question."

"And who will be your cast?" she continued, hoping to keep him in this lighter mood.

"Most of it will be local talent, with the two stars imported from Hollywood."

"Have you signed them yet?"

"Tentatively," Eric answered, realizing that the woman sitting across from him was as determined as she was beautiful.

"What's the play about?" she asked, leaning forward, the candlelight sparkling in her gold-flecked eyes.

As he told her the plot and listened to her intelligent responses, the bone-deep lassitude that had invaded his body seemed to dissipate. He found himself considering the technical aspects involved in changing the play to make it fit the open-theater concept. With an excitement he hadn't felt for a long time, he realized there was no reason for him not to go on with it. And since the play was about his and Stacia's life before Katie, maybe Aurora was right. Maybe it could help him and his daughter find a common ground—a place to build from.

"I did check into that beach property that Katie wanted," he admitted with a sheepish grin.

"Hey! Maybe you aren't so bad after all, Pop," Aurora teased, her smile shaping her full lips into a luscious crescent.

"Yeah." Distracted by her sophisticated appeal, he gave a short laugh. Aurora Duvall could make a fortune in one of those commercials that showed the many faces of a woman in an eighteen hour day. He was certain that no lighting, costume, or hairstyle could be unflattering to her. The beauty of her flawless complexion shone as radiantly by candlelight as it had in full sun. Yet he knew Aurora's day had been much longer than eighteen hours. She couldn't have had more than four hours sleep. "Just try convincing my daughter of that," he added, collecting his thoughts.

"I am," Aurora said, suddenly sober. "But there's something I need to tell you, and I'm not certain how you'll feel about me after I do."

He frowned. Was she going to set a limit on the amount of time she'd devote to helping him learn to cope with his daughter? If so, she didn't have to worry about his feelings about her. Suddenly he knew that even if that was what she intended, he'd still want her to be a part of his life. But would she want that, too?

"I took it upon myself to tell Katie about her mother this afternoon. Do you mind very much?"

"I'm relieved," Eric answered truthfully, feeling his pounding heart begin to slow to its normal pace. "Thank you. Could you make her understand?"

"It'll take a while," Aurora said, visibly relaxing against the back of her chair. "Mental illness is difficult for most adults to understand. But I think I made some progress. She wants to believe you love her, Eric. She's busy throwing obstacles in your path to see if you care enough to jump over them or go around them to reach her. Do you understand what I mean?"

"I'm slow," he said, with a nod of his head, "but I think I'm catching on. But does she have to be so obnoxious about it?"

"That's part of being thirteen, I'm afraid." Aurora's expressive hazel eyes shone with amusement. "Now, tell me about the beach house."

"I just called the realtor, so I haven't actually been in it, but it seems it's for rent with an option to buy. It's much bigger than I realized. There's even a separate apartment at the front of the garage. It might make a good investment.

And I was thinking that after I sell my house, it would be a perfect place for Bridey and Mac to retire to."

"Then you wouldn't be planning to use it yourself this summer?" she asked. Did he detect a shade of disappointment in her voice?

"You don't think you might find having the Thorpes as neighbors too burdensome? I understand the daughter's a perfectly obnoxious thirteen-year-old and that her old man is having trouble getting his head on straight."

"Is that so?" Aurora laughed.

"So I'm told," he said dryly. "How about it?" he persisted teasingly, wanting to hear once more the assurance that she intended to stand by her offer.

"I wouldn't mind as long as they had a dog," she said with mock solemnity. "A big dog. I really prefer animal lovers for neighbors."

DURING THE NEXT few weeks, Aurora's already busy life became almost hectic, but wonderfully so. Openly assuming a motherly role with Katie, she experienced a sense of fulfillment beyond anything that even her profession had ever inspired. Thankful that Paula hadn't referred again to her skeptical remarks after the early-morning delivery, she was grateful that her friend listened to her unending stories about Katie with at least feigned interest. She knew she was being as big a bore as most parents with their first child, but she couldn't seem to help herself. Her interest in Katie and in Katie's father... absorbed her.

On the evening of public tryouts for the play, she and Katie had sat on the grass watching as one would-be performer after another read from the comedy script. Caught up in the excitement, Katie had impulsively begged for a chance to read. Aurora had been pleased and proud when

Eric had given his daughter a small part in the production, as well as appointing her the company's official "go-fer."

Aurora had resisted Katie's pleas to try out, too, knowing that with her growing practice she'd have little time to commit to the play. But wanting to be a part of Katie's daily life, she'd admitted that her hobby was browsing secondhand stores and that she would enjoy looking for props and costumes. Seeming pleased, Eric had quickly accepted her offer.

What free time she'd had, she had spent on the set. She'd come to admire Eric more each day. He was a complete professional, showing no sign of the inward devils of indecision and guilt that she knew were still tormenting him. And Katie had taken to the stage like a duck to water. Aurora was certain that Bridey wasn't hearing anything lately about the teenager's fleeting ambition to be a doctor—Katie wasn't Stacia and Eric's child for nothing!

Katie had been dividing her time between her father and Aurora rather unevenly, going home with Eric nights after rehearsal, but spending as much of the weekend at the beach with Aurora as her schedule allowed. At times Aurora'd feared that with the added time Katie spent making shopping trips with her to neighboring towns to run down props, Eric might be feeling that his daughter was growing closer to her than to him. But he was busy, too, and the limited time the Thorpes spent together didn't seem to be bothering either one of them.

Perhaps, Aurora thought, their not being at each other's throats was as much as could be hoped for at this point. She'd known it would take time for the old wounds to heal. And since neither Katie nor Eric had brought it up, she was relieved to think that at least the rental of the beach house had stopped being an issue between them.

One night, during a particularly long rehearsal when nothing seemed to be going right, Katie began to act up. At first Aurora tried to cover for her, bringing Eric the things he asked for. But when Katie insisted on changing her lines in the short scene she had with Brook, who was playing a supporting role in the production, Eric became visibly rattled. Calling an abrupt end to the rehearsal, he stood alone on the lighted stage, his shoulders sagging.

Quickly arranging for Brook to take Katie home, Aurora went to him. "It'll be all right," she said softly. "It's just another bid for your attention."

"I'd like to believe that," he said morosely, "but she shuns like poison any attention I try to give her when we're alone. I've tried to keep your advice about dealing with her in mind, but I can't put up with insubordination at rehearsals. She's making the others nervous. I don't want to have to cut her out, but—"

"Don't," Aurora urged. "Something must be bothering her tonight."

"There is." He took her arm and walked her off the stage. "This evening when we were driving in she told me that she wanted her roommate, Jenni, to move in with us for the rest of the summer. I told her that was more than I could handle."

"I see," she said thoughtfully. "Jenni is lonely. She's used to having Katie with her, so I'm sure it's hard on them both."

"Are you saying I should have let Katie move back into the dorm for the summer like she wanted to?"

"No," she said firmly, stopping so that she could look up into his face. "You made the right decision. No matter what she said, she didn't really want to move back right now."

"Well, what about this Jenni business?" he asked. "Katie made me feel like a heel for not letting her invite the girl."

His hand on her arm tightened and she could feel the tension in him. She was acutely aware of each coiled finger encircling her bare flesh. "To tell you the truth," he continued, "no one in my life has ever made me feel as inadequate as that daughter of mine."

Aurora laughed lightly. "It comes with the territory. As for Jenni, I'll start taking her along some of the time Katie and I do things together. From what I understand, Jenni hasn't had the happiest of home lives either. Her father's older and a full captain for East-West Airlines, and her mother's a flight attendant who also owns a trendy women's apparel shop in L.A. They were divorced when Jenni was just a baby, and the dad remarried and started another family. From what Katie says, I don't think Jenni ever sees him."

Eric groaned. "Now I really feel like a heel. Why hasn't Katie ever told me all this?"

"I think—" she chose her words carefully, starting to walk again "—that in Katie's mind, Jenni's situation paralleled her own. It wasn't something she would have told you about."

"Then do you think I should reconsider letting Jenni move in?"

"No, I don't. You don't need that added responsibility. Just suggest that Katie invite her over to spend the night a few times. Has Katie ever had a friend over?"

"No," he said slowly, "I couldn't suggest it when Stacia was alive, and Katie never asked."

"Then I'm sure she'll enjoy it," Aurora said as they reached the car.

"What would I do without you, Doctor?" Eric murmured in the moonlight, smiling down into her eyes. "Do you make everyone who relies on you feel this good?"

"I don't know," Aurora said in a voice that came out in a husky whisper. "I'd like to think so."

"If your patients weren't all little people, I'm not sure I would." His intimate tone sent a rush of heat through her, making her excruciatingly conscious of his beguiling nearness. "Do you have any plans for tomorrow afternoon and evening?" he asked.

"Actually," she replied, her words almost as quick as the beat of her pulse, "I was just going to ask you the same thing. I'd like you and Katie to come to dinner before the rehearsal. I thought we could invite Brook and Jenni as well."

"That's very nice of you," he said with an enigmatic smile, opening the door to her car. "Of course we'll come. I might have a surprise ready by then."

Watching his solitary figure outlined against the night sky reflected in her rearview mirror as she drove away, Aurora wished she'd had the courage to find out what he'd had in mind before she'd blurted out her impulsive suggestion. Instinct told her he hadn't been planning on asking her for more advice about parenting.

Chapter Seven

The next evening, standing at the edge of Aurora's deck with his hand shielding his eyes, Eric peered down the beach. He spotted the figures of his daughter and his best friend running toward them, bathed in the crimson glow of the setting sun.

"They're coming back now," he remarked, "and Katie's in the lead. I'll put the steaks on."

"It's too bad Jenni came down with the stomach flu," Aurora commented. "I'm just glad Katie hadn't had a chance to ask her to come tonight before we found out she was sick. Knowing what she was missing out on, the poor kid would have been even more miserable than she is."

"Next time," Eric said with a smile.

Returning his smile, Aurora handed him the platter of steaks from the colorfully set picnic table, and sat down on one of the redwood benches, crossing her tanned legs. It was good having him to herself, she thought, enjoying the supple grace of his movements as he performed the simple task of arranging the pieces of meat on the gas grill. In the light of day, her reaction to his casual question of the evening before seemed like a major overreaction. She'd read far too much into it. He had probably just wanted some adult companionship, which she could understand. Even though they'd seen each other often during the past few weeks, it had been a long time since they'd had a real talk...and they'd never had one that hadn't centered around Katie and Stacia.

"How's your friend Paula doing these days?" he asked.

"She's busy dealing with the population explosion," Aurora laughed, "and still dating Bill Brady. Do you know him?"

"I think I've met him," Eric said, adjusting the flame. "If he's who I think he is, he doesn't seem like Paula's type."

"That's him," Aurora said with a wry grin. "His dad owns a chain of health spas and he manages the one here in Seahurst. The only thing those two have in common is a fetish for fitness. I don't mean to sound catty, but Paula was top in our med school graduating class. I'd be surprised if anything other than his athletic ability got Brady through high school. I can't figure out what she sees in him...other than his great body."

"Brook said more or less the same thing," Eric admitted with a grin.

"Now there's someone I can see with Paula," Aurora said slowly.

"Who?" Eric asked, turning to face her.

"Brook, of course," she said earnestly. "I don't see why it never occurred to me before."

Eric let out a hoot of laughter. "You've got to be kidding! Any woman with a 'fetish for fitness' would never be happy with Brook Oliver!"

"Oh, I don't know," Aurora hedged. "She's always been a sucker for lost causes. Actually, that may be why she's with Brady." Eric joined her in laughter.

"But let's talk about you. How did you manage to get Michelle Saunders and Tom Harris for your stars?" she asked, in awe of the names and the glamorous aura they projected. "I'm impressed."

He shrugged. "They've worked for me before and they owe me one," he stated unaffectedly, as though he was talking about run-of-the-mill employees instead of a pair of young Hollywood actors who were fast becoming hot box-office draws.

"Where will they be staying when they come to town Monday?"

"There've been so many offers to entertain them that I turned the job of choosing over to Brook. I think he's parceling them out between two of the academy's most generous patrons." He chuckled, sitting down beside her.

"Brook is ecstatic," she acknowledged, pleasantly aware of the arm Eric had placed behind her and of his long legs stretched out beside hers. "He said that all five nights are sold out. He's talking about making it an annual affair."

Before Eric could respond, Katie dragged herself up the steps. "Daddy, Daddy," she gasped, her thin chest heaving from the exertion of her long run on the soft sand. "Someone's rented *my* house! The sign is gone!"

Getting immediately to his feet, Eric put his hands on her shoulders, a wide smile lighting his face. "I rented it, Munchkin. Just like you asked me to. I have the key right here in my pocket. It was going to be a surprise for after dinner."

Aurora watched in dismay as Katie angrily wrenched herself from her father's light hold.

"I hate you!" the child shouted, her eyes narrowing to slits. "You always keep secrets from me! I never can trust you!" She stumbled backward down the steps, colliding with Brook who was just lumbering up to the house.

"Whoa, there," the red-faced man panted, settling her on her feet, before she ran off to the water's edge and dropped down on the sand. He turned a puzzled gaze at the two standing dumbfounded on the deck.

"Let her go," Aurora cautioned, catching Eric's arm as he started to move. "She needs to calm down before anyone can reason with her."

"She's upset about that house," Brook said breathlessly, as he dropped down onto the nearest chair.

"About that and a lot more," Eric murmured hopelessly, hanging his head and shaking it. His hand sought Aurora's and he gave it a squeeze before letting it go.

"She sure was disappointed," Brook commented worriedly, looking at the forlorn figure tossing pebbles at the quiet waves. Then, in an attempt to lighten the oppressive silence that hung in the air, he added, nodding toward the smoking grill, "That smells good."

Muttering a mild oath, Eric quickly moved to the forgotten steaks and turned them over, while Aurora busied herself uncovering the bowls on the table. She'd completely lost her appetite, and she suspected Eric had, as well. He had the look of a man who'd been punched in the stomach—bewildered and shaken. And it was hard for her to watch. She loved Katie like a daughter, and she knew she was falling more than a little in love with Eric, too.

It took every shred of willpower she possessed to keep from jumping in as a peacemaker. But she sensed this confrontation was a crucial moment in the Thorpes' lives, and she believed it was imperative that the two of them work through it on their own. As odd as it seemed, she knew it was common for a child who had lost one parent to exhibit open hostility toward the surviving parent— Katie had certainly demonstrated that response to Eric often enough.

But where they went from here was critical to their future. Eric had made a generous, caring gesture in securing the beach house for his daughter, even though he hadn't taken Aurora's advice about including Katie in the decision. Perhaps in experiencing the full force of the child's hostility, he would finally come to understand the extent of the problem. And, though angry that he'd kept his renting the house as a secret to surprise her, Katie needed to understand that he'd made a well-intentioned mistake, and more importantly that he'd done it out of love for her. Though it was painful to stand by while Eric and Katie were both hurting so badly, Aurora silently vowed to give them the time they needed to resolve the situation, themselves.

Still, before they sat down to eat, Aurora walked across the sand to invite Katie to dinner. She wasn't surprised and didn't press the issue when the young girl refused.

No one seemed to enjoy the meal, but they went through the motions of eating. Afterward Eric explained the true status of the house to his friend. Brook tried to keep up the conversation, but all their gazes kept straying to the lonely little girl silhouetted against the red ball of the setting sun.

After getting no response to his rehashing of the disastrous rehearsal of the evening before, Brook informed them, "With the extra monies already generated by Eric's play, I intend to follow through on my plans to implement a sex education program this fall."

"But you already tried to get that into the curriculum last spring and the headmaster vetoed it," Aurora reminded him, glad he had hit on a subject she could join in discussing.

Brook snorted. "How could I forget. He acted like I wanted to show pornographic movies to the girls."

"You mean…I mean…are you saying that Katie has no idea about sex?" Eric asked, drawn into the conversation in spite of his deep engrossment with his daughter's inexplicable reaction to getting what he'd thought she wanted.

"I'm sure it's been an all-consuming topic of great misinformation in the dorm for years," Aurora said with a wan smile. "But private schools are really a law unto themselves in many ways. Sometimes that's a plus. Sometimes it's a minus."

"That's for sure," Brook said vehemently. "But to be fair, many public schools have the same problem. I have public school colleagues who don't think the programs they offer are adequate. And some communities don't think sex education should be up to the schools. It's still a hot issue in many areas of the country.

"Frankly, I respect the rights of the parents involved to make the choice of whether the education should be done in the home or in the school. But I feel that since most of our girls are boarders, we have an obligation to provide the information the parents would give if they lived at home."

"I just assumed..." Eric started with a nod.

"You and most of the others, I suspect," Aurora interjected. "I think that if more of our parents were aware of what is—rather what isn't—going on, there'd be a clamor of protest. It's never been more important than it is now for our young people to have accurate and informative sex education. I feel Seahurst is inexcusably behind the times by not offering any such classes for the girls."

"Want to go to the board meeting with me Monday?" Brook asked hopefully.

"Definitely," Aurora answered. "And I want them to consider instituting a grief management course as soon as the regular term starts. All the girls in middle school will be touched to one degree or another by Katie's loss. Probably several of them have unresolved feelings about grief of their own. It's not fair to impose outdated taboos on them."

With the mention of Katie's name, all eyes at the table turned once more toward the motionless girl sitting at the water's edge.

WHAT DID SHE WANT, anyway? Katie asked herself. Why was she always so sad, except when she was with Aurora? And why did her father always make her feel so wrong about everything?

First he told her there was no way that he would get the beach house for her, and now without even giving her a clue, he said he had the key to it in his pocket.

Was she supposed to thank him for all the miserable days she'd spent wanting that house and thinking she couldn't have it, when all the time he knew she could? Did he think it was funny to torture her?

Why did everything have to be such a great big secret with him? She never knew what he was thinking, and when he did talk to her it was always about the wrong things, never about what was going to happen to them now that her mother was gone.

Why did things always have to go wrong? Why couldn't it be like it used to be when she was little and he'd liked her? She knew he had, because sometimes in her sleep she had dreams about how it used to be with them. When she'd wake up, she'd keep her eyes closed, wanting the dream to come back.

But it wasn't like that anymore. How could Aurora say he really loved her when he did things like this to her? And now Aurora was mad at her too. She could tell, because Aurora hadn't tried to coax her to come up to eat. She'd left her alone. She'd taken her father's side against her. Now everybody was against her.

Katie slowly got to her feet and brushed the sand from her shorts. What would happen if she just started to walk away?

She looked up the beach. That was where the house was. Her house. A thought flitted through her mind—maybe she'd even get a dog. Then she looked down the beach to where it curved away out of sight. A purple haze hung over the water and it would soon be dark. If she went that way, would they come after her and tell her they were sorry for treating her so mean?

Glancing at the group on the deck who were busy cleaning up the supper things, doubt began to grow in her mind. If she walked away, she'd hurt her father, she'd hurt Aurora—who must think he was right—and she might lose her house.

Suddenly, without further thought, she turned and ran to the deck.

"Daddy, can I talk to you?" she asked, not wanting anyone else to hear what she had to say.

"Of course," he answered. A special smile she seemed to remember from a long time ago lit his face as he came down the steps toward her.

"I'm sorry," was all she could get out before the tears came and she was engulfed in his arms, sobbing into the comfort of his knitted shirt.

BROOK LED THE WAY through the thickening fog, shining the beam from the powerful flashlight he kept in his truck. Eric and Aurora walked on either side of Katie. Knowing the electricity wouldn't be turned on until the next day, Eric had originally planned this trip to take place before dusk. But it was just as well this way, he thought, giving his daughter's hand a squeeze and feeling her brief answering clasp. He wondered if she'd passed it on to Aurora, with whom she was also holding hands. He hoped she had, since Aurora was responsible for this wonderful, newfound closeness between them. And even though they were all shrouded in mist, he felt that a dark cloud had lifted from his soul.

At the house he gave Katie the key, and after she'd opened the door, he took Aurora's hand while Katie and Brook led the way through the unfamiliar rooms.

"It's much larger than I thought," Aurora remarked as they walked through the living room and dining room and on into the kitchen.

"It's built on a narrow but very deep lot," he explained. "There are three large bedrooms upstairs."

"Let's go up there," Katie impulsively commanded Brook as his flashlight revealed a staircase leading up from the kitchen.

As Katie and Brook clambered up the wooden stairs taking the light with them, Eric and Aurora were left in the darkness.

"Alone, at last," he murmured the clichéd expression with a faint air of melodrama in a feeble effort to conceal the intense depth of his pleasure.

"Yes," she whispered huskily.

"I suppose we should go up, too," he suggested, not meaning a word of it.

"Hmm," she answered noncommittally, as his thumb found the rapidly beating pulse at her slim wrist.

"But then again, we might stumble in the dark."

"That could be a problem," she admitted breathlessly.

"Maybe we'd better not risk it."

"Maybe not," she agreed, her voice now barely audible, but intensely seductive.

Pulling her closer until their bodies touched, he inhaled her fresh scent, enticingly fragrant and sweet. He raised his hand to cradle her head, his fingers burying themselves in her thick silky hair. At the small of her back, his other hand traced the firm line of her spine, molding her tall, softly pliant body to fit his own length, until finally he held her head between his palms, his lips only inches from hers. She quivered beneath his touch, and her arms encircled his waist, causing a shudder of desire to course through him and an unbidden groan to rise in his throat. "I never knew there was really anyone as special as you," he murmured, and meant it.

He hadn't planned for this to happen tonight, yet he knew he'd been waiting, hoping this opportunity would come ever since that first morning they'd talked on the beach. Though he'd tried to deny it...tried to stifle his feelings... thoughts of Aurora Duvall had been central to his existence from that day until this one. He wished he could see her lovely face to find reflected in the depths of her clear eyes the same desire that was madly racing through his veins.

When the footsteps above receded, moving toward the front of the house, he lowered his face to hers, pressing his lips to her forehead, savoring its unlined smoothness. Then he brushed kisses along her cheekbone, reveling in the flaming warmth he knew glowed rosily there, until finally he found her full lips...open...moist...responsive.

Hungrily he invaded her warm mouth as wave after wave of pure sensation awakened every dulled fiber of nerve and flesh. He hadn't thought he'd ever be this alive again, ever be this demanding. The smoldering embers of his deadened emotions had been coaxed to white-hot flame by her wondrous receptivity. A part of him wanted the heady kiss to never end, wanted to fuse her to him, wanted to possess her as he had possessed no other.

Forcefully he pulled his lips from hers, afraid he'd frighten her with his intense emotional thirst. Holding her close, he nuzzled his face against her throat, letting his tongue touch the racing pulse at its smooth base, gratified that she'd been as affected as he.

"Let's wait for them outside," he whispered huskily, when he felt he could trust his voice. His eyes now adjusted to the darkness, he led her through the house to the porch, where they stood together, his arm around her shoulders as they breathed in the cool night air.

"Where did you guys go?" Katie asked, when she and Brook joined them only a moment later. "I thought you were right behind us."

"You took away the light," Eric said, as if that explained why they hadn't followed.

"You should have come with us," Katie said, locking the door. "I checked it all out and I've decided you can have the front bedroom. It has a bath of its own. I'll take the middle one, and Bridey and Mac can have the back one."

"There's a nice apartment in front of the garage," Eric laughingly corrected his bossy daughter. "Mac and Bridey can live there, that is if it's all right with you."

"That's fine," she agreed, handing back the key. "At least I'll have my own bathroom that way. And the view from the bedroom windows must be awesome. The house is at an angle, so I'll be able to see the ocean as well as you can."

"I know, honey. And that's yours," he said, refusing the key. "I have another one."

"What are we going to do for furniture?" Katie asked, immediately stepping into her established place between her father and Aurora, and taking their hands as they began walking back to Aurora's, Brook leading the way.

"You can choose whatever pieces from the house you want," he answered.

"Me? I get to choose?" she asked, sounding a little uncertain.

"Maybe Aurora would agree to help you."

"Oh, would you? I've never decorated anything except my dorm room, and all I do there is change the posters on my share of the walls."

Aurora laughed. "I'd be glad to help. We can start tomorrow, if you'd like. You have the whole weekend off before you have to practice again, and I don't have anything scheduled."

"That would be great," Eric agreed. "I need to get our stuff out of there if I want to sell the house. There's so much that needs to be gone through."

"Daddy," Katie's voice was suddenly hushed and sober. "Yes?"

"Could I just tell you what I want and then go spend the weekend in the dorm? I really don't want to be there when..."

"I was thinking this weekend would be the perfect time for you and me to take that camping trip to the redwoods, I promised you for this summer," Brook interjected, stopping so that they could catch up with him. "I think your dad and Aurora can get along without you this once."

So he hadn't missed a thing, Aurora thought with a smile. He was so intuitive and kind to understand Katie's feelings...and hers and Eric's. Did she glow in the dark with the almost electrical excitement Eric's kiss had generated deep inside her? Or had the heady aroma of unleashed passion wafted to him on the warm summer wind? Even in the dark she felt certain that these wonderful feelings...these feelings that she'd always imagined to be exaggerated by the world of lovers who claimed to have experienced them...must surely be manifesting themself in some form that could be perceived by the senses.

She longed to run free with the wind, with only Eric by her side, his long strides matching hers in perfect rhythm...to reach for the mist-obscured stars...to strive for the sublime release her body and soul had never known...but she forced herself to remember where she was and that they were not alone...forced herself to concentrate on the conversation instead of being totally preoccupied with the captivating memory of his demanding mouth and the promise of his long, sinewy body pressed to hers.

"Can Jenni come along, too?" Katie asked, dropping Aurora and Eric's hands to take Brook's. "She never gets to go anywhere. Aurora said she's just got a twenty-four-hour bug. She should be fine by then. Right, Aurora?"

"That's right."

"Say now," Brook said as he started once more down the beach, "that's my idea of camping. Two women to do all the work, cooking and cleaning. I think I'd like my breakfast served to me in my sleeping bag..."

As Eric's hand engulfed hers, Aurora's thoughts turned toward the weekend they would be spending alone together.

Chapter Eight

"I don't know where to start," Eric said Saturday morning, raising his hands in submission as he and Aurora returned to his large living room and stood among the jumbled spoils of Stacia's wild shopping sprees. The room looked more like a warehouse close-out sale than ever, now that she had time to inspect it. As soon as she'd arrived, he'd taken her on a tour through the numerous rooms in the huge house, wanting her to have some idea of what she'd gotten herself into.

"Did Katie have any suggestions?" Aurora asked, remembering the promise he'd made to his daughter.

He ruefully shook his head. "She was as baffled as I am. She wanted to keep everything that's in her rooms, and her bicycle and skateboard... they're in the garage. Other than that, there wasn't anything she cared about."

"How about Bridey and Mac?" Aurora asked, reaching up to push the fastener more securely in place around her ponytail. "Do you want to give them any of this?"

"Sure. Anything they'd like. I'll ask them to look it all over when they get back from cleaning the beach house," he said, glancing around, "but I doubt that much of this is to their taste. Bridey once told me she took a fancy to Early American maple furniture not long after she stepped off the boat from Ireland. And," he added, "I think that's one of the few types Stacia missed."

Aurora smiled, picturing Bridey and Mac in a home full of braided rugs, overstuffed chintz chairs and sofa, and warm maple furnishings. Bridey, she thought, would have been a wonderful mother. "Do she and Mac have any children?" she asked.

An enigmatic expression clouded Eric's eyes. "They have a son, Sean. He used to spend the summers here when he was attending the University of Southern California. He was a great kid. He planned on being a civil rights attorney."

"Planned?"

"He changed his mind."

"Obviously you didn't approve," she probed, wondering why she was having to drag the story out of him.

"I wouldn't say that exactly, but Mac and Bridey sure didn't. And I do feel somewhat responsible for what happened."

"What did happen?" Aurora persisted, keeping her tone light. "Nothing tragic, I hope?"

"No, not tragic," Eric said with a faint smile. "At least not yet. Sean had always dreamed of visiting Ireland . . . to see the land where his parents were born . . . the land of his ancestors. So, ten years ago I went in with Bridey and Mac to give him a trip back to the old country as a college graduation present.

"He sent us postcards saying he was having the time of his life. But the night before he was due to come home to start law school, they got a telegraph that was followed by a letter. He explained that he wasn't coming back. That he'd found what he'd been looking for all his life. A true cause. Something to believe in and work for.

"Bridey and Mac were in shock. They couldn't understand why he was deliberately involving himself in all the turmoil they'd tried to get away from. He's become quite a political activist. I know they're proud of him on one level, but they miss him terribly. And I know that they're a little bitter that their plans for him didn't work out the way they'd hoped.

"So, when Sean left, my relationship with them changed," he continued, his deep voice even lower than usual. "Oh, they still work for me, but they're far more than employees...and I like to think I'm more to them than their employer. If Sean had stayed here, he would have looked after them...as it is, I try to do that for him.

"That's why, if they're happy there, I plan to exercise the option to buy the beach property. Even if I decide to rent out the large house someday, they'll still have a comfortable place of their own."

"That's very generous of you," Aurora said, wondering how she could ever have thought, even for a moment, that this wonderful man could be cold or callous.

"No," Eric waved away her comment. "Generosity doesn't even figure into it. They'd do anything for me and Katie, and I know it."

"What about your folks?" Aurora asked impulsively.

Eric laughed and a genuine smile came to his face. "You're afraid I neglect them?"

"No..." she hedged.

"It's all right. With them down in Mexico and me up here, I can see why you might think that. But you don't have to worry," he said, coming to sit on the arm of a chair beside hers. "They're well taken care of and, as far as I've ever been able to tell, happy."

"Really," Aurora remarked.

"I'm only as far away as the phone, but they never call except on my birthday. And I call them on theirs, as well as on holidays. They'd think anything more was an unseemly display of affection. I have one of Katie's drawings framed for them each year, and send them one of Bridey's brandy-laced fruitcakes for the holidays. I've gotten the same thing for Christmas from them for the past thirty-five years.''

"What's that?'' she asked, warming to the humor in his tone.

"Five hardcover books and two magazine subscriptions. Only the titles have changed,'' he said poker-faced, though his eyes glinted with amusement.

"Didn't you mind?'' Aurora asked.

"I did when I was little,'' Eric admitted with a wry grin. "I used to lie mightily the first day back after Christmas vacation. The teachers must have thought I was one spoiled little kid. I waited until I heard what everyone else had gotten as presents, and then said I had one of everything, too.''

Aurora chortled with laughter. "I can't believe this!''

"Believe it,'' he said, his broad grin revealing his even teeth. "Don't get me wrong. My parents are good people. They saw to all my needs, and included me in their conversations as if I were an adult. The problem was they weren't the kind of people who should have ever had children. They didn't have any room in their carefully ordered lives for them.''

"I can't believe you can laugh about it,'' Aurora said. "You don't seem even slightly bitter.''

"I'm not,'' Eric assured her. "You see, I figured out a long time ago that I might never have become a writer if I hadn't had to use my imagination so much while I was growing up. Since my dad never played ball with me, I imagined all sorts of scenarios with a dad who did. I think I was writing complete scripts in my head by the time I was eight years old.

"But you're not here to hear the story of my life,'' he said, glancing askance at the room.

"I wouldn't mind at all," Aurora said sincerely. "But on the other hand, how can I be sure you're not just imagining and embellishing your past?" she teased.

He snorted as he grinned down at her. "Haven't you ever heard that truth is stranger than fiction? Not even I could make up a background as wacky as my own.

"I hate to say this, but we have to get to work. I may have been overly optimistic, but I called the movers before you got here and told them to come on Tuesday."

"Then let's start with the paintings," Aurora suggested, standing up and leaning back slightly with her hands on her hips. "They're very good. Do you think that Katie would like to have them sometime?"

"I'm giving them all to Brook. He helped Stacia choose them," Eric said as his gaze shifted to take in the large canvasses.

"How about Carla?"

"She asked for a couple of things... her mother's china... some family pictures..."

Sitting down again on the arm of the floral wing-backed chair, Aurora looked up at him. How little of the house seemed to be his. And, from what he'd told her, it must have been much the same for him while he was growing up in his parents' home. No wonder it was only in his office, with its burnished leather couch and chairs surrounded by walls filled with volumes of books, that she got the feeling he felt comfortable and at ease.

"Look," he said suddenly, taking her by her upper arms and pulling her to her feet, his dark eyes seeming to bore into hers. "I'm really sorry to be involving you in this. If I hadn't planned to have the stuff picked up so soon...maybe I should call them back...."

It was the first time he'd touched her since the night in the dark when his compelling kiss had stirred the embers of her suppressed passion. Conscious of his thrilling closeness and of the wild response her pulse was making to his touch, Aurora pulled her gaze from his.

"It's best to get it over with," she said as casually as she could, moving to stand, "and I don't mind helping in the least. Now, where are those stickers?"

"Out in the hall with the boxes," he answered, dropping his hands to his sides.

"Why don't you take a roll of them and mark the things in your office?" she suggested as she wove her way to the front hall, where waiting boxes were piled nearly to the ceiling. "I'll take care of the things in here and in the other rooms, and we'll leave the kitchen to Bridey."

IT WAS NEARLY DARK before the contents of the house bore their conspicuous marks: red for staying, yellow for storage and green for auction. The unmarked items would be moved to the beach house. During the long day, Aurora had made numerous suggestions that Eric had been quick to accept. The rattan family room furniture, along with the breakfast room set, would be used for the beach house. Katie's rooms, as well as Eric's study and the guest room he'd been using, were to be moved *en toto*. The deck and pool furniture would be sold with the house.

When she'd arrived home, Bridey's selections were modest, even though Aurora had encouraged her to agree to take the few additional items her gaze had seemed to linger upon.

Aurora hadn't had the heart to sell to the dealer a few simple, yet elegant pieces of particularly fine workmanship. Reasoning that Eric would only realize a fraction of their worth at auction, and that someday Katie might use them to set up her own first home, she'd marked them for storage.

Stacia's rooms had been the hardest to pack and mark. It was there that Aurora felt most like an intruder. Not wanting to take on the task alone, she'd waited for Bridey's help; but even so, several times she'd had to stop herself from going to find Eric to tell him that she couldn't do the job. She'd forced herself to go on with constant, silent reminders that there was no one else to do it. She hadn't wanted some stranger with no sensitivity to Katie's needs callously handling the girl's mother's most private possessions . . . and the kindly housekeeper, who was the obvious choice, hadn't been up to doing the job alone, either.

A tearful Bridey had nearly exhausted a box of tissue while she'd helped Aurora pack up Stacia's jewelry to keep for Katie. They'd sorted through closets stuffed with boxes of designer shoes, and holding racks that sagged from the weight of clothing which they moved to cardboard wardrobes to be sent to Carla in Texas. Coming across the gorgeous wedding gown that Stacia obviously had had professionally packed away and saved for her daughter, Aurora marked it for storage, even though Katie was clearly going to be larger than her petite mother.

They also carefully packed away Stacia's design books, diplomas, awards, picture albums and yearbooks from the schools she'd attended. Though Katie might not be interested in the mementos now, Aurora hoped that there would come a time when the girl would treasure them.

One item caused Aurora's tears to flow as profusely as Bridey's. It was a baby book, discovered in the bottom of one of Stacia's dresser drawers.

"She wanted that baby so bad," Bridey said sobbing. "Said it was the most precious gift God could ever give her. Took me back to the time I was carrying my own little Sean, she did. She loved being pregnant . . . said she'd never felt so good, or been so happy. We were so close during those happy months we were doing all the planning for that baby...she was like the daughter I'd never had. I'll never understand why she met such a terrible, cruel fate.''

Looking through the book, Aurora saw that it contained a detailed, upbeat record of Stacia's pregnancy, illustrated with pictures taken of her and Eric at various stages during the months, as well as some lovely poetry Stacia'd written to express her feelings about impending motherhood. The entries stopped abruptly after a jubilant—if scrawled—inscription announcing that labor pains had started and she was on her way to the hospital. Someday the book would provide poignant proof to Katie, that before tragedy struck, she had been a longed-for child. Aurora hugged the book to her chest for several long moments, giving herself up to racking sobs as she realized that Stacia had lost her child at birth almost as completely as she, herself, had lost hers.

"I don't know what we would have done without you today,'' Bridey said as the two women walked along the curving hall to Eric's study, when they were finally done. "It's a sad day, to be sure, but a good one, too. Already my heart feels lighter.

"This house once knew happy times, but they've long since been mucked up in misery. If only we could sort our memories out and put little red circles on the ones we wanted always to stay fresh and vivid in our minds, little yellow ones on those we wanted to store away for a while until we were ready to take them out and think about them and green circles on the terrible ones, to be packed off and sent away forever.''

"That would be nice,'' Aurora agreed with a sigh. "Misery is a heavy load. Eric told me about Sean,'' she added softly, reaching out to take Bridey's hand.

"Did he now,'' Bridey said, giving Aurora's hand a light squeeze. "It's just as well for you to know about our boy. I imagine you're about his age," she said reflectively. "He was a tall, strapping lad, with a smile that could break a colleen's heart. If he were here, he'd most likely be in competition with Mr. Eric for your attention."

"Thank you, Bridey." Aurora smiled. "That's the nicest compliment I've ever had."

Looking in at Eric's door, Aurora saw him sitting on the floor surrounded by stacks of papers and folders.

"It's hopeless," he said with a lopsided attempt at a grin. "I really don't want to get rid of a thing."

"Then don't," she replied, gingerly trying to find places to step amid the clutter.

"I'll set out a little supper," Bridey said from the door. "Come up when you're ready."

"Thanks," Aurora replied gratefully. Having made her way to the couch, she pushed aside some boxes to make room to sit down. "We'll be up soon. Would you and Mac join us?" she asked. "I think it would be good for us to all be together for a little while. This must be hard on him, too."

Seeing Bridey's tearful nod, Aurora knew she'd made the right decision. In breaking up the household, the older couple would be saying goodbye not only to Stacia, but to their last completely happy memories of their son, as well.

After absently flipping through a pile of bound manuscripts, Eric looked up at her with a thoughtful expression. "Going through this stuff has brought back so much that I'd forgotten. But it's funny...in a way I feel like all this happened to some other guy. I feel detached from the only part of myself that was ever really me." He wearily ran a hand through his hair. "I'm not sure I can ever get back where I was before...become that person again, and frankly, it scares the hell out of me."

"You mean not writing?" she asked, picking up and holding one of the three Oscars that had been on display in the room.

"Yeah . . . I guess. I mean, without it, who am I?"

"Eric," Aurora replied, compassion in her eyes. "Your writing didn't define you . . . you defined it."

He rested his elbows on his blue-jean-clad knees. "I don't know about that. I thought I knew where I was going once . . . what I was doing." Lowering his chin to his folded hands, he concluded, "Now I've lost it. And I don't know if I'll ever get it back."

Standing abruptly, Aurora held out her hands for him until he finally took them and she pulled him to his feet.

"There's no need to make any decisions now. All of this can go into storage until you're ready for it," she said quietly. "Come on, let's wash up. This isn't good for you. After we eat, let's get out of here. We can finish up tomorrow."

LATER, AFTER SUPPER, Eric drove her home in silence.

"I want to come in," he said, taking her hand and holding it under his chin, his words weighted with despondency. "I don't want to be without you . . . even for a moment."

"And I don't want to be without you," she confessed softly.

He let out a low moan and pulled her to him, cradling her in his arms. "I can't tell you what having you there today meant to me. It's hard to explain, but even though we spent most of the time in separate rooms, I could feel your presence. It kept me going."

"I'm glad," Aurora murmured, enjoying the warmth of his body close to hers.

"And I'm not sure how you feel, but right now," his voice took on a low, tender tone, "there's nothing I'd rather do than to spend the night making love to you."

Aurora tensed, but he continued, unaware of the conflicting emotions that warred within her. "But the timing is wrong. Today made me realize how much of the past is still with me. If we do have a future together, I want to be whole and free when I come to you, not half a man needing your pity."

"But..." she started, knowing in her heart it would be senseless to try to argue with him. How could she, when a part of her was still as afraid to commit as he? Still she declared, "It isn't pity I feel for you. I've never pitied you. You're a strong man."

Eric sighed and raised her fingers to his lips. "Right now you're much stronger than I am. I saw a little hermit crab sidling down the beach the other day, looking for the safety of a new shell. It struck me how much I was like him. Exposed, vulnerable... even scared."

I'm like that too, Eric. I may seem self-assured, but inside, I'm as frightened of love and commitment as you could ever be. Though she tried to say them, the words died silently in her throat.

He turned her hand over and gently kissed her palm, sending shivers of desire coursing through her nervous system... making her sway toward him.

"I understand," she whispered, perceiving his honesty and the promise behind all he'd said. She raised her other hand to brush the hair at his temples. "Right now, it's enough for me to be there for you and Katie."

"You're wonderful," he said, dropping her hand and putting his arm around her once more. "I wish I had more to give. All I seem to be able to do is take."

"If I've given you anything, I've given it willingly," she answered. "I know what it is to lose someone I love and to suffer from that loss. And I also know it takes a very long time to recover." She shuddered as the memory of that long-ago, terrible night threatened to inundate her mind. She felt her knees weaken.

"What?" he demanded, gravely concerned. His arms tightened around her, supporting her. "What happened to you? Who hurt you?"

"It was a long time ago," she said evasively, drawing in a deep breath and regaining her equilibrium. "It isn't anything that I want to think about or talk about. Maybe someday I'll be able to. I don't know." She abruptly stepped back, away from his grasp, appalled at how deeply he'd stirred her emotions. Shaken, she realized that she'd come close to blurting out her most closely guarded secret. "Good night, Eric."

"Good night, Aurora. If you need anything...if you decide you want to talk, just give me a call."

"I'll be fine," she assured him, forcing a smile.

Later, alone in her room, she sat on the side of the bed rethinking the scene at the door. She had been half hoping that he'd make love to her. Hoping that the feelings she had for him would overcome her inhibitions and drive away the revulsion she'd always experienced when she'd attempted the physical act of love.

But would they have? Was any emotion she could feel for a man...even for Eric...strong enough to block out the memories of degradation that she'd suffered? If they *had* slept together, would she have wanted to put him out of her life as quickly as possible afterward?

She didn't know, but she didn't want to find out...at least not yet. Even though her body ached with desire for him, she couldn't risk losing him or Katie. Before the Thorpes had exploded into her life, bringing with them an immediacy that she couldn't deny, and a depth of caring that had enriched her every moment, she had been a sideline participant in other people's lives...merely a supporting player who entered on cue, played her part, took her bows and walked off stage alone into the lonely darkness beyond. Now, with Eric and Katie, she longed to be a central player in the drama. But—she shivered as she slid between the smooth sheets of her bed—she was grateful that he'd turned away from her tonight. As much as she wanted the lead role in their lives, she wasn't sure she could ever be more than an understudy for some emotionally whole woman who might come along later to fill the part.

THE NEXT MORNING, after a troubled sleep, Aurora awoke as the first rays of the rising sun lightened her bedroom. Too restless to take advantage of the one day of the week when she could catch up on sleep, she showered and pulled on a pair of running shorts and a tank top.

After brewing a pot of coffee, she took her mug out on the deck where only the raucous cries of the gulls circling overhead broke the stillness of the dawn. The golden beach was dotted here and there with the solitary figures of early-morning surf-fishermen casting their bait into the swells of the gently rolling sea. Idly she wondered if they ever caught anything, and if they did, what sort of creatures they pulled from the sparkling waters.

Taking her mug, she walked down to the wet strand and strolled up the beach, mindful that in a few hours she would be joining Eric to finish the sorting job they'd begun the day before. As if to put off the actual moment when they'd meet again face to face, she slowed her steps.

"Good morning," she greeted the first grizzled man she approached. "Catch anything?"

"Not yet," the old man grunted without a glance in her direction.

"Do you ever catch anything?" she persisted, noticing that his bait can swam with herring, but that his stringer lay empty in the sand.

"Sometimes." His laconic reply was a long time coming.

"What?" she asked obstinately.

"Fish," he finally answered, fixing her with a gimlet eye as blue as the sea before him.

So much for that, she thought as she continued on her way, a smile lifting her lips.

It wasn't long before she stood in front of the house the Thorpes had rented.

Crossing the beach, she walked to the back of the house, where she was surprised to see Eric's convertible parked in the driveway in front of a second building nearly as large as the house itself. She had time to glimpse a broad lawn, bordered with flower beds, stretching back to the cliff on which the road ran before panic rose within her. Unwilling to abruptly confront him after the scene the night before, she stepped into the shadows of the garage, intending to circle the house and continue down the beach before he knew she was there.

A sharp rap on a newly awninged upstairs window drew her attention. She looked up as Eric struggled to free the window sash from the fresh white paint holding it fast. After a great deal of shaking and straining, he managed to open it far enough to call down to her.

"Come on in, the door's open."

This was the awkward moment she'd been dreading, and yet she'd known it was inevitable that they would have to meet again in the full light of morning. Their emotions would have to adjust to the rules of conduct he'd established the night before. They'd be civil friends, decorous and deferential. Nothing more.

"I've been going over the wiring," he said as they both stepped into the kitchen at the same time, he from the back staircase and she from the door. "I'm going to have to put in a few more outlets and string a two-twenty line upstairs for air conditioners. It's already too warm up there."

His smile, warm and sincere, enveloping her in its glow, spoke volumes, saying all the things that she wanted to hear, chasing away her fears. It acknowledged that there was something between them, something that had time and space to grow. Something that might overcome all the obstacles that had loomed so large in the darkest hour of the night.

"Come and see the rest of the house... in daylight," he invited, taking her hand, the twinkle in his eyes showing that he was remembering the kiss they'd shared in the pitch-dark kitchen. All the awkwardness that she'd envisioned was swept away by his casual acceptance of the attraction they felt for each other. His touch was as comforting as a caress.

The freshly carpeted and painted house was as charming as its comfortable exterior indicated. It would be a good place for the Thorpes to find each other. "I love it," she said enthusiastically, after they'd completed their tour. "Now all you need is a dog!"

THE NEXT EVENING, seated in the Seahurst Academy boardroom, Aurora scanned the gathering. She, Brook and the headmaster held down the faculty end of the highly polished table, while prominent members of the community filled the rest of the matching mahogany chairs surrounding it.

As the secretary read the minutes of the last meeting, Aurora mentally added up the pro votes she and Brook could count on for support for their proposal. A not too promising total, she feared, since an unusual number of members had shown up. She suspected they were there to give reports on the various committees they headed concerning the production of Eric's play.

In fact "old business" took so long, she was afraid that "new business" might be tabled until the next meeting. But she had reckoned without Brook's tenacity. As soon as the chairman asked for "new business" while pointedly looking at his watch, Brook stood to be recognized.

"Mr. Chairman, I would like to propose for the consideration of the board, some curriculum additions for the fall term. We are the only school in this county that does not offer to our middle and upper school students comprehensive drug education, information about AIDS, a course in human growth and development, or a grief-management seminar..."

An audible groan—low pitched and mannerly—but a definite groan, greeted his words. Undeterred, he carried through with his presentation, so articulate and convincing in all his arguments that Aurora could not believe that anyone concerned with the education of children could fail to grasp the significance of and the need for the programs he proposed.

"Young man," Mrs. Murray, an elderly woman who was the granddaughter of the founder of the school, addressed Brook after he had finished and she had been recognized. "The girls in Seahurst Academy are above such things! Drugs and AIDS are afflictions of the lower classes. Grief is a private matter. And if you are intimating that any of our girls might become pregnant out of wedlock, I would say that you are an unfit person to head our middle school!"

The boardroom was in an uproar before Mrs. Murray could sit down.

"Mr. Chairman, I'd like to speak in support of Dr. Oliver's motion..." Having no social status to protect within the community, Aurora felt she had nothing to lose by speaking out. By backing up Brook's presentation with actual anecdotes based on Seahurst girls' questions and the kinds of advice they came to her for, she held the floor for a full ten minutes.

"If there are no objections, I'd like a vote on this motion," the chairman directed when she took her seat, quickly squelching any further attacks.

The board split their vote—half in favor and half against Brook's motion. The chairman agreed to take the proposal under consideration.

"You know that means shelved!" Brook exclaimed later in the Jeep as they drove back to the beach.

"After the meeting I cornered the headmaster to talk to him about Katie. When I told him that at the very least we'll have to provide her classmates with some counseling on suicide and how to help her, he said we'd do no such thing. He said it would all blow over in time. He insisted that openly talking about it would only harm Katie more! I can't believe his archaic stance!" Aurora fumed.

"I can," Brook muttered. "I have to work with the guy every day...and he's scared to death of his shadow!"

"Mrs. Murray is a real problem, too."

"She can be," Brook conceded, "and she certainly attacked me tonight. But I've come to learn over the years that her motives are good and her interest is genuine. She really wants what she thinks is best for the girls. But she's far more reasonable than she seems, and she can be swayed by the facts. I've seen her change her mind before, when it seemed unlikely that she would. I should have approached her privately before bringing the issue up. But it's too late now. If I did it at this point, the headmaster would have my neck for insubordination."

"That man!" was all Aurora would allow herself on the subject.

When they pulled into her driveway, Aurora decided to ask Brook a question she'd been wondering about ever since she'd met him. For a well-educated, gregarious man, who she'd recently discovered held a doctorate degree from Stanford, to be forty years old and still employed as a middle school dean just didn't make sense. If he were independently wealthy and from an established family in the area, she could understand that he held the job as an avocation. But he wasn't, and still he stayed working for a fraction of what a man with his qualifications could command elsewhere. There had to be a compelling reason, and she'd recently become convinced that it had something to do with the Thorpes... though she couldn't say what.

"Why are you still here at Seahurst?" she asked, keeping her tone casual and light. The look of pain that crossed his rounded face on hearing her question made her wish she'd kept her mouth shut.

It was a long time before he answered.

"I've had plenty of offers over the years," he said quietly. "Actually, I have a letter right here in my pocket from a prestigious school outside of Chicago asking me to apply as headmaster. And you know, if things don't go right with the new curriculum proposal, I just might do it!"

"But those other offers... why didn't you explore any of them?"

"Because of Stacia Thorpe," he finally said with a ragged sigh.

"Stacia?" she repeated uncomprehendingly. "I don't understand."

"I fell in love with her the day Eric brought her to Seahurst," he stated simply.

Aurora's breath caught in her throat, and she took care to release it slowly, if painfully. "And she's the reason you've never married?" she almost whispered, wondering how she'd dared place herself in competition with memories of a woman who'd held two wonderful men captive to her spell even while ravaged by illness.

"Yes."

"But she was married to Eric," she protested, unable to imagine Brook in an adulterous relationship with his best friend's wife.

"That's right. And I never acted on my feelings for her, beyond friendship, but it didn't change them. Does that make me a terrible person?" he asked sadly.

"Oh, no, not at all," she said softly without hesitation. "None of us can help our feelings. Love doesn't seem to be something we can orchestrate or plan. I think it just happens or it doesn't. But Stacia..." She shook her head as if to clear her confusion. "Why don't you tell me about her."

"She was unique. One of a kind. There was no one in the world like her," he said as though lost in memory. "And then when she got sick, she needed me. With Ric gone to L.A., or on location so much of the time before she got really bad, she relied on me—made me promise that I'd never leave her. And I never did," he finished, tears threatening to spill from his eyes.

"Oh, Brook, I'm so sorry. I knew you were fond of her. But believe me, I would never have asked if I'd known. Eric has never mentioned..."

"I told you. There's nothing to mention," he interjected. "We were all friends, nothing more."

"Would you like to come in and talk about it?" she asked as gently as she could.

"No, Aurora, don't misunderstand me. I appreciate the offer and I know you're not trying to pry, but I don't need to talk about it. My feelings for Stacia were always private, and they'll stay that way. I accepted that and made my choices a long time ago. Believe me, I don't have any regrets for myself. It just wasn't meant to be any other way."

"But you deserve..."

"Happiness?"

She nodded over the lump that was forming in her throat.

He shrugged. "Maybe. I thought so at one time, but I'm not so sure anymore."

"It'll be all right, Brook, it really will," she offered, wondering whether she was trying to convince him or herself. Lasting happiness had eluded her as well.

"Well, I can't afford to make this a late night," he said, attempting a grin. "Tomorrow Ric's going to rehearse us with the stars instead of with the understudies. I need my beauty sleep if I'm going to make an impression on Michelle Saunders."

Feeling that she was somehow letting him down, yet respecting his right to drop the subject of Stacia, she let herself out of the Jeep. As she closed the door she responded, "I wonder how Eric and Katie made out at dinner tonight with her and Tom Harris."

"Good question," he quipped, "and one with no predictable answer. Katie can sure give her dad a run for his money."

Amen to that, Aurora agreed, her thoughts in turmoil as she watched the red taillights of Brook's Jeep disappear up the hill.

Chapter Nine

The following day Aurora knew she could put away her worries concerning any unpredictable behavior Katie might exhibit for the run of the play. Mesmerized by Tom Harris, the budding teenager was caught in the throes of an overpowering crush. After they'd shopped for and purchased a dress that was the exact color of her eyes, she'd spent hours trying different ways of arranging her hair, and had insisted on having full access to Aurora's cosmetics to do her face. Amused, Aurora knew that as long as the vibrant young actor was around, Katie would be thirteen, going on twenty-three.

And that night, while having a late supper at the country club with the Thorpes and the stars, Aurora found herself nearly as star struck as Katie. She could hardly pull her gaze away from the magnetic pair.

"What a hunk," she whispered to Eric as he held Katie's new camcorder to his eye, filming his enraptured daughter and a deliberately attentive Tom Harris on the dance floor. Katie had insisted on the purchase of the camera so that she could capture and keep every minute of the exciting week to watch over and over again.

"I noticed that you noticed," he said with a chuckle.

"Shh," she cautioned, "that microphone will pick up every word we say. I'm just as fascinated with Michelle as I am with Tom...well, almost," she conceded with a grin, as he raised one brow in amused objection. "They literally glow. I can understand now why they're called stars."

"You're pretty radiant, yourself," he said, turning to look down at her, the camera on his shoulder forgotten for the moment. "You sure do light up my life."

Hugging his words to her heart, Aurora gave herself up to pure enjoyment in the hours that followed. It was a kick when she had her chance to dance with a man who had just made the list of America's Ten Sexiest Men. But it was far more wonderful to be held in Eric's arms as they moved in time to the music on the dimly lit floor. She knew if she were polled, even though he usually spent his time behind the camera, Eric Thorpe would get her vote. And, she suspected, if Eric had ever chosen to cast himself in a movie role, she wouldn't be alone in her opinion.

Later, when Eric left Katie curled up in a small, sleeping ball of contentment in the back seat to walk Aurora to her door, she wasn't the least surprised when he stepped into the house behind her.

"I 'noticed' Michelle too," he drawled in a low, husky, teasing tone, "but I couldn't take my eyes off you." Pulling her into his arms, he gave her a gentle, lingering goodnight kiss.

While she dreamily got ready for bed, she ran the tip of her tongue over her lips, savoring the faint, delicious taste of him that she imagined remained. Why, she wondered, had she, who had carefully guarded her emotions all her adult life, chosen to fall in love with a man who was not yet free to love?

OPENING NIGHT was a gala affair for Seahurst, attended by the city's most prominent residents. Taking her seat in the front row beside Paula just before the lights dimmed, Aurora knew the butterflies in her stomach couldn't have been any worse if she had had the starring role. Though she knew it was foolish, she felt responsible... if she hadn't been so insistent that Eric carry through with his commitment to do the play, he might never have done it.

He was still so vulnerable.

The community had turned out in full force. But was it a show of support for him as a man and in recognition of his talent, or had they come out of some sort of ghoulish curiosity? Would his producing a play known to be about his life with Stacia be taken as a cold, opportunistic gesture, or as a tribute to her, as it was intended? Why, she wondered, her heart in her throat, hadn't any of these doubts occurred to her before?

Only moments later her fears dissipated. Dutifully filming the event for Katie, she was awestruck by the talent of the man who had written the uniquely original script. And the audience was with him every step of the way, she realized with a joy that took her breath away. It hadn't been a mistake to urge him to undertake the project.

"Isn't this fantastic?" Paula leaned over to whisper. Aurora could only nod in reply, too emotion-choked to speak.

As the crowd was moved to gales of laughter and applause by Eric's creative brilliance, Aurora refused to believe or accept that the plays he'd already written and produced would be the last he'd ever do. Perhaps, she allowed herself to fervently hope, given this boost, his confidence would return and his ingenious, artistic talent would flow once more.

Katie's performance was flawless. Aurora's maternal anxiety that the young girl would be intimidated and flustered by the large crowd faded into a warm glow of pride as she relaxed against her seat. As though she were a seasoned trouper, the thirteen-year-old timed her words perfectly around the mirthful response of the crowd.

When the final lines of the play had been spoken, the audience rose to its feet as one, calling the cast back time after time with the persistent sound of their clapping. When at last they called for the author, Aurora's tears of joy for Eric's success blurred the viewfinder of the camcorder.

Putting down the camera, Aurora joined in the applause for the handsome, intriguing man who took the stage hand-in-hand with his radiant daughter. There'd been surprisingly little of the negative publicity he'd said he expected in the press. Still, she wondered, what must he be feeling, making this public appearance before the people he'd feared would gossip about his wife's tragic death?

"Thank you for your wonderful reception," Eric said, his head held high. His words were lost to the thundering acclaim that greeted him. When at last after several bows the audience quieted for him, he went on. "I want to dedicate this opening-night performance to the memory of my wife, Stacia Hudson. This play was written about her, and for her, in a humble attempt to portray the unique quality of her laughing spirit and her abundant zest for life. She was always my inspiration."

There was a moment of hushed silence before the air around them was filled once more with cheering and clapping. Aurora was horrified to see Katie wrench her hand from Eric's. She watched helplessly as the child burst into tears and began to address him with furious gestures, seemingly oblivious to the crowd of onlookers.

"What on earth..." Paula started.

"I don't know," Aurora said frantically. "Take this for me, would you?" She handed the camcorder to her friend and stepped quickly to the edge of the stage.

"Katie, darling, Katie...come here," she directed, holding out her arms to the blindly weeping child who managed to stagger from the low stage. Cradling Katie against her body, she hurried her around the circle of the standing crowd, past the group of actors standing at the back, to the darkness behind the changing tent.

"What's wrong, honey?" she pleaded over and over again, but in her grief, Katie was beyond answering.

Quickly leading the pathetically sobbing child, Aurora helped her into the car and started for the beach house.

ALONE ON THE STAGE, feeling a painful pressure build and grow at the base of his skull, Eric continued to acknowledge the resounding applause with a smile so forced it was almost a grimace. He beckoned to the cast to join him for a final curtain call.

"Brook." He stopped his friend as he stepped up beside him. "Katie's hysterical. Take over for me as host at the cast party. I doubt I'll be back. Take Paula Sumner with you, would you?" he added as an afterthought. "I know she came with Aurora."

Then slipping into the darkness at the back of the stage, he ran for his car, knowing instinctively that Aurora had taken Katie and started for home.

For a moment on stage when his daughter had jerked away from him and her mouth had twisted as she'd shouted that she really hated him now, he'd been afraid that his knees would buckle. Plunging in a split second from the height of public acclamation to the pit of devastation had almost caused him to lose his balance.

Katie's irrational behavior had unnerved him...reminded him too much of Stacia. He didn't want to admit it, even to himself, but tonight had made him wonder if perhaps Katie's problems were more than he and Aurora could handle. As knowledgeable as she was, Aurora wasn't a psychiatrist...and she loved Katie like a mother, he was sure of that. Perhaps her love was blinding her to the full extent of Katie's emotional problems.

Anxiety gnawed at his heart, and his tension headache increased its pressure as he sped along the oceanside highway.

"I CAN'T GET HER calmed down enough to find out what triggered this outburst." A distraught Aurora greeted him as he ran up the back steps and into the house.

Hurrying to the couch where Katie lay curled tightly around a pillow, his heart missed a beat. How many times had he seen Stacia assume that same position? His mind raced ahead in a jumble of thoughts too terrible to allow to take form, as he forced himself to calmly kneel down beside her... forced himself to believe that she could be reasoned with and reached... forced himself to trust that his darling daughter was not becoming as ill as her mother had been.

"Katie," he said gently. He tried to take her into his arms, but she wordlessly resisted his touch and refused to look at him. "Katie," he repeated, "talk to me...say anything, darling, but talk to me. What have I done to hurt you like this?" he begged after an interminable wait, his voice cracking with anguish.

Just when he was close to giving up hope, Katie's muffled voice wailed, "Go away! Leave me alone!" before another outbreak of wretched sobbing shook her slight frame.

"I won't go away," he answered raggedly, gratitude for being able to elicit a response surging over him as he pressed his face against the damp hair of his perspiring child. "That's the one thing you can count on. And I'll never leave you alone. I'm staying right here tonight until I find out what's wrong."

Suddenly sitting bolt upright, her reddened face disfigured by its wrathful expression, she spat out, "You never told me the play was about my mother! How could you tell it to all those people without telling me first?"

Repelled by the venom in her tone, he sat back on his heels, trying to comprehend the meaning behind her words. Suddenly grasping the significance of her behavior, he realized she wasn't being irrational, but rather violently and even understandably disturbed by what had been a devastating revelation for her.

"But, Munchkin, everyone knows that my plays are mostly autobiographical," he answered in dismay, sheer relief warring with the stark guilt that overwhelmed him.

"Everyone but me!" she shouted. "I don't count as anybody to you, do I? I'm not even worth being told anything that involves you or your secret life!"

"Oh, Katie, Katie, darling," he said, rising on his knees before her, his arms helplessly reaching out in a plea for her forgiveness. "You're everything to me. You're my world...no one else..."

She pushed his hands away. "I suppose your next play is going to be about my mother going crazy and jumping off the Golden Gate Bridge!" The spite in her voice brought tears to his eyes.

"No, baby, you don't have to worry about that," he choked out. "Your mother's illness and death have hurt me so much I don't think I'll ever be able to write again."

Burying his face with its streaming tears in her lap, he slid his arms around his shaking child. "I don't have to use words to tell anyone what was best about your mother, you do that for me every day. I'm sorry I'm not good enough for you. I'm so sorry I've hurt you ... failed you ... misunderstood you ... when I love you so much."

Aurora stood rooted to the floor, her emotions so entwined with the father and child crying together on the couch, that she felt as though she were an impassioned participant sharing in their heartbreaking pain.

After a long while when Eric moved to sit up on the couch, cradling his daughter on his lap, Aurora sat down with them. Turning toward him, she placed one hand on his shoulder in a gesture of support, while softly stroking Katie's hair with the other. At long last, they'd openly mourned their mutual loss together, she thought with relief. The crisis had passed. The festering wound of grief had burst open with a searing episode of almost unbearable pain ... but it had been worth the cost. Now, the true healing could begin.

LATER, WHEN Katie's heavy sobs had subsided and the exhausted child lay motionless in Eric's arms, Aurora suggested that he carry her into bed.

"Daddy," Katie murmured as he kissed her good-night, after they'd gotten her into nightclothes and tucked her in. "I'm so afraid I'll lose you. I worry about it all the time."

"You don't have to worry about that," he said, his lips against her cheek. "I'm yours until Niagara Falls."

"How about until snowdrops?" Katie asked drowsily, a small smile curving her lips.

"Until then, too," he promised solemnly. "Now you get some sleep, precious."

As she watched them, and listened to the exchange that she knew must date back to the early days of Katie's childhood when she and her daddy had been close, Aurora felt her heart almost burst with boundless love for them both.

After Eric had washed his face, he joined her on the deck. He stood, his hands in his tuxedo pockets, breathing in the salt-tanged air of the balmy night. It was so still that the chirps of crickets in the grass by the road could be heard harmonizing with the lapping of the gentle waves at the shore.

It had been his incredible good looks that had attracted her first. Then his sensitivity, expressed in his willingness to admit his feelings of inadequacy when it came to his daughter, had rapidly compounded the attraction. But her attraction to Eric Thorpe was no longer based merely on externals, such as the way his body looked in a tux, or situational variables, such as his needing her help with Katie, Aurora realized. Now, when she looked at the man, it was his strength of character and nobility of heart that drew her to him like a magnet. She adored him, it was as simple as that.

"It's been quite a night for you," Aurora said softly, from where she sat in the double swing.

"That's for sure," he answered in the baritone voice that could be magnificently commanding, or stirringly emotional . . . but that never left her untouched.

"Two real triumphs . . ."

"Two?"

"The success of your production and the closeness you achieved with Katie."

He looked at her for a long moment before he sat down beside her. "The question is where do I go from here?" he asked, pushing back and putting his hands behind his head.

"I've been thinking about that," she said, slightly moving her leg to keep the swing going in a slow, gentle rock, "and I feel the next step is for you to really level with her tomorrow."

When he didn't answer but kept his eyes on the distant stars, she continued. "If tonight proved anything, it showed that no matter how well we may think things are going, Katie still feels like an outsider in your life. Actually, if you think about it, you raised her to be an outsider. You didn't want her to know what was really going on. That you did what was done in an honest effort to protect her is beside the point. Ultimately, not even you could keep the truth from her.

"She's been hurting for a long time. I suspect from the day you first sent her to the academy to board. She told me once that she never knew why she had to live at school when her home was in Seahurst...never knew why conversations broke off when she came into a room...never knew why her mother acted as though she didn't love her.

"I've tried to explain everything to her, but it isn't enough to have it come from me. You're going to have to answer all those questions, and you may have to do it again and again."

"Where will I start?" he asked.

"Start with Katie and keep your focus on her. Tell her the story of her life, from the very beginning. Tell her the little things like when you and she first started playing that word game I heard you play tonight. You two have a lot of past history that she needs to know about. She hasn't been in a family where she's had a chance to hear what her first words were...or, I don't know...whether or not she liked to have you sing to her before she fell asleep.

"Your plays show that you remember everything, Eric," she said, reaching over to entwine her fingers with his. "Just pour your heart out to her, a little at a time. Mix the big things in with the small ones so that you don't overwhelm her. But don't leave anything out that concerns her. Stress how much she is and has always been loved. She needs that reassurance from you.''

He drew in a deep breath and let it out slowly. "It's going to be hard to really let her in . . . I've kept my guard up for so long.''

"But don't you see? You dropped it tonight . . . and you don't ever have to put it back up. Katie is a part of you . . . you don't have to hold her at bay.''

"I think I've got it, Doc," he said after a long silence, getting to his feet and pulling her up beside him. "I'll start telling her everything over breakfast in the morning. And after that, I think we'll go on a little shopping spree . . . to buy a dog . . . together.''

"You've got it, all right," she agreed with an encouraging smile. And, she thought silently, I just might have a prescription for what ails you, too, Mr. Thorpe.

Chapter Ten

"Brook," Aurora began as soon as the secretary put him on the line. "Meet me for lunch? The German deli across the street from the hospital?"

"Well, let's see," he drawled, "have to check my social calendar..."

She could picture him leaning back in his chair to prop his feet up on his desk. His summertime duties at the academy were light, since most of the students attending enrichment classes were drawn from the local public school population. Only a few of the girls, like Katie's roommate Jenni, were, in essence, year-round boarders.

"Michelle Saunders is going to be awfully disappointed when I cancel out on having lunch with her," he chuckled. "I'll have to come up with a good excuse."

"Tell her you have to see your doctor," Aurora quipped.

"That should take care of it," Brook agreed solemnly. "Seriously, what time and why?"

"Twelve noon, and I'll tell you why when you get there," she said crisply, glancing at her watch. An epidemic of summer colds was sweeping the preteen set, and she'd have to hurry to see all the little people with stuffy noses and coughs who were cramming her waiting room. "It's just an idea I'd like your input on. It's too complicated to discuss on the phone, and I'm up to my neck in tongue depressors and cotton swabs.''

''Sounds kinky, if you ask me,'' he teased. When she didn't rise to the bait, he added, ''Can't even give me a clue, huh?''

''Nope,'' she said, with a grin on her face.

''I hope you know I won't be able to do anything the rest of the morning wondering what you've got on your mind,'' he warned. ''By the way, do you have any idea where Ric is? I've been trying to get hold of him, but all Bridey can tell me is that he left the house early this morning.''

''Katie slept over at my place last night,'' she explained, ''and he picked her up while I was in the shower. They're probably out making the rounds of all the kennels in the area by now.''

''Paula told me Katie fell apart during the curtain call last night...but I suppose you don't have time to tell me about that, either.''

''That's right,'' Aurora answered sweetly. ''Now I've...''

''So, she gets her dog,'' he continued in a pleased tone. ''Have you ever considered branching out into psychiatry, Doctor?''

''No. Now I'm hanging up before I have a mob of irate mothers in my office....''

''Ah, there are similarities between our jobs,'' Brook joked.

''Goodbye, Brook,'' Aurora said, hanging up the phone. She smiled. He was such a nice person and so much fun. It was no wonder he was popular among the students at Seahurst and in the community in general. Hearing a chorus of coughs, she quickly picked up a chart and opened the door to the first in a row of five small, colorfully decorated examination rooms. The more she thought of it, he was just the man Paula needed.

"WELL, WHAT DO you think?" Aurora asked before taking a sip of her lemonade. It felt wonderful just to be sitting down. She kicked off a shoe and wiggled her toes before reluctantly slipping it back on. The morning had been as hectic as she'd feared, and the afternoon was stacking up to be just as bad. She and her receptionist were two of a kind...neither one of them had the heart to refuse to squeeze one more sick child into the schedule.

"It's a great idea!" Brook said with genuine enthusiasm. "I wonder why I never thought of it."

"I can see why," Aurora commented. "Under ordinary circumstances it wouldn't be an appropriate suggestion to make to a three-time Oscar winner. But these aren't ordinary circumstances."

"You're right. But still, before opening night I would have been a little skeptical about acting on it," Brook answered, pulling at his ear the way he always did when he was thinking over a problem.

"Why's that?"

"The local gossip mongers," he replied, taking a bite of German potato salad. "Eric and Stacia never mixed much with the community, and Seahurst is still a small town at heart. Suicide casts a stigma on the surviving members of the family."

Aurora shuddered, causing the ice cubes in the drink she held to jingle. "I know. And I'll tell you I had a few anxious moments last night before the curtain went up. If the crowd had been hostile to him, I don't know what I would have done."

"You really care for Ric, don't you?" Brook asked softly.

"I do," she candidly admitted. "But I'm not sure there's any future in it."

"I can't believe that," he said, leaning forward and resting his lower arms on the table. "He's crazy about you. You're the only thing that's kept him going."

"That's one of the problems," she said, fleetingly wondering how she'd let herself become so sidetracked. "Maybe he just needs me . . . maybe his feelings are a reaction to losing Stacia."

"No," Brook said firmly, jutting out his lower jaw. "I know Ric as well as I've ever known anyone. He hadn't been anything but a caretaker to Stacia for years . . . a loving, devoted one, but that was it. He hasn't been in love like this for a long, long time."

It was on the tip of her tongue to ask Brook the question that still haunted her whenever she happened to wake up in the hours before dawn . . . If that were true, then why had Stacia been pregnant when she died . . . ? But she managed to bite it back. If anyone other than Eric would know, Brook might. But she'd resigned herself to never knowing the answer. And the longer she knew Eric Thorpe the less important it became.

"Ric showed a lot of guts going through with producing the play. He told me he would never have done it, if it hadn't been for you."

Aurora groaned and turned her face away before looking back to meet his gaze. "That's what I was afraid of. But what if the whole thing had flopped? What if they'd booed him?"

"That's just the point," Brook insisted. "It didn't flop. Your judgment was as right on the mark then as I'm sure it is now. And I felt that standing ovation he got was as much for the audience recognizing his courage and showing their acceptance of him, as it was for their appreciation of a damned good play."

"I felt that way, too," Aurora answered, amazed as always by Brook's keen perception. He was the one who would have made a fine psychiatrist.

"So," he continued expansively, "your idea couldn't be better. Taking Ric on as artist in residence at Seahurst will not only be a feather in our cap, but a public show of confidence in the man and his abilities.

"It should help Katie out, too," he added thoughtfully. "If any of the girls have negative opinions about Katie's family when they arrive back at school, it won't take long to get them to change their minds. Teenagers are easily swayed in their opinions. And Ric can be quite a charmer. They'll love him."

"Aren't we getting the cart a little before the horse?" she worried. "Eric hasn't even heard my idea, much less agreed to it."

"He will," Brook with confidence, taking a bite of his Reuben sandwich.

"I don't know," she said nervously. "Maybe I shouldn't have stuck my nose into his business again. It's just that I think Eric needs a chance to start rebuilding his life without feeling any pressure to write. If you'd seen how dejected he was Saturday trying to sort out his office for the movers, you'd understand why I'm suggesting this."

"Hey, you're talking about my buddy," Brook protested. "I know what he's been like."

"I'm sorry," she apologized. "Of course you do."

"Actually," Brook reflected, a faraway look in his eyes, "he held up better than most people could ever have done until about a year ago. We didn't talk about it, but I think it was about that time when he finally resigned himself to the fact that things weren't ever going to get any better.

"He seemed to lose hope after Stacia came back from that first cruise she took by herself, worse than she'd been when she'd left. The latest doctor had been so adamant that it would be therapeutic for her to be on her own in a relatively controlled environment for a few weeks, that he'd finally agreed to it. Ric let her go one more time after that at her insistence, but he knew it would be a disaster before she left.

"I loved Stacia," Brook said gently, "and I know Ric would never have left her. But I don't know what would have become of him if she'd lived. His mind just seemed to go blank and he lost his confidence. Sometimes I wonder if he'll ever get it back again. I know he does, too.

"So you see," he concluded, reaching over to pat her hand, "whether he does or not, your idea will give him a little breathing space. He can always go back to directing in time...but writing was his first love." He shook his head mournfully.

"Where do you think you should start?" she asked, nibbling disinterestedly at a large dill pickle. She knew she should eat, or she'd be sneaking one of the fruit sticks she kept in a jar for her small patients later in the afternoon. But she was interfering in Eric's life again, and though she believed her idea was sound, she was uneasy about it.

"I'll feel 'the old man' out this afternoon," Brook said after polishing off his sandwich.

"Do you think the headmaster will go for it?"

"Are you kidding? The timing's perfect. We'll capitalize immediately on the success of the play and the money it generated. Besides," he snorted, "you'd think, to hear the old goat tell it, that he'd been the prime mover behind the production!"

"He's a difficult man to work for," Aurora commiserated. "He thrives on control. He's the kind of person who gives the education profession a bad name. I wonder how close he is to retirement."

"Huh!" Brook let out a short puff of air. "He'll be squeezing every penny and making everyone jump to his tune until they carry him out someday on a litter. I've been tempted to take that job in Illinois, but I've got such a great staff that I hate to leave them without a sympathetic buffer." He laughed. "And if I go, it won't be this year. Ric won't jump to his tune. You can be damn sure of that. And I want to be around to see it."

"I wonder how Eric will take the idea," she said, becoming a little apprehensive as a disquieting thought occurred to her. "I hope he doesn't see it as a vote of no confidence."

"What do you mean?" Brook asked with a puzzled frown.

"Like teaching and directing at a girl's school is all we think he's capable of doing."

"Don't worry on that score. He'll understand."

"I wish I could be so sure. I hate to ask, but if you don't mind, when you approach him I'd like him to believe that it was your idea."

"Gotcha," he agreed with a wink.

"I just don't want him to think I'm trying to run his life..."

Brook held up a hand. "Say no more. I understand."

"Good," she said, giving him a grateful smile. "I've thought about it a lot, and I agree with you that another plus to his working at the academy is that it would be a wonderful opportunity for him to be involved in Katie's life. I think if he had the chance to work with other girls her age, he'd really understand that her behavior isn't unusual. I think it would help them become as close as they both want to be."

"I'll stress that," Brook said. "And after what you told me about what happened with Katie last night, I'm sure he'll go for it, if for no other reason."

"How do you feel the board will respond?" she asked, remembering Monday night's disappointment.

"More favorably than to our last proposal!" He laughed. "Don't worry about them. They'll be quick to see what a social as well as an academic coup it would be for Seahurst to have a nationally recognized playwright in residence. And with their eyes on the purse strings, they'll catch on real quick that this will be one way they can assure themselves of having another successful play next summer. We might even be able to ride our proposal in on the shirttail of this one. Maybe make it a contingency."

"You wouldn't do that... would you?"

"Not outright, but a word here and there might do it," he said with a sly grin. "Hey, Doctor, you haven't even touched your sandwich," he remarked, "and it's almost time for your afternoon office hours to start."

"I guess I wasn't as hungry as I thought."

He scowled. "I always thought you were a pretty good eater... not like that friend of yours."

"Paula?" she asked.

He nodded. "Eric asked me to take her with me to the cast party last night, and I'll tell you, she sure put a damper on things for me."

"Why's that?" Aurora asked, feeling her heart sink.

"Every time I popped a canape into my mouth I felt like she had the calories and cholesterol in it counted to the last gram."

Aurora laughed. "You just had a guilty conscience."

"No, I'm serious. I get the feeling that she and that Bill Brady eat lettuce and sprout sandwiches and drink wheat germ shakes. Where was he last night, anyway?"

Despite the fact that she knew Brook would heartily claim it wasn't so, Aurora detected a note of real interest in his seemingly casual question. The idea of pairing up Brook and Paula wasn't one she was ready to drop. No one got this worked up over someone who didn't interest him.

"His dad's chain was opening a new health spa in Vegas last night. He had to be there."

"It figures," Brook said glumly.

"Would you like my sandwich?" Aurora asked, as innocently as she could manage. "I could have the waitress put it in a doggie bag for you."

A flicker of temptation crossed his broad face, before he shook his head and placed a self-conscious hand on his midriff. "No, I think I'll pass."

DURING THE RUN of the play, Eric made no mention of her idea. Since she had assumed he would talk it over with her, she questioned Brook who assured her that the headmaster had been delighted with the suggestion and that he had insisted on being the one to approach Eric. As far as Brook knew, Eric was thinking it over.

But if he was giving it much thought, he wasn't letting on to her. Though she was anxious to know his decision, when she thought it through, she was relieved that he hadn't yet asked her opinion. She'd done enough by suggesting the plan to Brook...she didn't want to feel that she'd been a deciding influence in the choice he made. She didn't want to bear the heavy weight of responsibility that she'd experienced on opening night ever again.

THE WEEKEND AFTER the play had closed its successful run, Aurora and Paula were taking the rottweilers for their usual Sunday-morning romp on the beach when they decided to stop by to see how Eric and Katie were settling in. Katie and her roommate, Jenni, greeted them at the door, each holding one of Katie's two darling golden Labrador retriever puppies. Before they could get inside, Brook appeared with an invitation for everyone to join him at his house for an impromptu barbecue.

It hadn't been difficult to talk Eric out of his plans to spend the glorious day unpacking and putting his books in order on the newly installed shelves in his study, and Paula had agreed to go, but only for a while. She had a date for the evening. Piling into their separate cars, the group drove in a happy caravan up to the cliff house.

"It's fabulous!" Paula exclaimed to Brook as she got out of her car, looking around at the A-frame, then at the open field that stretched back to a stand of low, leafy trees. "It's heaven!"

"Would you like to come in and see the house?" he asked, obviously pleased with her reaction.

"You bet!" Paula agreed.

"Let me take Gretch and Gret," Katie offered, opening the rear door of Paula's station wagon.

"I haven't been here before, either," Aurora said, including herself in Brook's invitation, wanting to see where he'd hung the large paintings.

"You haven't?" he asked in a puzzled tone.

Shaking her head and giving him a smile, she knew what he meant. They'd become such close friends in the past few weeks that it did seem strange that she hadn't seen where he lived.

Glancing back at Eric, she caught the wave of his hand. "Go on," he said, "I'll keep an eye on the girls and the dogs."

Katie was already off and down the field with the bounding rottweilers, while Jenni had settled on the grass cuddling the two blond puppies.

"It's positively perfect!" Paula exclaimed with unusual enthusiasm as she strode around the open-beamed house.

"I'm proud of it," Brook admitted quietly. "Sometimes during the months when I was camping out and bedding down in that teardrop trailer, I didn't think I'd ever get it finished."

"You built this?" Paula asked in what Aurora could only label as a squeal of amazement. In all the years she'd known her, she couldn't remember Paula ever having been so openly effusive.

"Every bit of," Brook said, his face split by a broad grin. "Oh, Ric helped me get the beams in place...but for the rest of it, I was on my own."

"I can't believe it," Paula said. "I've never met anyone who actually built his own house. I think it's great!

"And those paintings! They're absolutely...well, fabulous!" She looked with new appreciation at the man by her side.

"You like them?" he responded in a pleased tone. His round face seemed fixed in a perpetual grin, as they stood at the deck end of the living room looking back at the long wall below the upstairs balcony. Hung side by side, the large canvases occupied almost the entire space.

"I love them! We must have very similar taste," Paula answered.

Aurora decided to leave the two of them alone for the rest of the tour and to go in search of Eric. The way things were going, she suspected her friends would never miss her.

"How are you enjoying your new house?" Aurora asked, when she found Eric standing at the cliff's edge, looking out over the ocean. Following his concentrated gaze, she made out the large, colorful sailing wings of hang gliders lifting and dipping on the air currents far to the south. For a moment fear gripped her heart. Was he thinking of Stacia?

But then he took her hand and said, "It's a great day for gliding. Maybe we'll unpack ours and take a spin. Would you like to try it?"

"I'll observe for a while," she answered with a cautious smile. "I'm not really that fond of flying. I like to have both feet on the ground."

He squeezed her hand, returning her smile. "Then don't ever think you have to try it on my account. Just don't try to get me down in a cave...I don't care how scenic it is. I have a terror of being underground," he confided.

"I'll remember that," she promised soberly, thinking how wonderful it was to be with him like this. Behaving like a future for the two of them was secured...certain. If only it were.

"To answer your question," he continued, walking her away from the bluff and back around the house. "Living on the water is wonderful. We're bumping into things, but I think that's as much because everything's in the wrong place as anything else...we'll get used to the smaller space in time. This week has been pretty hectic moving in.

"By the way, would you have time to make suggestions about the furniture arrangements?" he asked. "Bridey's wearing Mac and me out moving it every which way, and she still isn't satisfied. If you don't, I'll have to check into hiring an interior designer."

"Don't do that." Aurora chuckled. "I'll come over one evening this week, and Bridey and I can put both you and Mac to work."

"Thanks," he said sincerely. "It's tough trying to turn a house into a home. You know, I'm not concerned about this week, but I'm concerned about next week, and about all the weeks after that."

"Why?" she asked, alarmed at the sudden heaviness of his tone.

"The production kept me occupied for over a month. Moving will occupy a week or two... but then what?"

"Katie?" she suggested, not knowing what else to say. She was determined not to mention the job offer from Sea-hurst unless he brought it up.

He threw back his head and shrugged. "Katie's part of my life, a part that's with me always. I can't separate her from it for a single minute. But I can't occupy myself being a glorified nursemaid, and once she's back into the routine at school this fall, she won't need that from me. But I need to be doing something... growing, not stagnating."

"Are you thinking of going away?" she asked in a small voice, her throat constricting painfully.

"Oh, Lord, no," he murmured, gathering her close. "I couldn't leave you, Aurora, or Katie, either," he said against her hair. "The headmaster at the Academy has offered me a part-time job. Teaching. I've never thought about teaching. I don't know if I have it in me."

"Your father was a teacher," she reminded him.

"You're right," he said in amazement, holding her away to gaze into her eyes. "Maybe it's not such an alien idea after all. There must be something that's been passed down in my genes."

"What, exactly, would you be doing at the academy?" she asked, wondering what the headmaster had offered.

"Teaching a creative writing class. Perhaps an acting class. Directing stage plays. Nothing's been firmed up yet, because I haven't given him my answer."

"It would be a chance of a lifetime for those girls. You'd have so much to offer. Far more than anyone who hasn't had your experience."

"Think so?" he asked, uncertainly. "Even though I've never taught?"

"I'm positive of it," she answered. "Watching you rehearse for the play, it struck me that directing and teaching have many things in common. And not only that, they say the finest teachers are good actors. You qualify on that score, too. When you were rehearsing them, you showed that you could have played any part in that play as well as the actors who did.

"And," she continued enthusiastically, warming to her subject, "with writing up course objectives, selecting texts and content, and plotting out your weekly lesson plans, you'd have a full summer ahead of you."

"Hmm," he said, speculatively, putting his arm around her shoulders as they started to walk again. "Objectives. That's a good word. I think I need more of them in my life."

When they got around the side of the house, Aurora saw the girls and Paula gathered around Brook as he pulled a wheeled cart from the garage.

"He's getting out the gliders." Eric quickened his pace.

"Paula wants to see how it's done," Brook explained when they joined the group.

"Me, too." Katie's deep blue eyes sparkled with excitement. "I always wondered what those things were in the garage. I want to fly."

"Not so fast, Munchkin," Eric said, amused. "It takes a long time learning, and it's dangerous."

"Everybody does it," Katie insisted, tossing back her mane of dark hair. "They're always flying off the cliffs around here," she added in aside to Jenni. "Daddy, do you know how?"

"I used to," he admitted, taking a cart to pull it out into the yard. "But it's been a long time."

"Will you teach us?" Katie asked. "We want to learn, don't we, Jenni?" Aurora noted that though Jenni nodded dutifully in reply, she didn't seem as anxious as Katie.

The two girls were such a contrast in many ways. Aurora felt sure only their separate but mutual sense of alienation from their families had made them into close friends. They had both been so starved for affection that they had clung to each other. What, she wondered, would happen to that friendship as Katie began to trust in her newfound security? Would she leave the less fortunate girl behind?

Sitting on the grass with Jenni and the puppies, Aurora watched as Eric instructed Katie in the rudiments of the sport. Katie was one of those rare, golden girls who was making a graceful physical transition from childhood to adolescence. Everything about her had stayed lovely and in proportion. Jenni, on the other hand, was more typical of girls their age. She wore braces and even though she was a year older than Katie, her boxy little body had yet to narrow at the waist or to flare at the hips. Her nose, which would be attractive in a few years, seemed too large for her face, and her hair was a dishwater blond that Aurora knew would be lovely someday when lightened a few shades. Her hunched shoulders were a dead giveaway of a woman-child who was developing breasts, but didn't want the world to see this sign of her burgeoning sexuality.

Which type of child was hers? Aurora wondered with a pain so sudden and sharp that it cut her to the quick. Was her daughter now in the awkward stage where many girls felt unloved and unlovable? Why, God, she wondered in silent agony, had she been deprived of the right to help the child she'd borne get through this difficult phase of life? Did her daughter have a mother who was sensitive to her very special adolescent need for understanding and reassurance? Or was her own child stumbling and faltering, suffering from feelings of alienation and insecurity, at the very same moment when Aurora was spending her time with other girls her daughter's age? Almost strangling on a sob, and seeing the others turn their gazes toward her, she managed to fake a cough as she hurried toward the house. In the privacy of the bathroom, she gave vent to the gut-wrenching distress that shook her to the core.

Sometime later, after splashing cold water on her face and holding a cool compress to her swollen eyes, she slipped on sunglasses before rejoining her friends.

"Are you all right?" Eric asked, coming to meet her.

"Fine," she lied, wondering once again how he'd feel about her if he knew what a fraud she was. Who was she to give him advice on raising a daughter? "Did I miss anything?"

"Not yet, but I think Brook's about ready to take the plunge." Putting one arm around her shoulders, he gestured to where Paula and Brook stood by Brook's glider, poised on the edge of the cliff. "Shall we join them?"

Aurora nodded, managing a smile.

"This is a pretty nifty setup. I think I could get the hang of it." Paula's pun elicited groans of amusement from the other three, as the girls came running to join the excitement.

"Hey, Ric," Brook challenged, slipping a harness over his shoulders. "Let's try it."

"Yes, Daddy," Katie squealed delightedly. "I want to see you do it. Will you?"

"Not today, Munchkin," Eric replied. "I don't think I'm up to it. It's something you have to psyche yourself into."

"I don't think Brook should either," Paula said, earnestly appealing to Eric. "He says he can't remember when he last had a physical, and he can't remember ever having an EKG. That's ridiculous for a man his age. He won't even let me take his pulse! I told him that his body doesn't look like it's in good enough condition to take the exertion."

"And I told her, just watch," Brook interjected pointedly, lying down on the glider and adjusting the frame.

"Are you sure you should do it, Uncle Brook?" Katie said, suddenly anxious. "I don't want anything to happen to you."

He scowled. "Don't you worry your pretty little head about that. I don't want anything to happen to me, either. And it won't. Just ask your dad. He and I have even taken up jogging."

Eric rolled his eyes, but diplomatically kept his mouth shut. Aurora smiled. As far as she knew, Brook hadn't mentioned jogging again after the one time Eric had told her about. Still, she knew Paula tended to err on the side of overcautiousness. Brook wasn't that old, and one flight wasn't likely to do him in. Besides, she knew nothing any of them could do or say would stop him.

"Give me a shove, buddy," Brook directed.

After some preliminary checking and tightening, Eric helped Brook launch on an updraft, and for a few breathless minutes the group watched the determined man circle and soar out over the sparkling water before he returned, gliding over their heads to land on the green expanse of lawn.

Winded but triumphant, he shot Paula a look of pleased satisfaction.

"You'd better make your peace with him before he does something drastic to prove his physical prowess," Aurora whispered to Paula as they ran to where the pudgy man was struggling to get loose from his harness.

"That was wonderful," Paula gushed, when she reached him. "You were fantastic. After you get a routine checkup, I'd love for you to teach me. How many lessons will I need before I can actually try it?"

Aurora and Eric exchanged a glance. Neither one of them doubted that Brook would have a physical before the week was out.

THE REST OF THE DAY was perfect. After joining in a spirited game of volleyball, Aurora sat back enjoying the activity around her. She'd decided not to let her pervasive sense of regret spoil the day—reminding herself that she was not the only one in this small group who had to cope with loss and remorse—and she was managing to do a decent job of it. Brook and Paula had started up the grill and had dismissed her offers to help. She hadn't pushed the issue, not wanting to get into the middle of their heated discussion about the virtues of grilling red meat versus filleted fish. She was with Brook on this one. Those thick steaks looked delicious and they were beginning to smell even better.

Similarly rebuffed, Eric had joined her and they chatted as they watched the girls play with the dogs.

"Why two?" she asked, as Jenni rolled in the grass with the fat playful puppies.

"They were the last of the litter. Katie couldn't make up her mind between them, and frankly, I didn't want to separate them."

"That was a good decision," Aurora approved. "This way they'll never be lonely. They're adorable. I wonder what she'll finally name them."

"She's been in agony over that. You should see the lists of names she's compiled. She actually made me drive her in to Seahurst to buy a book of baby names. Said she didn't want to name them anything that she didn't know what it meant. It's a riot. She'll decide on a couple and go around the house using them for a while, then she decides they're not right. Those pups have been called everything from Pit and Pat to Homer and Hortense. Do you think they'll develop an identity crisis, Doctor?''

"I'm not a dog psychiatrist," Aurora said with a grin, "so I don't think I'll venture an opinion on that. Although, I understand professionals are available for consultation for a substantial fee."

Eric laughed. "I think I'll pass and let Dawn and Dusk, or whoever they happen to be today, take their chances, just like the rest of us poor suckers. She'll make up her mind eventually."

"Have you discussed the Seahurst job offer with her?" Aurora asked, glad of the opportunity to mention what had been on her mind most of the afternoon.

"I will tonight," he promised. "I'm not about to make the mistake of surprising her again. For all I know, she may hate the idea. She's been filling me in on how many 'embarrassing' things there are... like every other thing I do."

Aurora laughed aloud and leaned back, resting her weight on her outstretched arms.

"She may find the idea of having her old man teach at Seahurst too 'embarrassing' for her to handle." He grinned and shook his head. "What an age! I don't remember ever going through it. Do you?"

"Of course," Aurora replied. "I remember when my dad grew a beard. I couldn't believe he'd do that. I was mortified until he shaved it off a few weeks later. I thought it was a terrible reflection on me. I didn't want any of my friends to see him."

"You never talk about your parents...."

A loud bong interrupted him. The sound reverberated across the cliff.

"Good heavens!" Aurora exclaimed, when she could hear again. "What was that?"

Eric laughed. "That's Brook's idea of a dinner bell. I was in Chinatown with him one night when he saw that thing. I tried to talk him out of it, but he wasn't having any of it. It took both of us to get it into the car. I was afraid it would shatter glass. But so far, it hasn't even cracked a pane."

Aurora giggled. "He's quite a character, isn't he?"

"Yes," Eric agreed drolly. "That he is."

AFTER THEY'D EATEN and Paula had packed up her dogs and left, they sat on the deck enjoying the sunset while the girls, each blissfully cuddling a contented puppy, watched television.

"She sure reminds me of Stacia," Brook mused.

"Who does?" Aurora and Eric asked in unison, thinking he must mean Katie.

"Paula, of course," Brook answered, as if it were obvious. "So small and enthusiastic and full of life. I haven't had that much fun with anyone in years."

"You argued all afternoon," Eric remarked dryly.

"No, we didn't," Brook objected. "I don't know what gave you that idea. We just have a lot to talk about."

Aurora hid her smile by taking a sip of iced tea.

MENTALLY COMPARING Paula's freckled pixie face framed by its wiry strawberry-blond hair, with the picture of Stacia she'd seen in Katie's bedroom, Aurora couldn't think of two people who looked more unalike, unless it was Brook and Eric. Wondering if Eric had been struck by the same thought, later that evening she asked him about Brook's comment.

Eric laughed. "They were about the same height, but other than that I don't see any resemblance. If you ask me, the only resemblance is that Brook was attracted to both of them."

"They say everyone sees people from a different perspective," Aurora ventured.

Eric shook his dark head. "I know, but that's pretty farfetched in this case. Still, I think you missed your calling."

"How's that?"

"I didn't think there was a chance that Brook and Paula would hit it off. But she sure seemed interested. I think she would have stayed this evening, if she could have. And Brook told me he was going to make a play for her, and that if Brady got in his way he was going to punch the meathead's lights out!"

"Oh no!" Aurora chortled. "I hope Brook doesn't try that. He *will* need a doctor. Most likely a good plastic surgeon."

"I don't think it'll come to that," Eric said with a chuckle. "Verbal sparring is more Brook's speed. If they do get into an argument, which seems unlikely, Brook will win hands down."

"I'm really happy about this," Aurora admitted. "I worried for a while that if they did get together Brook might just use Paula to fill the gap left by his feelings for Stacia. But after seeing them together today, I'm not worried about that any longer. He likes her, he really does."

Later after Eric had gone, Aurora searched her motives for wanting him to accept the Seahurst job offer. Did she really believe that it would be the best for him and Katie, or was she thinking mainly of herself, wanting to keep the Thorpes near because she couldn't bear to think of life without them?

Chapter Eleven

Several days later an exhausted Aurora came home from work to find Eric and Katie sitting on the steps to her deck.

"We've been waiting for you. You're late. Guess what?" Katie greeted her, as she and her father both came to their feet.

"What?" Aurora said with a laugh, sensing it was going to be the announcement she'd been hoping to hear.

"My dad's going to be a teacher at my school!"

"That's wonderful," Aurora answered, giving the girl a hug. "And you're happy about it?"

"Of course," Katie said, as if Aurora's question were absurd. "He's going to have a cottage on campus where he can keep the puppies so I can see them every day. And I can stay in the dorm, or go to be with him anytime I want to, can't I?" She turned to her father for confirmation.

"You bet," Eric agreed.

The pure joy in Katie's voice caused tears to mist in Aurora's eyes. Father and daughter had come a long way. It seemed almost possible that their worst problems were behind them.

"I'm so glad for you both," she said, looking over the young girl's head at the tall man whose presence never failed to affect her. The white polo shirt and shorts he wore with casual ease set off the deep bronze of his mid-summer California tan, making her feel frumpy and anxious to get out of the short-sleeved blouse and functional skirt she'd worn all day.

"But we'll come to the beach on weekends so that you won't be too lonely," Katie assured her. "And we'll see each other at school, too. I'm still going to be your assistant, aren't I?"

"If you still have time," Aurora said. "Sounds to me like you'll have a lot to occupy you this year."

"I'll still have time," Katie said seriously before breaking into a grin. "Oh, I'm so happy! Everything's going to be so different!"

"Actually, we came down to invite you to dinner. We were going to break the news over Bridey's special lasagna," Eric said, stepping forward to lightly encircle both Aurora and Katie in his arms, his expression telling Aurora that he understood the reason tears were welling up in her eyes. "But Katie couldn't wait. You look terribly tired," he added with concern.

"I am," Aurora conceded, "and I'm glad you didn't wait to tell me. I needed some good news today."

"Did something happen?" he asked.

She nodded. "One of my patients had a bicycle accident this morning...." She sighed and lifted a tired hand to her forehead.

"Did a car hit her?" Katie asked, alarmed.

"No, dear, a dog ran out in front of her and when she swerved to miss it, she lost control of her bike...."

"Then she couldn't be too badly hurt..."

"Yes, she could. Bicycle accidents are one of the biggest killers among kids your age."

"Really?" Katie squealed in horror. "She's my age?"

"Thirteen," Aurora confirmed sadly.

"Is she going to be all right?"

"I don't know," Aurora admitted, swallowing over the lump in her throat. All day, thinking how she'd feel if it were Katie lying motionless in that hospital, she'd been filled with such empathy for the girl's poor mother that she'd had difficulty maintaining her professional composure. She knew that the odds were stacking up against the child every minute she remained unconscious. She just had to come out of it before morning! "She suffered some serious and unnecessary head injuries. She's still unconscious."

"Wasn't she wearing a helmet?" Eric asked.

Aurora bit her lip and shook her head. "They'd bought her one, but her mother said she wouldn't wear it because her friends didn't think it was cool." She took Katie by her upper arms and turned the child to face her. "Promise me you'll never ride your bike again without wearing a helmet," she insisted. "I couldn't stand it if something like that happened to you."

"Mine doesn't fit anymore," Katie said.

"We'll take care of that tomorrow," Eric promised.

"And you'll wear it?" Aurora persisted.

Katie scrunched up her nose. "It isn't cool...but I'll wear it to make you happy."

Aurora smiled down at her and gave her a loving squeeze of appreciation.

"AND I'M GOING to need some more of your help," Eric said almost apologetically as he walked her home in the silver light of a nearly full moon, long after Katie and her puppies, Michael and Mildred, had gone to bed.

"You should know by now that I like doing things for you and Katie," she answered, taking his hand, enjoying the cool breeze that touched her exposed shoulders and neck. Showering and changing into a pretty ruffled cotton top and matching gathered skirt had refreshed her and let her put the cares of the day aside for a few hours. "It's never any trouble. What is it?"

"Brook and I were up rummaging around in the attic of the academy's main building today, and all the furniture up there is broken down or moth-eaten. He's going to have it hauled to the dump. So it seems if I'm going to live in a house on campus, I'm going to have to furnish it," he explained. "Fortunately, it's small. A living room, a study and kitchen, with a dining area downstairs and two small bedrooms under the eaves upstairs."

"Sounds charming," she remarked, picturing the ivy covered stone buildings tucked away in the corners of the academy grounds.

"It seems foolish to be buying furniture after just getting rid of a whole houseful. I suppose I could get out some of the things we put in storage, but they aren't really what I have in mind."

"I'll take Katie and we'll have it taken care of in no time," she promised. "I want to take her shopping for her fall wardrobe, anyway. Is there any particular style of furniture you'd like?"

"I'd like it to look like your house," he said, "comfortable and functional."

"Secondhand?"

"If that's what it takes," he agreed, then added with a chuckle, "just not moth-eaten. And I want some dishes like yours."

"Fiestaware?"

"Yes," he said. "I enjoy eating off yours. Takes me back to when I was a boy."

"I'll start looking, but it will take some asking around and probably some time to get enough for you to use. You may have to settle for something a little more mundane in the meantime," she warned.

"I can handle that. You've already done so much by putting the beach house together for us, that I feel I'm imposing. You're sure you don't mind?" he repeated.

"Not at all. I've never had the chance to shop with someone else's money before," she joked. "That should really be fun. Seriously, I've had to curtail my shopping excursions recently, because my house is full. And I saw some things when Katie and I were out rounding up props for the play that I had a hard time resisting."

"I won't need too much," he said in an odd tone.

"Don't worry," she said, suddenly wondering if he might be thinking she was as compulsive about shopping as Stacia had been. "Shopping secondhand stores is my hobby, but I don't go overboard. Every once in a while, if I find something really special, I sell off a piece I already own to make room for it."

"Very sensible practice," he said approvingly, and she knew she'd been right about his concern. It would be a long time before he'd be completely free of the nightmare of living with Stacia. "I'd go with you myself," he offered, "but it might slow you down since I know nothing about furniture. I know how little time you have for yourself as it is."

"And I know how busy you're going to be mapping out your plans for the school year ahead of you," she countered. "Believe me, I'll enjoy doing it for you. Right now, though," she added regretfully, "I have to get back to the hospital."

"At this hour?" he asked, as they neared her bungalow.

"Uh-huh. I placed a quick call to the intensive care ward a few minutes ago, and there are signs that Allison is coming out of the coma."

"That's wonderful," he said sincerely, lifting her hand to his lips.

"Isn't it?" she agreed. "The sooner she comes out of it the better her chances are of making a complete recovery. You know," she confessed, "I've lost most of my objectivity this summer. Every time anything happens to one of my patients, I think how I would feel if it happened to Katie."

"I'm sorry," Eric said gently. "That must make it very difficult for you."

She nodded, biting her lip. A part of her wanted to blurt out the truth, to end the deception. To explain to him that having Katie in her life had brought to the fore all the feelings she'd suppressed about her own lost child. But she couldn't do it. "In a way it does," she admitted finally when her emotions were under control. "But I think having these feelings may have made me a better physician."

The day before the new term started Aurora and Eric moved Katie into her dorm room. Getting Katie ready for that day had been Aurora's first taste of back-to-school excitement from the vantage point of a parent. She'd loved the hullabaloo in the teen sections of San Francisco's department stores as mothers and daughters had exasperatedly tried to compromise to each other's tastes in selecting from the brightly colored, extreme styles packed tightly on the racks.

She and Katie hadn't had any problems, finding to their surprise and delight that their tastes ran along the same lines—bright, bold and sleek. She knew she'd been extravagant, had even gone overboard. But Katie had looked so cute in all the clothes she'd tried on, and the shadow figure of her own daughter her mind had projected into the mirror beside Katie's image had prompted her to deny the young girl nothing. She kept telling herself it was a textbook case of overcompensation. Yet she couldn't help it, knowing that she'd never have the chance to dress that other teenager, whom she knew was out there somewhere getting ready for her first day of a new term too.

And Katie had been genuinely grateful for her time and attention, saying that she and Bridey had always gone shopping together before, and that Bridey, in addition to being far too conventional in her taste, had always wanted to economize. Worse still, in her well-intentioned ignorance of pop culture, she'd insisted that they stay away from name brands! Aurora had laughed when Katie told her that there was no way to convince the kindly older woman that the brand was everything! This year, she'd confided, thanks to Aurora she'd have a closet full of really rad clothes to show the kids who were coming back to the dorm, and she wouldn't have to borrow from Jenni all the time.

Eric's house was ready, too, Aurora thought with satisfaction, as they left the pandemonium of the dorm floors and descended into the hushed atmosphere of the main floor with its offices and formal drawing room. It had turned out masculine yet cozy, just as she'd hoped.

"Come over to my place for a while?" he asked, as they reached the bottom of the brick building's broad front steps and started along the walkway that led to the campus's lower level. "I'll make some coffee with the housewarming present you gave me. That's about all I know how to do. Thankfully, I'll be able to eat in the dining hall."

"I wonder if you'll be so grateful for that by next week," she said drolly. "Spaghetti every Wednesday, pizza every Thursday, chicken every Monday..."

He laughed. "We'll sneak out for a good steak at the club when it gets too gross, as Katie says. And when she and I are home on the weekends, I'm sure Bridey will try to gorge us like geese."

"And, if I know her, she'll keep your refrigerator here stuffed with good things, too. How do she and Mac like waterfront life?" Aurora asked. "I've been meaning to stop by for a visit, but I've been on the run all week." The big house on the cliff had been sold to an area realtor, and the older couple had settled into the garage apartment the previous weekend.

"Mac is in his element. He's out there surf fishing every morning and he's already turned over half of the backyard for a vegetable garden."

"Does he catch anything?" Aurora asked with interest.

"So far, a few crabs, but he has high hopes of landing a big one."

"I hope it's not a shark."

"That's possible," Eric answered, grinning down at her.

"But I've never seen any large fish out there."

"They're there," he assured her. "They come in at night to feed on the small schools."

"That blows any plans I ever had for a moonlight dip!" she said with a shudder.

"Darn!" Eric exclaimed with a grin. "I'd been thinking lately about how much fun that could be."

Absurdly, Aurora felt her cheeks go hot. He hadn't said skinny-dipping. It was silly for her to read anything into his remark. But her body tingled with the intoxicating idea of the smoothness of her skin meeting with the hair-roughed texture of his as their legs entwined and her breasts encountered the expanse of his chest in the buoyant fluidity of the sea. Damn those sharks!

"Are you ready for tomorrow?" she asked, purposefully not attempting a response to his remark.

His face took on sober lines. "I've practiced my introductory speech until I could say it in my sleep, but I've got the worst case of opening-night jitters I've ever had."

"Why?" she asked, grinning up at him.

"Can you imagine facing a classroom full of Katies?"

She let out a hoot of laughter. "That's a succinct way of putting it. But relax. They're just little girls. They probably won't hear a word you say. They'll be busy falling in love with you." But hopefully not as completely as I have, she added silently, gazing with enjoyment at his unique profile.

"You're not serious!" he exclaimed, horror-stricken.

"Absolutely," she insisted, enjoying his discomfiture. "I still remember the crush I had on my ninth-grade algebra teacher. I knew he was married and had children of his own but I was mad for him. Even dreamed about him. Didn't Brook warn you about that?"

He shook his head and snorted. "He never mentioned it. I wonder what other hazards there are in the teaching profession he forgot to tell me about."

"You can clue me in on them Friday night," Aurora said, tucking her arm in his now that they were out of view of the main campus. Under the circumstances, it would be understandable that she'd helped Katie move into the dorm and get ready for the term, but she wasn't comfortable with the idea of rumors about her and Katie's father circulating among the school's students. Stacia's suicide was going to be enough for the girls to deal with. Eric didn't need for them to think that he was already involved with another woman. They were just too young to be expected to understand. "I'd like to have you and Katie come to dinner."

"I'm sure we'll be ready for some home cooking by then."

"What would you like? Spaghetti? Chicken? Pizza?" she teased.

"How about none of the above?"

"Picky!" she accused with a laugh. "Then how about Aurora Duvall's world-famous French onion soup?"

"World famous, huh?"

"Well . . . maybe I exaggerated just a little, but it's pretty good."

"I know I'd love Aurora Duvall's world-famous anything," he said gallantly.

"Not everything I make falls into the world-famous category," she confessed with a grimace. "I never learned how to make great gravy . . . mine always has lumps."

"Would you like Bridey to teach you?" he offered.

"Do you think she would?" Aurora asked.

He nodded. "Sounds like a plan. Any other terrible, dark secrets I should know about?" he asked in the same light vein.

Aurora's breath caught in her throat and her heart started to pound, but she managed to maintain her external composure. "Not that I can think of at the moment," she said smoothly.

"I'm sorry you have that seminar in San Francisco this week," he remarked. "After all you've told me about what to expect, I'm not sure I'm ready for this."

"You'll do just fine," she soothed, reaching up to pat his cheek. "Now, I'm going to have to pass on that invitation for coffee. I've got to head over to my office in the infirmary in case any of the parents want to see me.

"And I also want to get around the dorm this evening after things have settled down to talk with some of the girls about Katie and about how they should word their condolences. I've already mentioned it to her, and I feel fairly sure she can handle it."

"Do you think any of them will say something to me about Stacia's death?"

"Probably," she answered truthfully. "Kids this age are pretty forthright. It's something both of you are going to have to face."

"I think I'll walk back and stay with Katie for a while," he remarked with a worried frown, looking through the trees in the direction of the dorm.

"That's a good idea," she said with an encouraging smile.

"WHERE'S KATIE?" Aurora asked the following Friday evening, as an exuberant Eric bounded up her back steps, his arms full of champagne and flowers.

"She's gone to a dance! Can you imagine? My little girl grown up enough for a dance?"

"What kind of a dance? Where?" Aurora asked, her brow furrowing with concern as she took the bouquet from him. Her few days in San Francisco had seemed like a month. She'd felt as cut off from her real life as if she'd gone to the moon.

"One of the area high schools is holding a welcome dance for their ninth-graders and invited the Seahurst girls to attend," he explained.

"You don't know which one?" Aurora asked in alarm. "Who did she go with? How is she getting home? Who's supervising?"

"Relax," he said, parroting the advice she'd given him less than a week before, cleverly mimicking her voice. "They've gone as a group on a bus with Brook and Paula as chaperones. I'm sure that they'll see she gets home safely."

"Brook and Paula?" she repeated stupidly, feeling even more out of things than she'd imagined herself to be.

He grinned. "It seems they had a date for tonight until this came up."

"I must have a lot of catching up to do," she said, taking the flowers to the sink. Although she'd meant the statement to sound humorous, it came out grim. She hadn't realized quite how proprietary she'd become about anything that involved Katie. She'd come close to telling him that she should have been called and asked whether or not Katie could attend her first dance, but fortunately she'd managed to stifle the impulse. After all, he was Katie's father. But suddenly thirteen seemed far too young to begin going to dances with a high school crowd.

"Katie sent you a message," he said, opening the oven door to take a look inside where the cheese had just begun to bubble on the top of three individual stoneware soup dishes. "So this is where that delicious aroma is coming from. I don't think you were kidding. That soup looks like it could be world famous."

"Thanks, but what's the message?" she asked, brightening, though she still felt hurt and left out.

"She said to thank you for insisting that she buy a party dress."

"If I'd known what it was to be used for, maybe I wouldn't have been so persistent," she said peevishly. Turning her back to him, she reached into a top cupboard for a cut-glass vase.

"Hey," he said, his voice close to her ear as his arms encircled her waist and he pressed a kiss on her neck just below her jawline. "I know how much you worry about her. But it's just a dance. There's no reason why she shouldn't go with her friends."

After putting the flowers in the vase and filling it up with water, she turned, still in his light hold. "I'm sorry," she said sheepishly. "Of course there isn't. I guess I'm becoming too overprotective."

But she knew it was more than that. To have the Thorpes, both Katie and Eric, going their own ways independent of her, was unsettling. Really analyzing her reaction, it was more than unsettling, she decided. It was downright threatening.

"Come on," he said, smiling devastatingly, his deep-set eyes coaxing an answering smile from her. "Get some glasses and let's pop this cork. Then we can sit down and you can tell me about your week, and I'll tell you about mine."

After they were seated on her chintz slipcovered couch, she remarked, "I didn't even thank you for the flowers, did I?" Gesturing with her stemmed glass toward the bouquet of large yellow chrysanthemums on the coffee table, she added, "They're lovely, thank you."

"You're welcome," he said with a grin, raising his glass in a mock toast. "You're looking especially lovely, too. Did you find time to do a little shopping while you were in the city? I like that outfit. I know I'd remember if I'd seen you wear it before."

"Uh-huh. One afternoon there wasn't anything going on that I particularly wanted to attend, so I did run out to pick up a few things," she said, running a hand over the fabric of the crushed silk, copper-colored jumpsuit, glad that he'd noticed. "I stuck to buying for myself this time, but I couldn't resist making the rounds of the junior departments. I saw several new outfits that would look good on Katie... but I stopped myself just short of buying them."

"It's a good thing," he teased. "If she had any more clothes, we'd have to move her desk out to make room for them."

She smiled. "Get your priorities straight, Dad. What teenager needs a desk when she could have more clothes? Actually, I didn't resist completely. I did buy a few things for her hair. So, tell me about your week...every minute of it," she demanded, settling back.

"It was invigorating and exhausting," he said, arranging himself against the high arm of the couch so that he could look at her. "I don't know how full-time teachers keep going all day. By noon I'm ready for a nap!"

"You'll get used to it," she said with a laugh. "Kids are exhausting, though, aren't they?"

"Far more so than adults," he agreed with wonderment. "They're so eager and demanding...and stimulating. It's a challenge to keep up with them."

"They're a bright bunch," she commented. "I certainly enjoy the ones I meet in my practice. They're full of questions. They always want to know 'why.' It keeps me on my toes, though."

"I can imagine," Eric remarked. "Taking this job was the best thing I could have done for Katie."

"Really?"

He nodded, a pleased smile lighting his features. "Already I can see that she's typical of girls her age...everything that happens to them becomes a total crisis. They're either flying high or down in the doldrums. And they burst into tears at the most unexpected times with the slightest provocation!"

"I've been telling you that," she said, amused.

"Yes, I know you have," he conceded with a grin, "but I still had a hard time actually believing it. But I've never been around children, or should I say, adolescents, and believe me, it's a real revelation. They're astoundingly brilliant one minute and abysmally ignorant the next. Being in the classroom takes me back to when I was in high school...it's like I'm recapturing a life I'd thought I'd lost."

"That's what children do best," Aurora murmured. "They renew our lives. Let us see the world again through their fresh and eager eyes."

"Yes," he agreed, as though she'd said something deep and profound. "That's exactly what they do." He got up from the couch and refilled their glasses. "You should see their papers," he went on enthusiastically. "I'll bring them over so you can read them. I gave them a simple writing assignment and each of them approached it differently...originally..." He paced the floor in front of her. His excitement was contagious.

"What was the topic?" she asked, delighted with his reaction and tremendously relieved that her suggestion had been right. She'd worried while she was gone that he'd hate the isolation and routine of an institution. That he'd be as baffled and helpless with the girls as he'd been with his own daughter. But clearly, that hadn't been the case.

"Anger," he said, in answer to her question. "I want them to get in touch with their feelings and to learn to analyze them. I tried to write with them, and you know, I couldn't remember the last time I'd felt anger. I didn't realize how dulled my senses had become."

"But it's your sensitivity that I admire most about you," Aurora objected. "I like the way you show and express how you feel."

"With you, it's easy," he said, smiling down at her. "You and I relate to each other with our senses. But I stared down at that blank piece of paper trying to remember the last time I'd been angry. Nothing would come. The girls were busy, their heads bent over their desks, their pens moving, and I just sat there, panicking.

"Then I put myself back to when I was their age and I remembered a friend I'd brought home who broke one of my mother's lamps by throwing a baseball in the living room. I remember jumping on him and pounding him for all I was worth. I began writing about how angry I'd been with him, and after that it was like a dam had burst inside of my mind and it started to flow...how angry I'd been with the world when Stacia first got sick...how angry I'd felt each time I was told by a different doctor there was no help for her... how angry I'd been when I felt I had to send Katie away to school. It all came out... pure primitive anger that I hadn't even known was there.''

Aurora held her breath. She hardly dared to admit to herself the hope his words had generated.

''After that piece of catharsis,'' he went on, ''I began to wonder if maybe, in this different environment, completely removed from any I've ever lived in, I might be able to write again.''

''Oh, Eric,'' Aurora said, getting to her feet in excitement.

''I don't know if I'd be able to write the same kind of stuff I've written in the past... humor. But maybe something deeper... more expressive...''

''Why don't you write about Stacia?'' she asked impulsively. ''The final years of your life with her. It might never sell, but maybe it would help you put the past in perspective... and think how enlightening it would be for Katie.''

''It might be a place to start,'' he answered slowly, as though mulling the idea over in his mind. ''It's certainly dramatic... and tragic. It might make a good play.'' He paused, then shook his head. ''But I don't think I can do it. Do you remember when Katie accused me of someday writing about her mother's illness and her jumping from the bridge? I said I never would.''

''Of course, I remember, and Katie's feelings and your relationship with her have to come first. But things are very different between the two of you now,'' Aurora said, compassionately putting her hand on his upper arm. ''You'll have to be open with her and tell her what you're planning to do and why. I think she'll understand why it's important. And, of course, you'll have to promise that you won't make any decision about what to do with it when you're finished without discussing it with her. You can't be sure how you'll feel about producing it, either."

"You're right," he agreed thoughtfully. "I'll talk to her about it right away. Then, unless she objects, I'll give it a shot."

Later, after he'd gone, Aurora paced the floor, hugging her arms to her chest, filled with misgivings. Remembering the sparkle in Eric's eyes, as he'd kept telling her over and over at dinner how good it felt to be writing again, she knew she should be elated. But she wasn't.

When she'd met him, he had been like a man just emerged from a windowless cell, his mind, body and eyes dulled by the perpetual darkness of despair. She'd taken his hand while he'd been blinded by the brightness of his sudden freedom and guided him around the stumbling blocks of his perplexities. But now that his senses had adjusted to the world and all its promise, he was eager to take his place in it.

Her heart ached, and she felt miserably selfish and self-centered. But she couldn't seem to help herself. She had wanted him whole and well...she still did. But it was to be as she'd feared. Once he'd completely recovered, he wouldn't need her guidance. Wouldn't need her in his life.

She'd been looking forward all week to spending the entire evening with him and Katie. Instead, he'd gone home early, saying he needed to get some ideas down on paper...ideas that were crowding into his brain.... Soon, she feared, she would be written out of the picture entirely.

Chapter Twelve

"Brook certainly is trimming down," Aurora remarked to Paula as they sat on folding deck chairs close to the bungalow, shielded from the brisk wind that was carrying the colorful kites on the beach high into the late-October sky.

"It was his idea to cut down on his eating, not mine," Paula said defensively, shaking her head free from the hood of her bright blue windbreaker. "I've never made an issue of his weight. I fell in love with him twenty-five pounds ago."

Knowing that had been the case, but knowing, too, that wasn't the whole story, Aurora said, "He looks better this way, and I'm sure he feels better. Two months ago he wouldn't have had the stamina to get those three kites in the air."

"He is healthier now," Paula agreed, leaning forward to grasp one lean, jean-clad knee and to rest her heel on the webbed chair seat, "and I am happy about that. Every pound he drops means less strain on his heart."

Paula may not have mentioned his weight to him, Aurora thought with a wry smile, but she had put him through an exercise regime that would have daunted most forty-year-old, overweight men. If Paula wanted a measure of Brook's devotion, he could prove himself by the weight he'd lost.

"The kites are beautiful," Aurora said, watching the long tails of the elaborate dragons both Katie and Jenni held. The kites writhed sensuously, swirling vibrant colors above the white-crested waves, while the growing puppies romped at the water's edge with Gretchen and Gretel. "It was nice of you to get them for the girls. They're certainly enjoying them."

"Too bad Eric isn't here to fly his," the sandy-haired obstetrician replied. "It's a perfect day for kite flying."

"He's busy, as usual," Aurora said with a heavy sigh.

"You don't see him very much anymore, do you?" Paula asked. Though she kept her tone light, Aurora knew that her friend was worried about her. Since falling in love, Paula wanted everyone she cared about to have the happiness she'd found. But Paula and Brook didn't have the obstacles in their path that she and Eric had. As mature, caring adults who were obviously crazy about each other, their future should be smooth sailing. But, as much as it hurt to admit, Aurora wasn't even sure that she and Eric had a future.

After a long pause, she answered, "Only when I make a point of it. Whenever I stop in at his house on campus it's full of admiring young girls." She stopped, hating the jealousy she could hear in her voice. She was not by nature a jealous person, but lately she'd felt so incredibly insecure in her relationship with Eric that she'd come to resent any and everything that prevented her from seeing him. She couldn't seem to help it . . . she wanted some of his undivided attention.

"What are the girls doing at Eric's?" Paula asked, her brow furrowing quizzically.

Aurora shrugged and let out a deep breath, smiling in spite of herself. "Wonderful things. Just the sorts of things I had in mind when I first suggested the idea of his working at Seahurst." She knew Paula was aware of her involvement there. Brook and Paula already had the kind of open relationship that left no room for secrets. "They're practicing for the Thanksgiving play and getting tips on elocution, critiquing an old movie he's rented, or getting advice on the books they all seem to be writing.

"It's hard," Aurora confessed, her smile fading, "because on weekends he comes out to the beach loaded with papers to correct. Then he spends all Saturday night every week at his computer working on his play."

"And Katie?"

"I see her more often," Aurora said, brushing back a wisp of hair that the unruly breeze had caught and whipped in front of her face. "Usually just on the weekends like this. She doesn't work in the clinic with me anymore. She's so proud that her famous father has become a campus sensation. She loves being his hostess when the girls gather at his house. Bridey's got his cupboards stuffed with enough chips, dips, and sodas to last until the new year, and Katie oversees the get-togethers like she'd been entertaining all her life."

"Katie's quite different from the girl I met last spring," Paula commented pensively. "You've worked wonders with her."

"Eric's done his part," Aurora said with pride. "He's really pulled her into his life and involved himself in hers. From what Katie tells me, they no longer have any of the bitter disagreements they had this summer. She says that when they see things differently, they talk the problem over and work it out. I have to admit, I wasn't sure at first that that would ever happen.

"Right now, she's in charge of the sets for the Thanksgiving play and she's doing a fantastic job. Eric thinks she's showing signs of following in her mother's footsteps."

"That's terrific," Paula said. "If so, in time that may give her a tangible, positive link with Stacia's memory."

"That's the way I see it, too," Aurora said with a nod. "From what Brook and Eric have told me, Stacia was a natural-born hostess, too. I think Katie will gradually realize how many of her good traits she got from her mother, and when she does, I think a lot of her unhappy memories will fade."

As much as she loved Katie, Aurora had no possessive desire to weaken the girl's links to Stacia. Whenever possible, she believed those ties should be stressed. Katie needed to know that her mother had been a very special person before she'd become ill, and to really understand that Stacia hadn't been to blame for what had happened to all of them.

"What about Jenni?" Paula asked, as their gazes shifted to the stolid figure not far from Katie's side. "How's she doing?"

"Not very well, I'm afraid. Since Katie has started to bloom, Jenni has been outdistanced, just as I feared. Most of the time she clings to Katie like a shadow, but Katie's told me that they've had a few blowups lately, and that Jenni took off to town by herself a couple of times and arrived back after curfew, which is strictly against the rules. I know Jenni is unhappy. I just don't know what I can do...."

"You're doing enough," Paula interjected sharply. "You include her in everything. You can't personally take on every unhappy girl at Seahurst."

"I suppose not," Aurora said doubtfully, with another sigh. "But I don't understand her parents. How can they neglect Jenni?"

"Don't ask me," Paula said, shaking her head. "I deliver a lot of babies who I fear are going to end up like Jenni. And you see them later in your practice. Many parents in this upscale community of ours give their children everything except what they need most . . . time and attention. It really upsets me.''

"Me, too," Aurora said, rubbing her arms, feeling a sudden chill penetrate her salmon-colored jacket. "Have you and Brook done any talking about a family?"

"Didn't I tell you?" Paula said with a laugh. "He wants four kids, one right after the other. Like all men say, two boys and two girls. Says we'll have to hurry or he'll be too old to raise them."

"How do you feel about that?" Aurora asked.

"It suits me fine," Paula said, her eyes sparkling. "He promises that he'll be a full-time father. He doesn't want me to give up my practice, because he knows how much it means to me, but we have talked about my need to bring in another OB associate so I can cut way down on my load when the time comes."

"Oh, Paula," Aurora said reaching out to hug her friend. "I'm so happy for the two of you. Those will be four lucky kids!"

"I hope so." After returning the hug, Paula paused and looked away. "We've never talked about this, and it isn't a big issue because I'm sure Brook really loves me, but I know that he loved Stacia Thorpe. Do you think there's any chance that I should hold off for a little while, before I agree to setting a date? It's just that—"

"No," Aurora said firmly, reaching out to pat her friend's arm reassuringly. "Brook Oliver was in love with a phantom . . . a completely unattainable woman who didn't even really exist for most of the years he was tied to her. You came along and broke that spell."

"But don't you think that any woman who'd come along just then . . ."

"No, I don't," Aurora insisted. "If you're thinking that you were in the right place at the right time, forget it. Brook fell for you, no one else... and he fell hard.'' She lowered her voice confidentially to add, ''He told me the other day that he wished you'd come into his life before you did.''

''Really?'' Paula said, her freckled face brightening. ''While Stacia was still alive?''

''That's right,'' Aurora said solemnly, ''so you don't have a thing to worry about on that score. But,'' she said, changing the tone, ''how's old Bill doing since you dropped him?''

Paula giggled. ''He was never a keeper. He knew that, and he felt more or less the same about me. He told me right at the first that he liked the class that dating a doctor gave him.''

Now it was Aurora's turn to giggle. ''And all the time you had me worried!''

''Sorry,'' Paula said with a grin. ''But I think he's bearing up under the strain. That new aerobics instructor he hired has been with him everywhere I've seen him.''

''I've seen them, too,'' Aurora said. ''In a word—wow!''

''Yeah, she's built. They're a matched set! Enough about me,'' Paula said, changing the subject. ''We were talking about you and Eric.''

Aurora swallowed hard and looked out toward sea. ''I wasn't going to say this, but you might as well know. I'm not sure there is an 'Eric and me' anymore. I think he may have outgrown his need for me, just like you did for Bill.''

''Uh!'' Paula let out disparagingly. ''There's no comparison between the two relationships. You've always been one of the most rational people I've ever known... I can't believe you're talking like this.''

''I just don't understand him anymore,'' Aurora said in her own defense. ''I know that I shouldn't begrudge his immersing himself in the life of the school. Like I said, it's what I wanted for him ... and if I can't handle it, I know that's my problem.''

"I think I'd have to agree with that," Paula said, nodding her head. "So what's his problem? The one you can't understand?"

"He seems so happy. So well adjusted. He doesn't seem to be troubled by lingering doubts."

"Why would you worry about that?" Paula asked incredulously, crossing her arms across her chest.

Aurora hesitated. "It strikes an off chord with me, and I thought I was pretty tuned in to his feelings. After all, he is writing about his life with Stacia. It seems to me he'd be going through hell remembering all that happened. What I'm afraid of is that he's got his face-the-public facade back in place ... that he's controlling and suppressing his true emotions again."

"Maybe he's just busy and enjoying it," Paula said with a grimace. "I wouldn't worry too much about it. Give him time. What you need is a pet or two to lavish your attentions on, until he's ready to lavish his on you."

"No, thanks." Aurora smiled. "I have enough sand to clean out of my house after Katie and Jenni, and Mikey and Milly run through it all weekend."

ONE STORMY FRIDAY evening in mid-November Aurora stood before her large, plate-glass window watching the fury of the wind-whipped waves as they crashed upon the shore in a series of thunderous roars that shook the small house, causing her collection of china plates to rattle on the shelves. In the early dusk, the ordinarily brilliant landscape ... the sky, the sand and the rolling ocean ... was muted to a pearl gray. She loved the sound of the wind that lashed the house, reveled in the sight of the tumultuous surge of the surf, enjoyed the strange sense of exhilaration the turbulence stirred in her soul.

She stood there until the sky darkened into night and only the frothy luminescence of the storm-lashed waves could be seen. Then, after slowly drawing the drapes, she turned to replenish the fire glowing on the hearth.

She'd brought in a good supply of wood to keep herself warm in the long watch of the night to come. Worriedly, she thought of the two-year-old boy she'd seen in Emergency, carried in writhing in his mother's arms. After admitting the child to the hospital, she'd called in an abdominal specialist who'd tentatively diagnosed an intestinal obstruction. The case was now out of her hands, but if the specialist decided to operate, she'd made him promise to call her in to assist.

Placing a log on the grate, she sat back on her heels enjoying the fresh flames that leaped up with crackling warmth. Just as she pulled the fire screen shut, she heard a muffled knock on the back door.

"Eric," she exclaimed as a gust of wind nearly tore the door from her hand. "What are you..."

"...doing out on a night like this?" he finished the sentence for her while he quickly pushed the door shut.

"Yes," she answered, searching his wet face, sensing an exhilaration in him that matched her own.

Pulling a sheaf of papers from inside his jacket, he handed them to her.

"Read this," he commanded in a terse tone. "It's the first two acts of my new play."

While Eric hung his wet coat over the back of her kitchen stool, Aurora took the pages and walked over to the couch in front of the fire before curling up against the cushions. The script was untitled, giving no clue to its contents. But as she read the unfolding drama of a happy young couple whose lives began to crumble when the wife was stricken with manic-depression, tears sprang to her eyes. Heedlessly wiping them away with the back of her hand, she continued to read the compelling words until there were no more.

It was all there—the husband's initial anger, their child's bewilderment, and the unraveling of the emotional ties that had once bound them together in a loving unit.

"What comes next?" she asked, frustrated that the powerful story hung unfinished in midair.

"I don't really know," he answered, staring into the fire. "There has to be a resolution. I still have to tackle that. I can't leave the child and the father completely alienated at the end. No audience could stand that kind of heartbreak." The face he turned toward her was ravaged by anguish. "To think I'd almost done that to my own child," he whispered huskily.

"But it's all right now between you and Katie, isn't it?" Aurora asked, quickly moving to put her arm around his slumped shoulders. "She seems very happy."

"Yes, I think she is," he answered. "Thanks to you. But if you hadn't intervened, I would have sent her away." The words came out as a sob. Quickly he buried his face against her shoulder.

She let him cry, tears streaming unchecked down her own face until Eric finally sat up and pulled her close. Raising one hand, he smoothed her tumbled hair back from her face.

"You were like a guardian angel coming to save my daughter for me," he said, his voice shaking with emotion.

"I'm no angel," Aurora protested, lowering her lashes to escape his probing gaze.

"To me you are," he whispered, pressing his lips to her brow.

Dear Lord, she thought in alarm, if he only knew. What would he think if he knew the truth about her? She may have saved his daughter for him, but how would he feel if he knew she'd given her own away?

Struggling to her feet, she choked out, "Let's go for a walk."

"A walk? Tonight? In this storm?"

"Yes," she insisted, quickly turning to take her waterproof jacket from the oak stand by the door and to pick up her pager from the table. Only out in the violence of the storm, the cold rain pelting her flushed face, the fierce wind whipping at her hair, her body grappling with the wild elements, would she find a tumult to equal the torment in her soul.

They walked in silence, their voices too weak to combat the bluster of the furious squall enveloping them. Barely conscious of Eric's strong hand on the small of her back and his protective body between hers and the relentless onslaught of the pounding surf, Aurora let the salt from her tears mingle with that from the storm-whipped spray. With ominous foreboding she knew the time was approaching for her to reveal the painful secrets of her own past. Safe for a while in the darkness, she gave free rein to her tortured thoughts as the driving rain found its way down her open collar and trickled chillingly into the cleft between her breasts.

Suddenly Eric stopped. Taking her into his arms with a gesture as powerful and rough as the storm, he pressed his lips to hers. His moving mouth forced hers open to meet the sweet invasion of his searching tongue. Immediately her shivering body warmed as liquid fire surged through her veins, dispelling the cold remorse that had gripped her heart.

"I love you, Aurora," he said breathlessly, his lips against hers. "I need you. I want you."

"Yes," was all she had time to answer before his mouth was on hers once more, offering wordless solace to her tortured mind. Locking her arms around his slim waist, her body arched against his with erotic longing as the kiss deepened into arousing, consuming desire. The roar of the storm was overridden by the wild pounding of her pulse as wave after wave of sweet ecstasy engulfed her.

How long they stood on the drenched sand, pelted by the soaking rain, she didn't know. She only knew that in that eternity where time stood still, she had given her heart and soul up to him as completely as though the kiss had been a consummation of their love.

Later in the cottage, while playfully toweling each other dry between long languorous kisses, Aurora abruptly returned to reality.

"Eric," she said regretfully, pulling her wet blouse together over her exposed lace bra. "We can't make love now."

"Why not?" The look of sheer disappointment on his face made her want to bite back her words.

"I'm going to be called to the hospital any minute." As she explained the plight of the child and the necessity for her to be there, a devilish grin spread across his features.

"Let's see how far we get," he said, taking her hands from her blouse and slipping it off.

But he'd only dropped her bra onto the pile of damp clothing beside the couch when her pager sounded. Expecting it to be the hospital, they were both surprised to hear Brook's worried voice.

"Jenni is very ill. She's vomiting continuously and is hysterical about the idea of having to go to emergency."

"I'll come get her," Aurora said quickly. "I have to go to the hospital anyway."

"I'll drive you," Eric offered, grabbing up his woollen shirt.

"I'll need my car," she said reluctantly. "I don't know if I'll get home tonight at all."

"Well, if you need me for anything, I'll be at the cottage."

"You're not going to stay at the beach?"

"No, if there's anything seriously wrong with Jenni, I want to be close to Katie. She'll be upset."

AT THE DORM, Brook answered Aurora's ring at the back door and hurried her up the stairs to Jenni's floor.

"The only reason I'm still here is that the girls had a pizza party tonight, and I've been busy putting everything away," he explained.

"You said she was vomiting. Is anyone else sick?"

"No one seems to be. I asked around about that myself, thinking it might be food poisoning. But Katie said Jenni didn't even finish one piece. The poor kid just can't seem to stop crying. My second thought was that she might be upset about something, but no one has come up with any explanation for that, either."

When they reached the room, Aurora smiled a reassuring greeting to the anxious-faced group of girls standing vigil at Katie and Jenni's door.

"Now, you go back to bed," she told them. "I'll take care of Jenni."

"But she's really sick," one girl answered.

"I know," Aurora soothed, "I'll do my best." Then, meeting Katie's frightened gaze she turned to Brook saying, "Why don't you take all the girls down to the kitchen for some hot chocolate?"

"She's really scared," Katie whispered to Aurora. "She hates hospitals."

"Thanks for telling me," Aurora whispered back, giving Katie a quick hug.

Holding Jenni in her arms, Aurora managed to calm the hysterical child enough so that she could examine her. After probing her abdomen and questioning the girl, she was able to rule out appendicitis, which had been her first guess, and a ruptured spleen, which had been her second one. But noting several suspicious symptoms, she told Jenni she needed to see her in her office the next day. After administering a mild stomach sedative, she sat by the girl's bedside, cooling her forehead with a damp cloth until she fell asleep.

THE CALL Aurora had been expecting came just as she was driving into the hospital parking lot. Giving her keys to the parking valet, she hurried in.

His life signs erratic, the child's condition had deteriorated to critical and the specialist had decided to operate immediately. After scrubbing up, Aurora went to the operating room to study the X rays and the results of the hourly physiological tests. She could see that the operation was a necessary one, even though the surgery itself could be life threatening to so young a child. Gritting her teeth, she mentally prepared herself for the ordeal to come.

During the procedure, she found herself admiring the skill and deftness of the surgeon she'd called in. Little Travis Worth was in good hands.

Too wired up to go to bed after the surgery, and concerned that the child might need her before the night was out, Aurora decided to wait in the staff lounge.

"I heard you were in here," Paula's voice penetrated the sleepy haze clouding Aurora's brain.

"What time is it?" she asked, squinting at her watch.

"Nearly seven. I've just delivered twins. See what I do to increase your practice for you?"

"You are a great help," Aurora conceded, straightening in her chair. "And when you have your four, that should help even more."

"Can't we work out a cut rate?" Paula teased.

Aurora shook her head. "It takes an even dozen before my rates go down," she said facetiously.

"Don't tell Brook that!" Paula exclaimed in mock horror. "Coffee?" she asked, bringing the pot over to fill Aurora's mug.

"Thanks," Aurora said gratefully. "Do you happen to know if it's still raining?" The lounge was located behind the elevator shaft on the inside of the building, totally isolated from the elements.

"The storm blew itself out by three," Paula said, sitting down. "How's your love life? Any improvement since we last had a real talk?"

"Definitely improving," Aurora answered. She could feel a silly grin curling her lips.

"Good!" Paula laughed. "Whenever I see that dimple in your left cheek, I know you're very pleased with yourself."

"I don't have dimples," Aurora protested.

"Yes, you do," Paula asserted. "One. And it's a dead giveaway."

"Well, there's one thing I'm definitely not dimpling about," Aurora said soberly. "I'm going to bring Jenni in first thing this morning. Fortunately the medical release that boarders' parents sign for the school's records covers a GYN exam. I want you to take a look at her."

"You don't think she's . . ." Paula asked, startled.

Aurora nodded, her teeth tugging at her upper lip. "I just hope I'm wrong."

Chapter Thirteen

"Katie...Katie...help me...please...I think I'm dying," Jenni panted out in the darkness of the small dorm room.

Katie's bare feet hit the floor before she was fully conscious. "What...Jenni...what did you say?" she asked, snapping on the reading light above her bed.

"I...I...hurt so bad," Jenni moaned, sweat pouring off her face and soaking her long brown hair. "My insides...are trying—" her face contorted and she gasped as if in great pain "—to come out."

Even in the dim light Katie could tell that something terrible was wrong with her friend. Jenni lay jerking around as if she couldn't hold still in the twisted pile of bedclothes, her head thrown back in an unnatural position. Her pillows had fallen to the floor and the fitted sheets had pulled loose from the mattress.

"What do you want me to do?" Katie asked, paralyzed with fright, wondering how long Jenni had been like this before she'd wakened her.

"Get help," Jenni managed to choke out before her body started to shake so hard that the bed rattled against the wall.

Hurrying into the hall, Katie spent a split second trying to decide whether to go downstairs to get the house mother, or to call her daddy. Her daddy. He'd come the quickest, and she wouldn't have to explain as long to get him to do it. Pulling the receiver off the hook, she dialed rapidly, remembering as she hit the last digit that it was Friday night and he was probably at the beach house.

"Daddy," she whimpered, leaning against the wall in relief over his having answered on the first ring. He was at the cottage, that was all that mattered.

"Katie?" he asked, alarm in his deep voice. "What's wrong?"

Her words came out in a sob. "You've got to get up here right away. Jenni's dying, and I don't know what to do."

"Calm down, sweetheart," he urged, his voice terse with tension. "Go back and check on her. If you really think she's that bad, call 911. I'll be right there."

Hanging up, Katie took a deep breath before starting back to her room. She knew there were other girls sleeping behind the doors she passed. All she had to do was knock, and she wouldn't be alone. But somehow she couldn't do it. All they could do would be to crowd into the room to stand and stare, and feeling an intense protectiveness for her roommate, she knew she didn't want them there. She'd stay with her friend until her dad came. She could last until then, and he'd know what to do.

Jenni wasn't any better. In fact, she seemed worse. She was making awful noises that seemed to come from someplace much lower than her throat. Not knowing what else to do, Katie crept to the side of Jenni's narrow bed. Wringing her hands, she looked helplessly down at her friend, now thrashing from side to side in torment, as jointless as a rag doll. Jenni's familiar face was so twisted out of shape that she could hardly recognize her. Wanting to offer what comfort she could, she leaned down to straighten the balled-up quilt.

"Oh my God!" she nearly screamed, when her fingers encountered a sticky wetness. The bed was soaked with blood. Running from the room, she grabbed the phone and dialed 911, managing to get out a strangled plea for help.

What she did after that, she didn't know. All she could remember was that it seemed like hours before she heard heavy footsteps running down the hall. Seconds later men burst through the open door of the room with a stretcher. Somehow her father was with them, lifting her from the floor where she must have fallen. He helped her pull on some clothes over her shorty pajamas, before they ran down the stairs and out into the night. Seeing the revolving light on top of the emergency vehicle streak the trees and the building in a crimson as red as Jenni's blood, Katie shuddered with horror and almost collapsed against her father.

"Hurry, hurry," she mindlessly begged, after he'd half carried her to the waiting convertible and put her in. At last, giving in to the panic that rose like vomit to her throat, she screamed hysterically, "Just don't let her die!" Her father gunned the engine, and their car took off into the blackness of the night after the swiftly traveling ambulance.

"UNFORTUNATELY you were right," Paula said, her ordinarily cheerful face wan with dejection as she pulled off her surgical gloves before dropping them into the step can under the stark white hospital sink.

"Oh, Lord! How could this have happened right under our noses? She's just a baby!" Aurora exclaimed, exhaustion seeping into her soul as she leaned against the wall for support.

"Babies having babies," Paula responded woodenly. "A thousand teenagers get pregnant each and every day in this country. And worse yet, six hundred of them go full term and give birth."

Aurora rubbed her fingers over her forehead, trying to erase from her mind the picture of Jenni running on the beach that day that seemed so very long ago now, taking innocent joy in flying the beautiful kite Paula had given her. "I know the statistics, and they're appalling. But my mind slides over them until I'm forced to face reality every time I see it happen to one of these little girls.

"But Jenni...of all people." She let out a ragged sigh. "I blame myself for this. I should have insisted...even put my position at the academy on the line for some sex ed for those girls."

"It's not your fault," Paula objected wearily, resting one hip on the counter. "I blame her parents. Jenni was a statistic waiting to happen. The child is starved for affection. But she's going to be all right ... physically, anyway. I honestly think she doesn't even know what happened. Do you want me to talk with her about it?"

Aurora shook her head and straightened to her feet. "I'll come in this afternoon and do it. It's my responsibility."

"Are you sure you can handle it?" Paula asked with concern. "I know this is hitting awfully close to home for you."

"Thanks," Aurora said, attempting a smile, "but I owe it to her. In the meantime, I've got to come up with a plausible story for Eric and Katie."

"Just say Jenni's in a lot of pain and we've admitted her for observation."

"It'll take more than that. Katie saw the blood. Eric said she was almost in a state of shock by the time he could get to her. I checked her over and then gave her a mild sedative. She didn't need this, either. Eric said she was positive Jenni was going to die, just like her mother did."

"Poor kid," Paula sympathized, pulling her close-fitting cap from her head, and running her fingers through her hair. "Some of these economically 'privileged' kids sure have it rough."

"Speaking of 'economically privileged,' someone's got to get hold of Jenni's parents," Aurora added, not bothering to hide the contempt she felt for them. How could two mature individuals, blessed with the gift of a daughter to raise, blind themselves to her emotional needs. It was beyond her comprehension.

"I'll call Brook and fill him in. He can do that," Paula answered, reaching up to give Aurora an encouraging pat on the back.

"Thanks." She squared her shoulders before going out the swinging doors to catch the elevator down to the waiting room.

Seeing Aurora enter the temporary quiet area, Eric rose to his feet, a question in his eyes.

"How is she?" Katie asked, coming to a sitting position from where she'd been curled up on a vinyl-covered couch. Her eyes were glittering, blue coals in her white face, framed by her mass of tousled hair. "What took you so long?"

"We had to run a lot of tests," Aurora lied smoothly. "Right now we have Jenni under observation. She's going to be fine. Don't worry."

"She was in awful pain," Katie said, wrapping her arms around Aurora's waist to snuggle her face against Aurora's shoulder.

"I know, sweetheart, you told me," Aurora said, stroking her hair.

"And she was bleeding so bad," Katie continued, as if she hadn't heard. "She thought she was going to die, and so did I."

"I know," Aurora soothed, wishing she could erase the terrible memories from the child's mind. "But she isn't going to die. She's going to be fine. She's sleeping peacefully right now, just like you need to be."

"I didn't know what to do...."

"You did everything right," Aurora said, taking the child's face between her hands and kissing her forehead, before Katie burrowed back against her shoulder. "What you've got to do now is stop worrying about it. It's all over." But above Katie's head, she answered Eric's questioning gaze with a long solemn look.

"Come on, Munchkin," he said, pulling Katie away from Aurora and tucking her under his protective arm. "We need to get home and get cleaned up. I don't think we'll have any trouble talking Bridey into whipping up your favorite breakfast, Belgian waffles with strawberry topping, before I tuck you in bed. Aurora's right. You need some rest."

"When can I see Jenni?" Katie asked, refusing to be sidetracked.

"I'll let you know the minute she can have visitors," Aurora promised as she walked with them toward the door.

"Is there anything I can do?" Eric asked. His jaw was covered with a dark stubble that Aurora found surprisingly endearing. She'd never seen him less than impeccably groomed, no matter what the circumstances. This small evidence of how quickly he'd responded to his daughter's need touched her deeply.

She gave him a warm smile. "Not right now. But before you leave, Katie and I really need to take a minute for a girl talk."

"Of course," he said, releasing his daughter.

Taking Katie by the hand, Aurora led her to a secluded corner and sat down beside her on a brown vinyl couch. She couldn't put off giving Katie an explanation, but she still wasn't sure what to say to put the young girl's mind at ease.

"Jenni is having some unusual trouble with her period," she said tentatively, though not untruthfully, "and we're going to get her all straightened out. I know it seemed like she was losing a lot of blood, but it wasn't life threatening. Honey, you did a wonderful thing for her by staying with her until help came. You're a good friend, and I know she'll never forget it."

"Is that ever going to happen to me?" Katie asked fearfully.

"No, darling," Aurora declared vehemently, clasping the young girl close to her heart, worried that her attempt at explaining had added to Katie's concerns. If only she'd admitted Jenni when she'd first become ill, Katie wouldn't have had to go through any of this! In that dark moment, it seemed to her that her life was a series of regrets... a whole string of *if onlys!* Shaking off the momentary lapse into self-pity, she said with conviction, "Believe me, you don't have anything to worry about on that score. I'll make sure it never happens to you. Now, you go home with your dad. You need some sleep and so do I."

At the door, Eric took both of them into his arms for a comforting hug. "You and I are due for a heavy date tonight," he whispered into Aurora's ear. "Dinner first and then I'm taking you up on last night's rain check."

"What are you two whispering about?" Katie asked, pushing them apart, her pale inquisitive face turned up toward theirs.

"I'm taking Aurora out for dinner tonight," Eric explained lightly, "and you're staying home with Bridey and Mac."

"That's okay with me," the young girl responded nonchalantly. "Bridey's going to teach me how to make fetballs."

"Fetballs?" Aurora and Eric asked in unison.

"You know, those fluffy kind of raisin doughnuts without holes that you like so much," she said with a toss of her head, stepping onto the black rubber mat to slide open the automatic door. "She was going to teach Jenni, too," she added wistfully.

"Jenni will be better real soon, and then you can help Bridey teach her," Aurora said, wondering if it were true. Jenni's future was uncertain right now. Aurora had no idea how the girl's parents or the headmaster would react to the girl's situation.

"About seven?" Eric asked with an intimate smile, before following his daughter.

"Seven will be fine," Aurora assured him, conscious that her answering smile undoubtedly displayed her one-sided dimple. A thrill of anticipation rippled down her spine. One thing was certain—tonight she was going to give herself to this wonderful, caring man...heart, body and soul. This time she knew the morrow would bring no regrets.

AWAKENING FROM a deep sleep a few minutes after noon, Aurora immediately lifted the receiver from her bedside phone and called the hospital. After learning that Jenni had recovered from the anesthesia and was sleeping peacefully, she called Brook.

"I haven't been able to get hold of her parents yet," he answered worriedly. "The father is on a flight to Tokyo and the mother is on a buying trip to the Far East. The father's airline has promised that a message to call me will reach him the minute he lands, and the mother's store manager in Beverly Hills is trying to reach her for us."

"Let me know as soon as you find out when they'll be here," Aurora said. "I want to see both of them before they see Jenni. Have you told the headmaster anything yet?"

"No, and I'm not going to until the last possible moment. He's so unpredictable there's no telling what he might do. We, by that I mean you, me and Jenni's parents, need to close ranks before we confront the bastard," Brook answered heatedly.

"I feel the same way," Aurora said with relief. "I was sure I could count on you."

"How is she?" he asked with concern. "Paula said she came through the procedure okay."

If Aurora hadn't been so upset, Brook's slip into medical jargon would have amused her. Brook was going to make the kind of supportive husband that a woman in Paula's position needed. "Out of the anesthetic and sleeping. I'm going up to the hospital right now to see her."

"Good. Let me know when you think it's all right for me to visit. I hate to think of her lying there all alone. I'll tell you, I've been racking my brain trying to think how and when this could have happened. We've had a couple of pregnancies over the years in my tenure at Seahurst, but they were in the upper school, never in the middle school, or with a girl this young. I thought we did a better job of supervising them than this."

"You do a good job," Aurora said vehemently, "but you can't watch them every moment. They need sex education. I hate to use a cliché, but in this case, ignorance isn't bliss."

"I don't know what the hell we're going to do," Brook said dejectedly. "I'll get canned for it, but I'm ready to be openly insubordinate and blitz these kids with the facts."

"As soon as we get past this crisis, count me in. I don't care what kind of ramifications there are. I just can't help thinking what if it had been Katie?"

"I know what you mean. I keep wondering who the boy could have been."

"That child has been so lonely, that I'm sure she would have done anything for someone who seemed interested in her. We don't know though, the boy may be as lonely and emotionally vulnerable as she is."

Brook groaned. "It was tough being a teenager way back when I was one. And I think kids today have an even harder time than we did. Those hormones kick in long before the brain is mature enough to deal with the problems they can cause."

"That's for sure. Listen, I've got to get going. I need to talk with Jenni, but there's a chance she may not want to see anyone else until her parents get here. If that's the case, we'll keep her here as long as that takes."

"I sent her flowers...from me and from the girls in the dorm," Brook said. "It seemed pretty feeble, but I couldn't think what else to do."

"That was very thoughtful of you. I'm sure that Jenni will appreciate every blossom," she answered before ringing off.

Brook was such a caring person, she thought as she got out of bed. If only he were the headmaster of Seahurst! The staff were by and large a great bunch of people. With a little encouragement and the opportunity for some specialized training, she suspected they'd be fired up and ready to implement some innovative programs. Teachers were always a major influence on a child's life, but teachers of boarding school students played an even larger role. At times, they were almost surrogate parents. It was a shame this terrible episode with Jenni had to be the catalyst to spark the needed change!

All the while Aurora showered, her spirits vacillated between soaring elation and deep despair. Tonight would be the most special of her life. In Eric's loving arms, the curtain would come down on years of frustration and uncertainty. Eric was the miracle she'd thought would never happen...the man who had made her believe she had the capacity to be a complete, fulfilled woman. But, ironically, she wondered if tonight would also be the beginning of years of unhappiness for the little girl lying alone in her hospital bed. Unless Jenni got the right kind of help...the kind of help that had been denied Aurora...the girl might never be whole again. Aurora vowed she would not let that happen.

But she had to put Jenni out of her mind at least for a little while, she decided as she toweled herself dry. There was nothing more she could do for Jenni today, and she wasn't going to let that sad fact cast a cloud over the evening ahead. This night belonged to her and Eric alone.

After pulling on a pair of stone-washed jeans and a sweatshirt, she took her Icelandic knit jacket from the clothes rack and quickly stuffed her arms into it before slipping on a pair of ankle-high boots. Although the storm of the night before had blown over, it had left behind an unusual chill in the coastal California air.

She wished she had time to shop...she would have liked to have worn something brand-new tonight...something symbolic of the fresh direction and purpose Eric had given to her life. Wait a minute, she thought, hurrying back to check her closet. She'd picked up a dinner dress at a little specialty store while at the convention in San Francisco, and then hadn't worn it. Pulling the dress from its bag, she lovingly laid it out on the bed. It had been an extravagance, but she didn't begrudge a penny of it now. It fit to perfection, and she knew she wanted Eric to always remember the way she'd look tonight.

Chapter Fourteen

While Aurora drove the short distance to the hospital, she let her mind dwell dreamily on Eric. She loved him so. All the while she'd doubted his commitment to her, he'd been working to rid himself of the past...working to build an unencumbered path to their future. She'd had so little time to adjust to the fact that he truly loved her that she was almost afraid it was all a wonderful dream from which she would awaken to find herself alone and unloved.

But it was not a dream...it was her new reality. She could have it all...everything she'd ever wanted and thought fate had denied was now within her grasp. Only one obstacle lay in their path—she hadn't yet been honest with him. She hadn't shared her secret...and as much as she dreaded doing it, she knew she would have to tell him tonight after they made love. She'd never thought she could tell her story to any man, fearing rejection and even revulsion. But Eric wasn't just any man...and she knew he would never turn from her in disgust. Eric had lived through his own hell and had come out the other side into the sunlight that she vowed would characterize their lives together. It was possible...just possible, she thought with a surge of hope, that he'd be able to help her to a safe haven, far away from the shadows of her past.

Driving onto the hospital grounds, she reluctantly shook off her sense of euphoria and concentrated on Jenni's plight. After entering the building she stopped by the gift shop just long enough to pick out a pair of pretty earrings she thought might appeal to Jenni. Material offerings were valueless in themselves, Aurora knew well from her own experience, but she hoped Jenni would recognize and appreciate the earrings for what they were—a token of her concern and affection. She also made a quick stop at the flower stand before taking the elevator up to the third floor.

As she rounded the corner and approached the hall outside Jenni's room, she was surprised to see Eric.

"What are you doing here?" she asked, her heart skipping a beat. "Is Katie all right?"

"She's fine . . . sound asleep at home. As for me, I'm sort of standing . . . or sitting . . . vigil, I guess," he answered, stepping forward and lightly taking her by her upper arms. "Brook filled me in on the real story. He wanted to be here, but he and Paula had an appointment to pick out her rings. I told him to go ahead. That I'd stand in for him. Neither of us wanted to think of Jenni up here alone.

"Besides," he said, dropping his voice confidentially, "I knew you'd be coming and I was having a hard time waiting until seven to see you."

He took the vase of yellow rosebuds from her hand and put it down on the lamp table beside the couch. Turning back to her, his dark eyes sparkled with a special joy she had never seen in their depths. Taking her in his arms, he kissed her. She melted against him, all reserve gone as her lips softened and opened to the probe of his tongue. After a long moment, they reluctantly drew apart with an unspoken understanding that the encounter had been only a brief prelude to the wonderful evening to come.

"I know what you mean," Aurora confessed breathlessly, her heart soaring.

"Let me open the door for you," he murmured, handing her back the vase.

"Eric?"

"Yes?"

"I'd like to see Jenni alone . . . first."

"Of course," he answered, pushing open the door. "I'll wait for you out here. I—"

"Yes?" She paused, waiting for him to go on.

He shook his head. "Nothing. I'm just so sorry this happened to her."

She nodded, feeling a lump rise in her throat. "We all are."

She crossed the quiet room and set her gifts on the elongated surface of the serving table before speaking to Jenni. The girl was lying on the white bed, her face buried in a pillow.

"Jenni, are you awake?"

"Yes," came the muffled answer.

"I brought you a couple of little gifts I thought you might like, dear."

"Thank you," the girl answered dutifully, still not turning over to look at her visitor.

Aurora walked over to the large window and pulled open the drapes letting the sunlight spill into the room in stark contrast to the cheerlessness she felt in her heart. This was going to be a difficult encounter, but for Jenni's sake she had to do it. She didn't want to risk letting the girl bury her feelings, only to find years later that she still wasn't free of them. Pulling up a chair beside the bed, she took Jenni's listless hand from where it lay on her hip.

"You certainly have a lot of flowers. It smells like a summer garden in here." Prominent among the bouquets was a vase with a dozen long-stemmed roses.

"Mr. Oliver sent some. The housemother sent the plant. And Katie and her father sent the roses," Jenni responded, gingerly rolling over onto her back.

"Everyone wants you to get well as quickly as you can," Aurora said, giving Jenni's hand an encouraging squeeze.

"I want my mother," the girl whimpered. "Is she coming?"

"The manager of her store is trying to get hold of her. She's on a buying trip to the Far East. But I'm sure you'll hear from her before evening. How are you feeling?"

"I don't know," Jenni answered groggily. "I ache all over and I still have some cramps every once in a while."

"That's normal. They should stop soon."

"What happened to me?"

"You had an operation," Aurora said softly. "It's called a D and C. It means that Dr. Paula had to scrape out your uterus."

Jenni's eyes widened. "Dr. Paula did it?"

"That's right."

"I'm glad it wasn't anyone else," she said, reaching up to move her pillow to a more comfortable position. "Will I have a scar?"

Not one that shows, Aurora answered silently, before saying, "No, dear."

"What was wrong with me? Is it ever going to happen again?"

"You were pregnant," Aurora said as gently as she could. "You had a miscarriage." Because of its emotional weight, she didn't want to use the technical term *spontaneous abortion*, though the fetus had been lost before the ninetieth day of development. "Under the circumstances, the operation was necessary. But don't worry. You'll be just fine. There was no damage to your internal organs."

"I couldn't have been pregnant," Jenni said with alarm, her startled eyes searching Aurora's face. "I'm not married."

Oh, Lord, it was going to be even more difficult than she'd thought. It was hard to believe that any girl Jenni's age could be so naive, but in her sheltered boarding school existence, even Jenni's exposure to television was very limited and controlled. Silently cursing the Seahurst school board for the child's ignorance, Aurora persisted. "You don't have to be married to conceive. You just have to have sexual intercourse with a male."

"You mean like making out? But I only did it once," the child declared. "And he said you couldn't get pregnant just doing it once."

"Then he was lying or misinformed. Once is enough," Aurora assured her. How well she knew. "Jenni, who did this to you?" The room felt stifling, the perfume from the flowers overpowering, as Aurora experienced a sudden sense of déjà vu. The words coming from her mouth could have been those coming from her own mother's fourteen years ago.

"I'm not going to tell you," Jenni stated flatly, turning her head away. "And please don't tell Katie that I was pregnant."

"I won't tell Katie, or any of the other girls. No one will know about it besides Dr. Paula and me, your parents, and..."

"Not my parents!" Jenni shouted. "You don't have to tell them!"

"They have to know," Aurora said as calmly as she could, "in order to get you the help you need. Jenni, dar-

ling, you've suffered enough. You don't have to be alone
this anymore. Now, tell me, who caused your pregnancy

"Why?" Jenni asked, her dark eyes wide with fear. '
isn't any of your business! I don't have to tell you."

"Yes, you do, dear, you must," Aurora gently insiste
unsure how best to approach the woefully ignorant g
"Has anyone ever explained to you about sex?"

"No," Jenni said, her body going stiff as she stared up
the ceiling.

Aurora just managed to hold back a sigh, thinking wh
an incredible position a combination of neglect and na
row-mindedness had put the poor child in.

"Jenni, when two people love each other, sex can be
beautiful extension of that love. But sex isn't something
be taken lightly. It carries with it a responsibility to you
self and to the other person. Sex without love can be ve
damaging..."

"But there was love!" Jenni protested, suddenly comi
to life. "He loves me. He said he did. And I love him too

"Who, dear, who do you love?" Aurora pressed, hopi
to capitalize on the momentum created by the girl's stro
feelings.

A strong emotion flashed in Jenni's eyes as she bare
mouthed the words, "Mr. Thorpe. It was Mr. Thorpe."

Not believing she could have heard right, Aurora c
manded, "Who? Who did you say it was?" Her pulse w
pounding so violently in her ears she thought she was goi
to faint.

"Katie's father," Jennie whispered again.

"How? When?" Aurora stammered hoarsely. Rising
her feet, she tried to fight off the revolting memory of t
drunken neighbor who'd forced himself on her when she
been a teenage babysitter for his children... the horrifyi
nightmare that still insidiously invaded her sleep from tir

to time, leaving her shaking uncontrollably in the dark, cringing with fear. His contorted face . . . the one she would never forget . . . superimposed itself over the image of Eric's that rose to her mind in response to Jenni's words.

"At his house on campus one night," the child replied, a faraway look in her eyes and a singsong quality to her voice. "When I went to tell him that Katie was being mean to me."

"Have you told anyone else about this?" Aurora asked, imposing a tenuous hold on her shattered emotions. Feeling the blood in her veins turn to ice, a chilling numbness holding her in its grip.

"He told me I couldn't, or he wouldn't love me anymore. I wanted him to love me. Nobody else did. Not even Katie."

Not Eric! Aurora's heart screamed. It wasn't possible! But while her heart protested, her treacherous mind produced damning evidence. What was his real reason for sitting outside Jenni's room? Had it been Brook's idea or his? Was he afraid of Jenni telling? And the intimidating bouquet! Were the red blossoms supposed to signal a warning to the child? Its opulence suddenly sickened her! And why would an innocent child lie?

Realizing she was having trouble remembering how to breathe, Aurora tried to calm herself without success. Had his self-imposed celibacy become too much for him? Had he lost control and preyed on Jenni's pitiful need for affection? Had he forced himself upon his daughter's friend as her own father's business partner had forced himself on her?

Stunned by the child's shocking confession and identifying her own brutal violation with Jenni's experience, Eric Thorpe assumed the proportions of a vicious monster in her mind. A monster who she'd see destroyed!

Tearing open the door, she plunged out of the room, catching only a glimpse of Eric's startled face as she began to run down the hall. The sight of him nauseated her, and she gasped for huge lungsful of air. She had to get away... she couldn't breathe... she couldn't think. Reaching the stairway door, she opened it and blindly began to stagger down the steps.

"Aurora," Eric called behind her, his voice echoing menacingly in the stairwell. "Aurora, wait! What's wrong?"

When he caught up with her outside the building he grabbed her arm, swinging her around to face him.

"How could you have done this to Jenni... to me?" she demanded, her voice full of loathing, her free fist pounding viciously against the hardness of his muscled chest, tears of blind rage flowing down her heated cheeks. "How dare you show your face? You belong behind bars, and I'm going to see that you're put there. You're not going to get away with this, this time. You... you... child molester!"

"Wait a minute!" he said from between clenched teeth, his dark face close to hers, his hand closing on her arm in a painful grip. "What are you saying? What are you accusing me of?"

"Jenni told me that you were the man who raped her!" she hissed, fighting off the dreadful blackness that threatened to envelope her, her eyes glittering with an unnatural light.

"And you believed her?" he asked incredulously, a stunned expression on his face.

"Why shouldn't I?" Aurora spat out, wrenching her arm free.

"Because it isn't true!" he shouted, as she ran heedlessly for her car.

Chapter Fifteen

Desperately fumbling in her handbag for her keys, Aurora found herself possessed by a primitive anger. Her cheeks and the back of her eyelids burned fiery red, though her fingers felt numb and useless. Hatred seared and choked her reason, reducing her mind to operating on the level of barbarous rage... rage against the man who'd taken Jenni's irreplaceable innocence...rage against the other man who'd drunkenly and brutally taken her own.

Unaware of the sound of screeching tires as she backed from the parking spot and raced out into the street, the hideous memory of the night she'd conceived her child played again in her mind—a scenario in which the image of Eric Thorpe now intermingled with the image of the man who'd raped her. Her body alternated between fierce heat and teeth-chattering cold as shame and fear swept over her as forcefully as if she were actually reliving the months of isolation she'd spent afterward in a private seaside home in the northern part of the state.

A scream died in her throat as her sense of loss hit her as devastatingly as it had the moment her mother had turned and walked away, leaving her emotionally bereft in the care of strangers, unprepared for and undeserving of the sudden, wrenching break of family ties.

Failing to see a stop sign, she careened through an intersection, narrowly missing a collision with a car that had the right-of-way. Its horn blared, but she didn't hear it as she remembered again her terror and pain during the difficult, seemingly endless hours her girlish body had struggled to give birth . . . with only the support of her physician and the hospital staff. Scorched into her mind's eye was the only—forbidden—glimpse she'd ever had of her daughter . . . a tiny, red, wailing speck of humanity with a tuft of coal black hair.

A fog of despair descended on her spirit as she remembered the depression and the disorientation she'd plunged into after the birth. She'd struggled for direction . . . purpose . . . a reason to go on living, unaware that her worst hell was yet to come. As the months and years had passed, her mind and emotions had matured. She'd become haunted by guilt and filled with an enormous sense of loss. She'd come to realize that the child she'd given birth to was an integral, irreplaceable part of herself. The knowledge that her daughter would live a life totally separate and apart from her was a reality too awful for her mind to accept. That knowledge had stunted her desire to lead a full life . . . until last summer.

She sped through the small town out to the coastal highway, heading her car north toward San Francisco. Driven by instinct to find the key to the present situation that was more tragic in its implications than anything she'd ever had to face, she sought a target for her fury. The man who'd violated her had gotten off unscathed. Incredibly he remained a respected community leader. She doubted he even knew that he'd impregnated her. Yet, she'd paid and continued to pay the price for his vile moment of sexual urgency. Many times during her months of exile she'd wanted to contact her own father, to draw on his strength, to feel the warmth of his unconditional love. Only her mother's frightened warnings and her own strong belief that if he'd found out the truth he would have killed the man who'd attacked her, had kept her from it.

Now she knew the full depth of the murderous wrath her father would have experienced. Well, Eric Thorpe was not going to get away with it, she vowed, tears streaming down her contorted face as her fists pounded the steering wheel. He'd tried to claim he was innocent, but why would Jenni lie? Kids rarely lied about their attackers. There was no way she was going to believe him. She was not her mother! This man was going to pay!

Once in San Francisco she would confront her mother with the long overdue condemnation she had coming to her, and she'd tell her father the real reason their relationship had become so distant. Then, her feverish mind hoped, she'd be free of some of the emotional baggage that had plagued her all these years, and she'd be able to deal rationally with the problem of Eric Thorpe.

It was nearly six when Aurora turned onto the quiet tree-lined street where she'd grown up...where she'd lived a happy, normal existence until her seventeenth summer. Fearing the facade of composure she'd managed to impose on herself might crack, she didn't chance a look down the block at the house where her father's business partner had lived with his family that long-ago evening, and where, before the night was over, her life had been shattered. Gritting her teeth, she swung into the familiar driveway of a large low house set back from the other Spanish-styled homes on either side of it. After getting out of her car, she ran across the well-manicured lawn and pulled open the grilled gate to an artfully landscaped garden courtyard and ran a few more steps to pound on the heavy door to the house.

"Aurora," her mother exclaimed in surprise a momen later as her daughter pushed past her into the tiled hal "Why didn't you call to tell me you were coming? I woul have made something special..." Her pleased expressio changed to one of alarm when Aurora turned to face he "What's wrong?" she asked, her hand raising to cover he mouth in the familiar gesture Aurora recognized as fearfu confusion.

"Where's Dad?" she demanded, refusing to waste a mo ment in tea-party talk with her mother. Never a strong per sonality, the once-pretty woman had been coddled an protected by her husband throughout her entire married life It was time, Aurora thought grimly, way past time for Che Duvall to grow up.

"He's gone hunting...in Canada," the older woma stammered. "Please, dear, tell me—"

"No! You tell me," Aurora interrupted bitterly, flingin her handbag down on the entry hall floor, "how you coul have let me be the scapegoat when I was the innocent vic tim of a vicious rape."

"Oh, dear," her mother said fearfully, her hand flutter ing at her breast as she cringed against the wall, her frigh ened eyes staring at Aurora like those of a bird hypnotize by a snake. "I don't see what good it will do to bring all thi up again now..."

For once, determined not to let herself be daunted or de terred by her mother's helpless stance, Aurora shouted "We've never brought it up! We've never had it out! Yo swept it aside like dirt under the edge of a carpet. You mad me feel like I was filth that had to be hidden away from th light." Her voice dropped, "Well, I wasn't filth, Mother, was a hurt, devastated child who needed your help. But didn't get it."

"I tried to do..."

"What was best for me," Aurora finished the sentence for her mother. "I've heard that line before. Well, it wasn't best for me. Bruce Douglas should have been arrested! Put behind bars! Publicly exposed for his crime! You were my mother, you should have seen to it! Instead, you treated me like I was the criminal . . . like I was the one who had to be locked away."

"Come in, sit down," her mother urged in a shaky voice, "let me get you some hot tea."

"I don't want any tea," Aurora protested, stubbornly refusing to let herself be disarmed by her mother's passive manner. This time Cheri Duvall wasn't going to diffuse her anger, or turn her away from her purpose. This time the woman was going to admit responsibility for what she'd done, as surely as Eric Thorpe was going to pay for his own treachery.

Following the slender woman into the kitchen, Aurora dropped down onto a chair at the table set for her mother's evening meal.

"I'm so sorry about what happened," the older woman said softly, timidly placing a hand on Aurora's shoulder.

"You're sorry?" Aurora mimicked disbelievingly, forcing herself not to pull away from her mother's unwanted touch. "You're sorry? Is that supposed to mean something to me?"

Her mother bit her lower lip and averted her eyes. "No . . . I suppose not. I had no idea it would be like this. I thought in time that we'd recover from it and that we could go back to the way it had been before . . ." Her fingers slid down Aurora's arm and came to rest on her hand as she took the seat next to her daughter.

"I've cried until I have no more tears," she went on, her hand tightening. "I've gone over and over it in my mind . . . there's never been a day since that terrible night that

I haven't thought about it. And I know, my darling, that what's happened since then has to be my fault. I don't blame you for hating me," she swallowed hard, "I hate myself."

"You were a bright child, Aurora. No one had to tell you that your father always made the important decisions in our marriage. I've always been weak, and I've depended on his strength. I guess when I had to make the most important decision of our lives without him, I wasn't up to it. I made a terrible mistake—one we've all had to live with—but I still can't bear to think of the alternative. Having your father behind bars for murder... and he would have killed Bruce, you know that... and the business he'd spent so long building up lost in a morass of court actions and debt..." Her voice trailed off, as her hand gestured at the lovely room. "I didn't care about having things... you must believe me. But your father had poured his life's blood into his invention and getting that patent."

"I know all that," Aurora said, beginning to see her mother in a new light. "And I know that Bruce Douglas's partnership with Dad was based on his providing the financing to back Dad's idea. But how could you face him after what he did to me?"

"I hated him as much or more than you did," her mother answered in a whisper, her eyes cast down. "I couldn't stand the sight of him. After I had you settled in, and I knew you wouldn't be involved, I went to him and told him that I knew what he'd done."

"Did he admit it?" Aurora asked, wondering what kind of confrontation her mother could have possibly had with the arrogant, overbearing man.

"He didn't have to," Cheri said, a look in her eyes Aurora had never seen before. "Remember, I was the one you came to that night... I was the one who held you in my arms until morning. He knew I knew. I gave him six months to arrange to sell out the business to your father.''

"Or what?'' Aurora asked, feeling an unbidden sense of admiration. She'd always wondered about the abrupt break-up of the partnership. Her father's invention had been certain to make everyone involved in it wealthy, and Bruce Douglas was not the sort to walk away from a sure-fire investment. Shrewd and unscrupulous, he'd parlayed his wife's modest inheritance into a small fortune by repeatedly backing the right horses.

Cheri straightened her spine. "Or I'd go to the police with the whole story.''

Aurora looked at her mother. She knew how hard it must have been for the timorous woman to take a courageous stand. "You never told me that.''

"I had to get him out of our lives. I felt the less said about anything that had to do with him the better.''

"You were wrong,'' Aurora forced the words from her lips. "I needed you. I needed Dad. I was all alone.''

"I know...and I should have been there for you. I should have come up with some excuse to get away. But your father thought you were spending your last year at a private school in Europe. It was so difficult for me to arrange all the details of the deception as it was. How would it have looked if I had gone running up to see you all the time?''

How would it have looked! Aurora thought with dismay. Her mother's code of ethics! The phrase by which she'd been brought up! The words that had kept her isolated from her parents when she'd needed them the most!

Her anger rekindled, she lashed out, "You prefer false appearances to the reality of our miserable relationship?''

"No,'' Cheri Duvall admitted humbly...placatingly. "How can you even ask?''

"Because you've put me through hell," Aurora accused raising her voice. "I've had to live with the choice you made for me every day of my life! Somewhere out there, I have daughter. She's my flesh and blood. I've lost her. Every day I wonder where she is. What she's doing. Whether or not she needs me. You'll never understand what torment you've inflicted on me."

"You're wrong, Aurora," Cheri's hoarse voice caught tearfully. "Every day I mourn the loss of *my* daughter, too We both know I lost you then, almost as completely as you lost your child. And your child," she whispered, "is my only granddaughter."

Moments passed and the only sound in the room was th ticking of a wall clock. The two women sat silently, as i neither knew where to go from there.

Finally Cheri spoke. "Your father is heartbroken. H doesn't talk about it anymore, but he used to agonize ove what had happened to estrange you from him. The two o you were so close when you were growing up. He neve wanted a son, you know. Even before you were born he wa hoping for a daughter. And, whatever you may think of me you have to admit that he was the perfect father. No matte how busy he was, he always had time for you.

"He couldn't understand it when you became so cold ar distant. He never knew what turned you into a polit stranger...and I couldn't tell him for fear of tearing all ou lives apart.

"I never told you, but that first Christmas when yo called from college and told us that you were going to spend the holidays with your roommate's family—" her voic broke, and she made a visible effort to gain control befor going on "—I thought his heart would break. We didn' even put up a tree. I knew all he could think of was thos yearly trips he'd made up into the hills with you to cut down a fresh one, and the happy times we'd all shared putting them up.

"Even so, he was so proud when you graduated from medical school. So ready to have you back in our lives. I think until then he'd allowed himself to believe that it was some kind of phase you were going through. But when things didn't change after that, he finally gave up." She lifted her head, and her pleading gaze sought Aurora's. "This house isn't much of a home anymore... hasn't been since you left... for either of us.

"He blames me. He doesn't know what I did, but I know he believes I'm responsible. He finds every excuse he can to get away... without me."

For a long moment the two women searched each other's faces for an understanding of the other's sufferings. "I did what I thought was the best thing to do at the time," her mother said beseechingly. "I didn't know it would turn out like this. Can you ever forgive me?"

Though tears welled in her faded blue eyes, Cheri continued to look at her daughter with a resoluteness Aurora would never have given her mother credit for having. Touched by her mother's plea and by the similarity of their losses, Aurora searched for words to answer, "I'm not sure.

"Even though I can accept that you were doing the best that you could...I really can...I can never agree with what you did. There was too much risk to other people. As hard as it would have been on all of us, we didn't have the right to remain silent. How do you know that Bruce Douglas didn't do what he did to me to other girls?"

"Of course, I can't know," Cheri admitted, "and you don't know how I've worried about that...but I don't think he did. You see, everyone in our circle knew what a skirt chaser he was." Her face darkened. "He'd even made a silly pass at me one night at a party. But you see, after he hurt you I told him that if anything ever got back to me again...even a breath of scandal...I'd go to Madeleine with the whole story." Her voice dropped reflectively, and she let out a ragged sigh. "Poor Madeleine, married to an awful man like that. And those lovely children of theirs."

"If you knew that about him, why did you let me baby-sit his children?" Aurora asked hotly.

"How could anyone guess that he was dangerous?" her mother asked in a shocked tone. "We thought no one we knew would ever do a thing like that! He was your father's business partner! We had baby-sitters for you when you were a child. Do you think I should have worried when your father took them home?"

"Of course not!" Aurora answered scornfully. "Daddy's too good, too kind, too decent..." She stopped herself mid-sentence, staring vacantly into space. How could anyone know the truth about anyone? Was every man a potential rapist? Brook? Bill? The headmaster? Her father? Of course not, she answered her own question. Then why had she been so quick to believe that Eric was? The man who'd gained her respect and trust through his actions and his attitudes? The man who'd humbled himself to meet the needs of his demanding adolescent daughter? The man who'd been honest enough with her to not take her love until he was free to offer himself completely? The man whom she'd trusted and come to love?

The images of Bruce Douglas and Eric Thorpe, which had been so hideously superimposed on each other in her mind, suddenly separated, and she saw them each for what they were. Eric Thorpe had no need to assert some distorted version of his masculinity on a poor, innocent child. He didn't have the capacity to commit such a heinous act. He was decent to the core.... She'd stake her life on it.

Confused, she rose to her feet. Then why had Jenni accused him? There had to be a compelling reason for her to lie. But loving Eric as she did, why had she been so quick to believe the child's words without further investigation? Why hadn't she listened to and believed his denial? Was she so flawed and unstable that she'd never be able to really trust a man again?

Chapter Sixteen

Eric sat slumped in his car in Aurora's driveway. Isolated from the world by the dense fog that had rolled in with the setting of the winter sun, for hours he'd had little to occupy his mind, other than the incredible accusations the woman he loved had flung at him before she'd torn out of the hospital parking lot. But worry about Aurora had robbed him of the ability to think rationally for more than a few minutes at a time. His anxiety had increased with every moment that passed, and rapid, disconnected thoughts skittered wildly through his brain. Where could she have gone? he wondered with an edge of desperation.

He should have tried to follow her right then, but he'd been thrown by her accusation, and by the time he'd recovered, it had been too late. Shifting in his seat, he tried to find a more comfortable position for his long legs. Like the rest of him, they were beginning to feel stiff and badly in need of exercise. But he wasn't budging from behind the wheel. He wasn't going to risk having her drive up and decide to leave again before he could follow.

Where could she be? He'd thought that she would eventually have to come home, and he was willing to wait for her no matter how long it took. But glancing at the luminous dial on his watch he began to wonder if he could afford to wait much longer. Something could have happened. Perhaps, he worried, he should alert Brook and Paula and wake Mac, and they should all go out to look for her. He'd give it another ten minutes, he decided, trying not to give in to his growing sense of panic, then he'd have to try to do something. He couldn't stand to think of her out there alone somewhere in her precarious state of mind.

How could everything he touched go so wrong? he wondered bleakly. And why was the wonderful woman he loved more deeply than he'd ever loved anyone—the woman who'd had the strength to help Katie and him regain their emotional equilibrium—behaving so irrationally? Lord, where was she?

Agitated and alarmed, he tried to focus his thoughts. He wasn't concerned about what she'd called him. His conscience was clear on that score. But he had to know what critical factor in Aurora's own background had triggered the hysteria that still twisted his gut to remember. He couldn't stand to think of her hurting that badly! Thinking back over the past few months, he realized that he'd had occasional clues that something deep and significant was troubling her. And he should have picked up on them and insisted on some answers. But he'd been so damned wrapped up in his own problems that he hadn't bothered to find out about hers. It had something to do with her family, he'd concluded hours ago, remembering how she'd always shied away from any mention of them or of her childhood.

His weary eyes blinked and hope surged over him as headlights from behind flooded the interior of his car with a sudden brightness before they were snapped off. Instantly he jumped out and had his fingers on the handle of Aurora's door before she could open it.

"I've been so worried about you," he said, helping her out. "Where did you go?" His gentle question was filled with loving concern.

"I had to go to San Francisco," she answered stiffly. She hadn't been prepared to see him here, and for just a moment she'd considered throwing her car into reverse and taking off again into the black night. She hadn't wanted to face him . . . at least not yet. Shaken, unsure and emotionally depleted, she'd thought she wanted to be alone. All her soul-searching on the way back from the city had not yet led to any conclusive answers to the questions still haunting her. Her mind had gone around in never-ending, senseless circles like a mechanical wind-up toy. Realizing there would be no answers without him, she decided to stay.

"I'm glad you're back," he said, walking with her to the door.

He followed her into the house after she unlocked the door. Wanting only to throw herself into his arms and to pretend that nothing had gone wrong between them, she steeled herself against the attraction his body held for hers, knowing that the way matters stood between them she had no right to seek comfort from him.

"You must know that whatever Jenni told you wasn't true," he said after snapping on the light.

"Oh, Eric, I want to believe that it isn't," she said with a sob, deliberately avoiding his gaze. "And I know that it couldn't possibly be. But . . ."

"But what?" he insisted, cupping his hand beneath her chin and raising her face so that she had to look at him. "Tell me why you believed her without asking me if it was true."

He was so caring, his dark eyes so filled with solicitude, his words so free from resentment, that Aurora could no longer keep her secret from him. In a rush of barely articulate words, punctuated by her exhausted sobbing, she blurted out the story of her own past.

He held her, smoothing her hair and murmuring words of comfort, until she was calm enough to talk again.

"I don't know what I would have wanted done differently," she confessed, after noisily blowing her nose on the handkerchief he offered. "I wouldn't have wanted to destroy my father. I certainly wouldn't have wanted my daughter to know that her father was a drunken rapist. And I wouldn't have wanted to destroy the lives of that man's wife and children, either. But still . . ."

"You want justice," he stated as though he understood completely.

She pondered his words. Could it be as simple as that? "Do you think that's what it is?" she asked finally.

He nodded. "We're taught from the time we're children that things should be fair . . . just. That right triumphs over wrong. And it's hard to accept when things don't work out that way. All we can do is accept what we must and forgive what we can. You're the one who's helped me understand that."

"Have I been so blind?" she asked in a small voice, as her mind sifted quickly through the evidence swirling there. Pulling away from his loose embrace, she walked into the darkened living room to stare unseeingly out the window. The mournful wail of a foghorn sounded in the distance, its low tones magnified by the thick mist blanketing the sea.

She gave a mirthless laugh. "You're right. I've always been the one to advise others not to wallow in self-pity. I've told them to face up to their problems. To get on with their lives. I should have followed my own prescription. I'm the one who clung to the past, allowing it to overshadow my future."

Sensing Eric's presence behind her, she turned. "I love you," she declared simply, looking up into his eyes, seeing an acceptance there she wasn't quite sure she deserved. "I was so happy this afternoon thinking of spending this evening with you. So happy that I'd finally found someone I could trust."

With a low moan, he gathered her into his arms holding her tightly against him.

"No, wait," she whispered against the warm skin of his throat. "I have to think this through. I know now that you're not the person who took advantage of Jenni. I know you couldn't possibly have done such a thing. But why didn't I know that when she told me that you had? Though it's rare, I've seen a couple of cases before where young girls named men other than the ones who'd actually fathered their children. Why didn't I even consider that possibility with Jenni? Why was I so quick to believe her when I love and trust you? What's the matter with me?"

"There's nothing the matter with you, darling," he murmured. "It's not hard to figure out what happened. Being close to Jenni, with your own history, you immediately identified with her as a victim. You got the man Jenni named confused with the man who'd raped you."

"That's exactly what I did," she confessed. "But you're nothing like him." Looking at Eric's dear face, she let her fingers trace his strong features. "He was an arrogant man...with a need to dominate everyone and every situation. He had no regard for anyone else's feelings. You're his opposite in every way. How could I have confused you with him?"

"My darling, darling Aurora," Eric said with soothing conviction, "you're a deeply passionate woman. Stories like ours have played to audiences for centuries."

"Will ours have a happy ending?" she asked, wanting to ear his assurance that it would.

"I hope so, but there is something you have to know," he nswered instead, his eyes taking on a guarded look.

"What?" she demanded, her heart pounding with fresh larm.

"There's no easy way to tell you this. I can't father any hildren."

"You can't..." she stared blankly.

He shook his head. "I had a vasectomy not long after Katie was born. Stacia's doctor told me that another pregancy would never be advisable for a woman in her cond.ion. At that time, I couldn't ever imagine wanting another hild, so it seemed like the right thing to do. But now, I'm o sorry... knowing how much you miss your own daugher, I can understand that you'd want to have another aby."

"No," she answered truthfully without having to think bout it. "No. I can see why you'd think that I would, but don't. I love Katie as though she were my own. She's all I'll ver want and need. But I don't understand... tacia...wasn't she...?"

"Pregnant?"

She nodded.

"Yes," he answered after a painful pause, "but not with ny child. We hadn't slept together for over a year. It must ave happened on that last cruise she took before her leath."

She breathed the final question, wanting to leave nothing nspoken between them. "Do you think that was the cause of her...?"

"Suicide? I don't know. I hope not, but that's something we'll never know," he said with finality. "It belongs with the past."

"And we," she said with newly born confidence, "b
long to the present."

"And to the future," he murmured against her hair.

Longing for the next few moments to completely free he
from the stranglehold of the past, Aurora raised her hand
to Eric's strong neck and pulled his face down to meet he
tremulous lips.

Though her tentative touch elicited a surge of passio
more powerful than any he had ever known, he kissed he
gently, with caution, knowing how much it had cost her t
reach out to him. Feeling her stiffen and pull away, he qui
etly held her in the circle of his arms. Realizing how deepl
her ordeal had scarred her, he pushed down futile, murder
ous thoughts of the man who had hurt her. All that mat
tered was his responsibility to this incredibly wonderfu
woman... a responsibility to use his overwhelming love fo
her to make her whole again.

"I'm so frightened," she confessed after a long momen
her throaty voice shaded with uncertainty.

"Of what?" he asked in a deliberately light tone, bend
ing his head to kiss the rapidly beating pulse at the base o
her slender throat. "Of me?"

"Never of you," she breathed, hesitantly meeting his ga
as he raised his face to hers.

"Then of what?" he repeated with a slow smile, gentl
moving one hand up into the thick mass of silken hair at he
nape, encouraged by the involuntary shiver of response he
body made to his touch.

"Of not being good enough for you." She worried he
full, lower lip with her even, white teeth in an endearin
gesture that caused him to feel an almost incapacitatin
sense of protectiveness. "Of not being able to...to make yo
happy," she finished in a whisper, averting her eyes.

"You don't ever have to do anything more than you've already done to make me happy," he answered softly, frustrated with the inadequacy of his response. Always so glib with words, suddenly they failed him. Nothing he could say could express the depth of his feelings for her. In the months that he'd loved her, he'd relied on her strength, taken it for granted . . . had never imagined a time could come when she would be as openly vulnerable as she was now. He knew she had never loved before, and though he had no doubt of her love for him, he suspected that unless she came away strengthened by their lovemaking, he might lose her forever. Feeling a stab of something akin to panic, he realized that this was not the time for either of them to think . . . he couldn't allow her insecurity to color the moment. She needed to feel absolutely secure and unconditionally wanted. "You, my darling, are all I'll ever want . . . all I'll ever need. I couldn't go on without you in my life."

Closing her beautiful hazel eyes and letting her body sway toward his, she murmured, "Make love to me, Eric . . . please. Tell me what to do to make you happy."

A groan rose unbidden from deep in his throat as his lips found hers. Desire tore through him with the force of a red hot flame . . . desire tempered only by the need to protect this incredible creature who was willing to risk everything in his arms. An unbearable ache to fulfill her needs, to end her pain, possessed him as his mouth searched the open, pliant softness of hers.

As his strong hands explored the contours of her supple back and rounded buttocks, melding her length to his, Aurora didn't know when her anxiety was replaced by a rocking sensation so giddily wild that she had to cling to Eric for support. Her mouth began to move, not mechanically in a forced response, but with a will of its own. The taste and texture of him became her world, as she sought a release her body had never known.

Without taking his mouth from hers, he swept her up into his arms and cradled her close. Her fingers found the button at his neck and worked under the fabric of his shirt, enjoying the feel of his taut masculine skin, before moving up his throat to brush against the stubble on his chin and jaw. She felt his body quiver and her heart was filled with a melodic joy to know that she had caused his response.

Her eyes opened wide, and she momentarily felt bereft and alone when he pulled his lips from hers and gently placed her on the couch. He knelt beside her, and when she dared to look at him, the light shining in his eyes left no doubt in her mind that she was all he desired . . . all he wanted. She made a move to reach up to caress him, but was stopped by his husky words.

"No, don't move," he gently commanded. "Lie still. Let me undress you."

She did as he asked, though a nervous tension built within her at his every touch. She'd never known such sweet torment as he unbuttoned her blouse and unfastened the front of her lacy bra, his mouth leaving a trail of burning kisses down her breastbone and midriff. Then his tender hands moved in a circular pattern, pushing back her garments to reveal her high, full breasts. She stifled a groan as his fingers continued to knead her sensitized flesh, and she gasped for air when his moist mouth captured one hardened nipple. The other ached for his touch until he claimed it in turn. She arched her back and his dark eyes met hers with a knowing smile.

When his fingers found the buttons at her waist and pushed under the fabric of her slacks and panties, her breath caught in her throat, and a gasp of pure pleasure escaped from her lips. A white hot, throbbing sensation began to grow in the very center of her, and she began to move her head from side to side as she wordlessly begged with soft cries and moans for his body to take hers.

"Help me, darling," he ordered in a husky whisper, and with her willing compliance it took only a few deft moves to strip her arms and legs free from the constraints of her clothes. She shivered uncontrollably when he leaned back slightly and gazed adoringly at her exposed form. Her eyes shimmered through a haze of passion, reflecting the longing in his.

Leaning forward, he sought her lips with a searing urgency. She reached up to embrace him, and her mouth clung to his in a soul-stirring kiss as he moved to strip off his own shirt and jeans. In an instant he was beside her. Every fiber of her being was in an altered state of absolute sensation as the world became only the two of them. Her breasts moved against the hair-roughened texture of his chest and responded as if they had been made only for this meeting. Her long, smooth legs wrapped themselves around the textured surface of his, and a raging fire threatened to consume her as his hands stroked the skin of her buttocks and thighs before he gently shifted one of her legs, exposing the very core of her to his sure, knowing fingers.

She moaned, thrashing and writhing under his touch, but still he held back, denying the explosive force of his own desire, knowing that he had to wait for the perfect moment. The moment at which she could not turn back.

"Are you still afraid?" he whispered at last.

"No," she answered breathlessly. "No...no..."

"I am," his voice was muffled against her heated flesh. "I want to be everything for you that you've become for me. I want to fulfill your wildest fantasies."

"You do," she gasped, feeling his fingers and mouth everywhere at once, raising her passions to a delirious fever pitch. "I want you, Eric...you're all that I want."

He was in control, commanding...but she was completely unafraid, her resistance overcome by the tender gentleness of the man. Her trust was absolute as she gave herself to him, body and soul.

When he moved to enter her, she instinctively rose to meet him in sweet surrender. The pain of uncertainty that had haunted every moment of her adult life, that had made her doubt her ability to be woman enough for him was replaced with an exploding, colorful ecstasy more brilliant than she'd ever imagined. Her emotions were a swirling kaleidoscope that drew her deep into a vision of love more wonderful than she'd ever believed could be real.

She met each velvet thrust, her body molten, trembling...totally alive...wondrously abandoned. He lowered his desire-darkened face to hers to claim her mouth in a kiss, no longer so gentle, but demanding, urgent, compelling. He thrust more deeply still, and mindless sensation was all she knew as she clung desperately to his shoulders, gasping for breath as shockwave after shockwave rocked through her, electrifying every nerve as her senses and her emotions melded in blissful harmony with his shudder of release.

Passion spent, they clung to one another, savoring the moment as their breathing slowed and their racing hearts grew calm with the certainty of their love.

"Are you cold?" he asked, as he moved to settle them on their sides.

"No," she murmured, her eyes shining with a golden light. "I don't think I'll ever be cold again as long as I have you."

He reached out to reverently trace the lovely outline of her jaw and cheekbones. "I know I should wait to ask this on bended knee, after surrounding you with candlelight and flowers. But I can't wait. Will you marry me, Aurora? Will you be my wife?"

She smiled. "You don't even need to ask." Tears of joy threatened to spill from her eyes as his mouth claimed hers, and the blood began to race through her veins once more, heated by the warmth of her one true love.

Chapter Seventeen

The sun was streaming into the room when they finished showering. The fog of the night before had been blown away by the brisk wind stirring up the sand of the beach, scattering it in puffs against the windows. Humming, with her mouth fixed in what was rapidly becoming a habitual grin, Aurora did her hair and dressed while Eric made breakfast.

"My," she exclaimed when he pulled out her chair and seated her before a plate filled with bacon and scrambled eggs. "You've developed quite a repertoire."

"Actually," he said with a smile, "this is about it. I eat a lot of scrambled eggs."

"They're very good," she complimented after taking a bite. "I'm starving. I haven't had anything to eat since yesterday morning."

"Do you want me to go with you to see Jenni?" he asked as he rose to get the pot of coffee that had finished perking.

"I think I should see her alone," Aurora answered, sobered. She bit off a piece of toast. "Your being there would probably embarrass her."

"I suppose you're right, but I still can't understand why she named me. I thought she knew I cared about her. I can't imagine her wanting to hurt me."

"I can't, either," Aurora confessed. "It just doesn't make sense. But maybe there's some sort of explanation we haven't thought of. I don't know. I just have to get her to tell me who did do this to her, in case it was someone over eighteen."

"Then while you're at the hospital, I'll go with Brook to call on the headmaster in my role as an irate parent. When Brook told him what had happened, his first reaction was to expel Jenni."

"That awful man is absolutely predictable!" Aurora exclaimed with vehemence.

"Don't worry, we're not going to let him get away with it. But I'm not going to leave you alone to face Jenni's parents, either. I'll meet you at noon for lunch and we'll wait for them together."

"As Jenni's doctor, I'll have to talk to them by myself. But it'll be a big help to know you're near by. I love you so much," Aurora declared, tears of happiness swimming in her eyes. "You can't know what it means to me to have someone to rely on."

"Yes, I can," he answered softly, taking her hand. "Without you I could never have faced the past months." He leaned across the table inviting the kiss she stretched forward to share.

The insistent ringing of the phone caused them to reluctantly pull apart. "It's Brook," Aurora whispered to Eric after she'd answered.

"You're home," Brook exclaimed, a note of relief in his voice. "Does Eric know?"

"He's right here," she said, as strong arms encircled her waist and a stubbly cheek rubbed against hers.

"Good. I wanted to let you know that Jenni's parents will be in sometime today. The father was going to wait for the mother to join him in Tokyo so they could take a flight out together.''

''I hope they're still speaking to each other when they get here,'' Aurora remarked with a cheerless laugh.

''Under the circumstances he was very reasonable,'' Brook assured her before Eric took the receiver and held it between them.

''Hi there, Buddy!''

''You sound a lot happier than you did the last time I saw you,'' Brook answered with a chuckle.

''You might say that. In fact, you're talking to the happiest guy in the world,'' Eric declared. ''Aurora and I are going to be married.''

''That is good news! Congratulations! May I tell Paula?''

''Of course,'' Aurora put in. ''And tell her I'm on my way to see Jenni.''

''Will do.''

Then, after giving Eric a quick kiss and whispering her thanks for the breakfast, Aurora went to get her coat and handbag while Eric continued his conversation.

Putting his hand over the receiver as she went out the door, he called out, ''Good luck.''

''You, too, darling,'' she answered with a wave, fearing they were both going to need it.

BREAKFAST WAS being served as Aurora entered Jenni's room.

''Hi, honey,'' she said, hiding her nervousness as she sat on the bed beside the young girl who was investigating the covered serving dishes on her tray. The next few moments were so important. Jenni just had to tell the truth. If her unwarranted accusations got out, they could cause a terrible scandal that would result in a hurtful invasion of Eric's privacy.

"Hi," Jenni answered shyly, not meeting Aurora's steady gaze.

"We need to talk."

"Yeah, we do," Jenni said so quietly Aurora could barely hear her.

Feeling a surge of hope, Aurora kept her voice even as she asked, "Mr. Thorpe wasn't the person who impregnated you, was he?"

"No," the girl answered in a whisper.

"Then who was it?" Aurora persisted, taking Jenni's hand and holding it tightly. "I need to know."

Jenni lifted her gaze and looked at Aurora a long time before answering. "It was just a boy I met at the first dance. I sneaked out to meet him a couple of times after that. Is my mother coming soon?"

Aurora let out the breath she had been unconsciously holding. "Yes, dear, she and your father will be here today. They're coming as fast as they can."

"Does Katie know what happened to me?"

"No. Doctors keep their cases confidential...you can tell her if you want to." Aurora flushed hotly. "But Mr. Thorpe knows. I was so upset when you said he'd done this to you, I couldn't keep from telling him."

"He called Dr. Paula and she explained that to me. She said that he wasn't mad at me about it, either," the child said with trembling lips, innocently unaware of the havoc she'd caused.

"Of course he's not. He's just very concerned about you." Someday, when Jenni was old enough to understand, Aurora decided, she'd share with her the effect that accusation had had upon her own life.

"I'm glad he's not mad."

Aurora hesitated. "There is one thing Mr. Thorpe and I would both like to know. Can you tell me why you said he was the one?"

Jenni dropped her gaze and nervously fingered the sheet. "It's going to sound really stupid."

"That doesn't matter," Aurora assured her.

"He's the nicest man I know and..."

"And what?" Aurora prompted.

"And I thought it would make me seem important if he loved me," Jenni got out before bursting into tears.

"Oh, honey," Aurora quickly moved the breakfast tray and gathered the sobbing girl into her arms, "you are important. And you are loved. We all love you. And don't you ever forget it."

Pulling a tissue from the box on the bedside table she dried Jenni's tears. "Now, you settle down and when you feel like it, see if you can eat a little of your breakfast. I'll call Katie. She's anxious to come see you. I have a patient to visit right now, then after I'm done I'll come back to sit with you for a while."

The grateful smile on Jenni's face tore at Aurora's heart-strings.

"BROOK CALLED. Jenni's parents will be in around three," Aurora said as Eric joined her at the restaurant.

He nodded. "I know. I just dropped Katie off at Jenni's door. She brought so many things to keep her little roomie entertained, I had to help her carry them. She thinks you're a miracle worker who saved Jenni's life. I told her I agreed you could work miracles," he said with a grin so filled with intimacy it left her dizzy.

"Did you tell her about us?" she asked, not wanting to take her eyes from his.

He shook his head. "I thought we could save that for dinner tonight...at my place. Bridey seemed very pleased when I asked her to fix something special. I'm sure she and Mac won't be a bit surprised at our news. I invited Brook and Paula over, too. I thought we could have a little impromptu engagement party."

"But we have Katie to think about," Aurora said cautiously. "Don't you think we should wait a while? You and she have just found each other. I don't want her to feel I'm intruding on her relationship with you. Girls her age can be very possessive of their fathers. And we haven't been very open with her about what's been going on between us. She may need time to get used to the idea of us being a couple."

His raised eyebrow gave his face a rakish look. "Now who is it that doesn't want to level with her?" he teased.

"But..." Aurora began, before she dropped her gaze in surrender.

"We are a couple. And my daughter loves you. Nothing's going to change that. Do you think she'd ever forgive us if everyone else knew and she didn't? Besides, I want to shout it from the cliff tops."

"You're right," she said, her happiness overflowing.

It was almost three before they left the restaurant. They'd been so involved in making plans that neither of them had realized how much time had passed. Hurrying back to the hospital, hand in hand with Eric, Aurora barely felt her feet touch the pavement.

The awkward moment when Eric entered Jenni's room passed with Katie's innocent suggestion that the four of them play cards. His hearty agreement, followed by a fatherly hug for Jenni, brought a tentative smile to the young girl's face and filled Aurora's heart with pride. They'd been there only a little while before Brook's greeting from the door drew their attention from a rousing game of hearts.

"Aurora, may I see you for a moment, please?" he asked.

After putting down her cards, she joined him in the hall where he introduced her to Jenni's weary and obviously distraught parents. Both the woman, who wore a stylish but crumpled silk jumpsuit, and the uniformed man carried airline flight bags. Their faces showed enormous strain.

"Go in and play my hand," she said to Brook before ushering the Reynoldses to the couches in the small waiting room.

"We got here just as quickly as we could," Mrs. Reynolds stated apologetically. "How is Jenni, Doctor? Mr. Oliver said she's all right, but I want to hear it from you."

"She's recovering well from her miscarriage, but she's going to need a lot of counseling before she understands and deals with what's happened to her."

"Miscarriage," the slender woman repeated with a gasp that ended with a sob. "I still can't believe this!"

"I don't understand how this could have happened to our daughter," Captain Reynolds said gruffly, although Aurora could see he was as affected by the word as his ex-wife was.

"Now, Howard," Mrs. Reynolds warned. She wiped her eyes with a tissue before she turned to Aurora. "We've had a long trip. A very long trip. We argued for hours already, blaming each other and blaming the school. But we're past that point now. We know that we're equally to blame. Neither one of us has given Jenni the time and attention she deserves. We've left our daughter's care up to others far too much." She pointedly looked back at Jenni's father.

"We're in complete agreement on that score," the silver-haired man interjected with a nod. "But Mr. Oliver told us the trouble you've been having with the headmaster and the board about teaching the girls about their bodies. We're very angry with the headmaster for insisting that we take Jenni out of school. Nothing like this is ever going to happen to her again. We'll see to that. Our little girl is going to have all the loving care she needs!''

"Now, Howard," the woman said again, standing, "I told you I'm giving up my traveling and taking Jenni home for a rest until after winter break. And that's not the doctor's problem. Right now, I just want to see my daughter."

"Of course," Aurora said, getting to her feet. "You can go right in."

"Thank you," Mrs. Reynolds said, as her ex-husband pushed open the door and waited for the two of them to enter before him.

"Mom! Dad!" Jenni called out, throwing her cards onto the spread before opening her arms to her parents.

"My baby!" Mrs. Reynolds cried, rushing toward the bed.

All the Reynoldses' attention was for their daughter. Realizing it was not the time for social amenities, Aurora held the door while the other three visitors hurried from the room.

In the hall Brook's tone was serious, although his eyes twinkled. "Katie, I need you to help me out."

"Sure, what can I do?"

"This is a little anniversary for Paula and me," he explained. "I want to get her some flowers, and I'd like to take a bouquet to Bridey, too. I want your advice at the florists, then I'll take you back to your house in time for dinner."

"Sounds like fun," Katie said happily. "What do you think about one of those helium balloons? Or..."

After they'd gone, Eric and Aurora settled back onto the couch, and he put his arm around her shoulders.

"How did it go?"

She shrugged and lifted her eyebrows. "I've got my fingers crossed. It looks promising. I'm very sorry all this happened, but it may be just the jolt they needed. I'm hopeful that they'll carry through and do the best they can for her."

"I'm glad to hear it," Eric remarked.

"Captain Reynolds is going to protest Jenni's expulsion. I never asked how you and Brook made out with the headmaster this morning. I was so wrapped up in thoughts about us, I—"

"It wasn't pleasant," Eric cut in, tracing the lines of her face with his finger. "He accused Brook of insubordination and threatened to take it up with the board."

"What did Brook say to that?"

"He said that was exactly what he had in mind, himself."

"Then . . . ?"

"We went over to Brook's office and put in a call to Mrs. Murray asking to see her immediately."

"And . . . ?"

"She agreed. So we went over to her house . . . that Victorian mansion hidden in the high firs behind the campus. It was like stepping into the eighteen-nineties, uniformed maid and all. Mrs. Murray greeted us in the front parlor."

Aurora's brows knit in a frown. "Brook told me she could be receptive to change if she was approached correctly, but I sure didn't see any signs of it at the board meeting."

"We were prepared for a showdown," Eric admitted, "a genteel one. But we were both so angry about Jenni's expulsion and the probability of something like this happening again to another one of the girls, that we were ready to take the headmaster and the board to court."

"Did she throw you out? Genteelly?"

"Surprisingly, she was very receptive. Remember the board had been split and had decided to take the matter under consideration?"

"Yes..."

"Well, it seems she'd been getting pressure from the consenting half who'd done some spade work. When Brook offered to tender his resignation she became indignant. She felt it was the headmaster who'd overstepped his bounds. Anyway, the upshot was that there's to be an emergency meeting of the board Monday night. 'Full of surprises' were Mrs. Murray's own words. And Jenni, she assured us, will not be expelled. 'Over my dead body,' is another direct quote."

"Jenni's parents will be happy to hear that," Aurora said, relaxing against Eric's chest as she took his free hand and kissed it.

"Let's talk about us," he murmured, pulling her closer. "When do you want to shop for your rings?"

They were deep in conversation when Jenni's parents came out of her room.

After introducing Eric, Aurora asked them how long they planned to stay.

"How soon do you think Jenni can leave the hospital?" Mrs. Reynolds asked.

"I'd like her to spend another night here," Aurora answered. "But she can be released tomorrow provided her activity is limited for a few days."

"Then we need to find a motel and rent a car," Captain Reynolds put in. "We thought we'd drive her down to L.A. instead of flying. It will give some time for us all to be together and make some plans for her future."

Mrs. Reynolds reddened. "We talked about it a great deal on our way here, and we agreed that it's important for Jenni to know that though things didn't work out the way we hoped between us, we once loved each other. And she's the very special product of that love. We've been very foolish to think because she was just a child she didn't need to know how things really stood between her parents."

"It boils down to priorities," the captain said. "And my little girl has just moved to the top of my list. Right where she always should have been. Now, is there any place close to here to rent a car?"

"I'll be glad to help you out there," Eric offered.

"Thanks," Captain Reynolds answered. "And I need to get in touch with that headmaster as soon as possible. He has some accounting to do. And I want to find out on what grounds he thinks he can expell my daughter!"

"You're not going to have to worry about that," Eric said. "Brook Oliver and I have already seen Mrs. Murray, the most influential member of the Seahurst board, and she assured us that she isn't going to allow that to happen."

"That's good to hear," the captain said in a slightly mollified tone. "For Jenni's sake, I don't want this to be blown up into a big row. But I still intend to make that headmaster account for himself."

Eric nodded. "Speaking as a father of a daughter, myself, I have to agree he's got it coming to him."

"I'd like to see both of you tomorrow before Jenni's released," Aurora said to the girl's parents. "Could we meet for breakfast? Around nine?"

"Of course," Mrs. Reynolds agreed. "And please call me Audrey. You've been so kind, Doctor. Jenni seems to adore you. She's written so many times about the wonderful way you and Mr. Thorpe have included her this summer. She and his daughter Katie have been close friends for a long time."

"Yes, they have," Aurora said, thinking sadly of the years when the two girls had had very few people to depend on in their lives other than each other. "We can meet in the hospital cafeteria in the morning."

"Thank you again," Audrey Reynolds said, extending her hand to each of them before picking up her bag. "We'll have to go pick up some of Jenni's things before we leave."

"Katie can help you do that," Aurora suggested. "I'll bring her with me tomorrow. She can keep Jenni company while we talk, then she can go over to the dorm with you."

After taking Mrs. Reynolds's bag, Eric gave Aurora a quick kiss on the cheek. He whispered, "I'll pick you up around seven," before leading Jenni's parents to his car.

"BRIDEY'S DONE IT AGAIN," Brook declared, laying down his dessert fork and patting his stomach. "That woman is a real gem."

"Yeah," Katie said, suspiciously. "But I want to know just why we're having this special dinner."

"Oh, you do, do you?" Eric teased, before rising from his chair to stand by hers. Putting his arm around her, he waited while Aurora rose to join them. Then he said, "Because Aurora and I have something to tell you. We're getting married."

"Oh, Daddy!" Katie exclaimed joyously, jumping up to hug them. "When?"

"As soon as possible," he told her.

"Probably in two weeks," Aurora added.

"But you can't do that!" Katie declared in a stricken tone.

Taken aback, both Eric and Aurora asked at the same time, "Why not?"

"Because Jenni and I have your wedding all planned out and she won't be here! You said she was going home with her mother."

"Then you're not even surprised?" Eric asked.

"Of course not," Katie said matter-of-factly. "It's what I've been hoping would happen ever since you two met each other. But Jenni and I've been at the bridal store every weekend, and we have all the dresses for your wedding picked out."

"That's wonderful," Aurora quickly said, pulling the girl close. "It will save me time. Next weekend I want to take you and your father to San Francisco to meet my parents, and then we'd like to be married at their house... my... home."

"Your parents? Your home?" Katie asked, looking up to search Aurora's face. "I thought you were mad at your mother."

"I was," Aurora answered solemnly, "just like you were mad at your dad. Remember?"

Katie nodded, her eyes wide.

"Well, you made up, didn't you? And that's what happened with me and my mom. My parents are going to be very happy to meet their new granddaughter."

"But Jenni and I wanted your wedding to be even bigger than Aunt Paula and Uncle Brook's," Katie said in a thoughtful tone, as if her words were an afterthought and her mind was already mulling over Aurora's latest statement.

"Your father and I prefer a much smaller one," Aurora said with a smile at Eric over Katie's head, thinking of the enormous guest list the other couple had compiled.

"If Jenni's going home tomorrow until the new semester, will she still be in the weddings?" Katie asked with alarm as a new worry assailed her.

"No reason why not," Aurora assured her. "But, you'd better add two names to our invitation list. I think we should invite her parents."

"Things really do change around here," Katie declared shaking her head.

"For the better?" Aurora asked.

"Better than I ever dared hope," Katie said, tears of happiness swimming in her eyes.

"For me too," Aurora said with a glorious smile, looking up at the man who'd brought the illuminating light of love to her life, to dispel the deep shadows of her past.

Epilogue

"Will it be all right?" Katie asked in a hushed voice, as Aurora snipped the fishing line twisted around and embedded in the bright orange-colored leg of the seagull that Eric held with a firm grip.

"Will it be able to fly?" Jenni added.

"I think it'll be just fine. It seems to be more exhausted than injured," Aurora answered the anxious questions. The rays of the morning sun shot incandescent sparks from the wide wedding band of diamonds and rubies circling the ring finger of her left hand, as she quickly worked to free the frightened bird.

"I never saw one this close before. It's so beautiful," Katie remarked, awe apparent in her tone. "The same color as our house, isn't it?" She looked up toward their newly remodeled home with its wide, double set of decks running around three sides of the imposing structure.

"The stain was called Gull Gray," Eric offered with a chuckle.

"There," Aurora said, as she untangled the last piece of fishing line. "Let's take him closer to the house and put him on the sand. He'll fly away when he's ready."

Together the concerned group followed Eric up the beach and dropped down on the warm sand around the injured bird he placed before them.

It was the last holiday of summer before the new school term began, and relaxed contentment glowed on all the suntanned faces.

"Yo, Katie . . . Jenni," an adolescent male voice called.

Looking up, Aurora saw two of the teenaged boys who lived in nearby homes walking toward them. The taller one was spinning a volleyball on the tip of one finger.

"Want to come over and play a game or two?" the shorter boy asked, a friendly grin on his open, freckled face.

Both of the girls got to their feet, brushing sand from their tanned legs as they looked down questioningly at Eric for approval.

After only a slight hesitation, he nodded. "Go ahead. We'll watch the bird."

"We'll be back before everyone comes," Katie promised, shooting a last reluctant glance down at the gull before she ran to join the others.

Watching them walk away, four abreast, with the girls in the middle, Aurora felt Eric stiffen. "They'll be all right," he said calmly, putting a hand on his arm.

He frowned. "I can't help but think of . . ."

"I know," she said, moving over to sit close to him. As his arm came around her shoulders she snuggled against him, planting a kiss of gratitude on the warm skin at the base of his neck. "It's been hard for you to allow Katie the freedom she has to have in order to become a strong, happy woman, but you're doing a great job. And you don't need to worry. Nothing's going to happen to Katie or Jenni again. They've both got their eyes wide open and their heads on straight.

"I'm really glad Jenni decided to share her story with Katie . . . it has let me be frank with both of them. Jenni understands now that the boy she met at the dance was able to manipulate her because she felt so unloved. She doesn't feel that way anymore."

"Yes," Eric agreed, "you just have to look at her to see that. She's taking so much pride in her appearance that you'd never know she was the same girl she was last summer. You have to give her parents credit for coming through when they realized how badly she needed them. It's just unfortunate that she had to go through so much to get their attention."

"Sometimes it takes a crisis to pull everyone together," Aurora said softly. "It's so strange . . . miraculous, really . . . how things work out, isn't it? If Jenni hadn't chosen you as the father figure in her life to replace the one whom she believed had abandoned her . . . 'The nicest man in the world,' she called you, and I agree with that," Aurora said with another kiss. "And if she hadn't named you as the one in her grief and confusion . . . I might never have gotten over my past. And we'd never have been this incredibly happy, if I hadn't been able to forgive my parents and have them back in my life."

"Happiness rises like a Phoenix from the ashes," he mused, half-jokingly, his lips on her forehead. "Sounds like a theme for another play."

"Not from the ashes," she corrected. "From the embers of smoldering love."

"Yes," he answered after a long while. "Jenni and her parents . . . Katie and me . . . your parents and you . . . Brook and Paula . . . us . . ." He looked down at her with a smile so fond and full of love it seemed to encompass all the goodness and promise she'd ever dared to dream of actually having in her life. "With all this material, I'll never run out of ideas again, will I?"

"Never," she assured him, gazing long into his dark eyes.

"My only worry left is whether the public will take me seriously as a dramatic playwright."

"Huh!" Aurora said disparagingly. "With production companies bidding for the rights to your play, and top-flight actors scrambling for parts in it, I don't think you have anything to worry about there. Your work is wonderful, darling . . . a whole new dimension."

"I wish you were a critic," he joked, but she could tell he knew she was right.

"You know, my darling husband, today seems more like a celebration of beginning for all of us than just a house-warming for our new home." She began to tick off her own list. "Brook's new position as headmaster for the school . . . now there's another good thing that came out of Jenni's ordeal. The shake-up that her crisis caused in both the board and the administration is going to make Seahurst an exciting place for me to work and for the girls to go to school. I can't believe those two are starting upper school already."

"They're growing up fast, that's for sure," Eric agreed. "A little too fast for me."

Aurora laughed, a rich warm sound that bubbled freely from her throat. "Well, Brook and Paula are doing their best to provide us with some little ones to love . . ."

Eric grinned. "They sure didn't waste any time getting started, did they?"

"No, and if they have the four they want, being godparents to them all will keep us busy for years to come. I can hardly wait for that baby to arrive."

"I always wanted to be an uncle," Eric admitted.

"Did you? You never told me that. The truth is, I always wanted to be an aunt. And speaking of that, my parents adore being grandparents. If we don't watch it, they'll spoil Katie rotten."

"I know," Eric commented. "But I feel like I'd be letting your dad down if I didn't let him."

"You would be," Aurora affirmed. "He still feels he has to make up to me for what happened, although I've tried to help him understand that it isn't necessary. I think he's beginning to believe that I love him as much as I ever did. And Mother told me that they're becoming close again."

"I'm glad to hear that," Eric said. "They've made their mistakes, like the rest of us, but they're great people."

"They are, aren't they?" Aurora said with a sense of pride. Coming to terms with her mother, and seeing her long-ago decision through the eyes of maturity, had been critical to her current happiness and to her sense of well-being. "And don't forget, we have to celebrate the production of your new screenplay. As I said, today is the start of a real celebration."

But what about my daughter, she wondered suddenly, as the shadow of the child she had never known flitted across her thoughts like a vaporous cloud intruding on the clear blue sky of the promising day.

"Not for me, it isn't," he stated simply, causing her to pull away in surprise. Gathering her back into his arms, he whispered against her lips, "My celebration started the moment I met you."

Lost to the world in their rapturous embrace, they didn't see the wounded bird on the sand struggle to its feet to take a few tottering steps.

"Hey there," the deep voice of Aurora's father called from the lower deck of the house. "Save a kiss or two for me!"

Laughing, Eric pulled Aurora to her feet as they both waved to her mother and father who'd come down from the city for the day.

Then, remembering the gull, Aurora turned in time to see it stretch its wings and lift off into the sun-warmed air, rising higher and higher until it banked and flew out over the waves of the rippled sea.

Suddenly she understood the words to the lesson her heart had learned. Life must be lived and enjoyed in the present. The past must never be allowed to dominate the future.

With a new hope that her own child was being raised with a love equal to the boundless love she had for Katie, Aurora let go of the last worries she had for that other young girl, letting her love fly with the gull, free on the wind.

HARLEQUIN
Romance®

This September, travel to England
with Harlequin Romance
FIRST CLASS title #3149,
ROSES HAVE THORNS
by Betty Neels

It was Radolf Nauta's fault that Sarah lost her job at the hospital and was forced to look elsewhere for a living. So she wasn't particulary pleased to meet him again in a totally different environment. Not that he seemed disposed to be gracious to her: arrogant, opinionated and entirely too sure of himself, Radolf was just the sort of man Sarah disliked most. And yet, the more she saw of him, the more she found herself wondering what he really thought about her—which was stupid, because he was the last man on earth she could ever love....

Coming Soon

Fashion A Whole New You in classic romantic style with a trip for two to Paris via American Airlines®, a brand-new Mercury Sable LS and a $2,000 Fashion Allowance.

Plus, romantic free gifts* are yours to Fashion A Whole New You.

From September through November, you can take part in this exciting opportunity from Harlequin.

Watch for details in September.

* with proofs-of-purchase, plus postage and handling

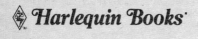 **Harlequin Books**

HQFW-TS